MW00354309

THE POLLY PRINCIPLE

SOMETIMES LOVE IS UNPREDICTABLE

DAVINA STONE

FEATHERS & STONE PUBLISHING

Copyright © 2021 by Davina Stone

All rights reserved.

No part of this book may be reproduced in any form or by any electronic or mechanical means, including information storage and retrieval systems, without written permission from the author, except for the use of brief quotations in a book review.

This is a work of fiction. Names, characters, places, and incidents are products of the author's imagination or are used fictitiously. Any resemblance to actual events, locales, organizations, or persons, living or dead, is entirely coincidental.

Print ISBN: 978-0-6450065-2-0

Ebook ISBN: 978-0-6450065-3-7

Cover design by Bailey McGinn, Bailey Designs Books

Edited by Abigail Nathan, Bothersome Words

Proofread by Vanessa Lanaway, Red Dot Scribble

PREFACE

Polly Fletcher has one guiding principle in life... NEVER FALL IN LOVE.

~

Dear reader,
This novel is set in a Covid Free world. Which means all kissing and what-not between these pages is allowed!

CHAPTER 1

With her champagne flute poised, it flashed through Polly's mind that she should be paid for delivering couples to the altar. Would a wedding planner hire her? Or a swanky venue? Her track record for pairing bridesmaids off with stray guests was impressive. She could single-handedly keep the bookings up for cakes, dresses, hire services... honestly, the list was endless.

"Please raise your glasses to the beautiful bride and the ugly groom." The best man's words cut through her brilliant career plans. Laughter, murmurs of *"Jake and Lou"*, and the clink of glasses filled the room. Jake kissed his bride, the couple wearing matching only-have-eyes-for-you smiles.

Usually Polly's heart did a happy dance right about now, so why was there a stabbing sensation just above the waist of her Suzy Perette dress? It couldn't be the food. She'd been super careful not to overdose on smoked salmon blinis and chocolate-drizzled profiteroles. She might as well be wearing a hair shirt instead of her Spanx, as far as self-denial was concerned.

She took a gulp of champagne. And then it struck her.

Polly Fletcher, you are jealous.

Which was patently ridiculous. Sure, she could get a PhD in match-making, but all this commitment crap was never going to be her gig.

"Piss off, I am not."

"Excuse me?" The woman next to her said in a shocked tone. Polly grimaced. Clearly another of her brain-to-mouth malfunctions. More than three glasses of champagne and they became a regular occurrence.

"Sorry," she hiss-whispered. "Emergency call from my brother. Amazing things, smart watches, aren't they? I'll take it outside."

Wrist held to her ear, (it was actually a fake Patek Philippe she'd bought in Bali for two dollars, but who'd know at a distance?), Polly squeezed through the crowded room. Stumbling onto the hotel patio, she heaved a sigh of relief, downed the rest of her glass, and muttered, *"Idiot."*

"Who's an idiot?"

The voice was husky, male and very close to her ear.

Polly swung around. Luminous silver eyes fringed by black lashes stared back at her, crinkles of amusement fanning the tan skin at each corner. Quick as a flash she took in the rest of his face. Not exactly handsome. Short, dark hair, nose a little crooked; a lean jaw shadowed with stubble, but add in a mouth that looked like it was made for plea-suring a girl and Polly's powers of speech sank to a spot well below her waist.

Hot. As. Hell.

The guy cocked an eyebrow, brought a cigarette to his lips, and took a slow drag.

Hot he might be, but a vice like that was too good to miss.

"You are, clearly." She smirked.

Both eyebrows shot up this time. "Why?"

"For smoking, Mr *Dinosaur.*"

Hot-as-hell turned his cheek, and exhaled, which gave her time for a once-over of his bod. Polly's mouth went dry at the vision of broad shoulders gift-wrapped in leather, long denim-clad legs, and dusty biker boots.

When she dragged her gaze back up he was pointing at her cham-pagne. "Why's that stuff any better?"

2

"*Hel-lo*. You don't see smoke coming out of my glass, do you?" Polly wiggled her glass in his face.

He grinned. "Just a different choice of poison."

Polly narrowed her eyes. "Meaning what, exactly? That we're all stuffed up?"

"That's an assumption that says more about you than me."

"Oh, very clever." Polly huffed.

"What?"

"The way you turned the tables so it looks like I'm the one with the problem."

Hot-as-hell laughed and tapped ash off his cigarette. "You're a guest at the wedding?"

"And clearly you're not."

His pupils dilated, black blotting out silver. "How do you know?"

She allowed herself another lightning-fast scan—purely for research purposes, of course. "You've got oil stains on your jeans, and filthy boots," she said airily. "Not exactly hard to work out. Besides, I get paid to observe people."

He dropped the cigarette butt and ground it under his heel. "Really? What do you do?"

"Why would I tell you?" That was snarkier than she'd meant; blame it on rampant lust.

"No reason. Except I asked."

"If you want me to enter into a conversation, a name would help."

"Solo."

"Ha-ha, where's R2D2?"

He dead-panned her. "Yeah, I get that a lot. More often Luke Skywalker, but that's the name I go by."

Polly propped her butt on the wall and crossed her arms. It was just too... *arousing,* standing facing him. He must have noticed her nipples like little bullets pointing at him from under the flimsy fabric of her dress. "Do you live up to it?"

He sat down next to her. "What do you mean?"

"Do you fly solo?" It was out of her mouth before her brain cells could engage.

3

He chuckled. "Are you hitting on me?"

Fuckity fuck. "God. No! I just meant, are you a loner?"

"That depends," he said. "And you?"

"After that apology for an answer, I'm not telling."

"Ah, right. So, if a woman wants to ask personal questions, that's fine, but if the guy makes a move, he gets a bad rap."

Holy shit, is he making a move?

A quick sideways glance snagged on a muscular thigh almost nudging hers and it took all her energy not to whimper.

Solo gave an exaggerated sigh. "Anyway, when I said *and you,* I meant what's your name? Only fair—I told you mine."

She hesitated. "Polly."

"Nice."

She gave a snort.

"I mean it. I like your name. Come on, you've just ridiculed mine and I'm being genuinely complimentary about yours. Why are you so tetchy?"

He had a point. She was being a prize cow. Too much alcohol because her fuck buddy had got married when she'd come to the erroneous conclusion he'd always be single, and now her complete mess-up of an introduction to the sexiest guy she'd encountered in months, possibly years, wasn't something to be particularly proud of.

Pushing off the wall, she shoved a curl off her forehead and gifted him her best apologetic smile. "Okay, I admit it. Champagne makes my tongue muscle misbehave. Let's start again. My name's Polly and I'm here at my friend Jake's wedding, and when I'm not being a complete bitch to men I've just met, I work as a social worker."

She thought a brief shadow passed over his face, then his lips tipped into a grin. "Nice to meet you, Polly. Passing through on my way to take up a three-month contract in Perth. No offence taken. I quite enjoyed sparring with your bitchy alter-ego."

"Thanks, I aim to please. What are you doing in Perth?"

Again that misting of his features. "Working on a building project."

"Designing?"

"No, labouring."

Polly frowned. Somehow it didn't add up. Sure, he looked fit enough to do all kinds of manual work but... the way he spoke... he sounded as if he was more, what...? *Educated...?* Hell, she was grossly stereotyping, wasn't she? A sudden vision of Solo naked to the waist and glistening in sweat as he heaved girders over his shoulder sent her into another near-meltdown.

On second thoughts, manual work it most definitely was.

Flustered, she turned and leaned her elbows on the wall. Beyond the hotel's reticulated gardens, great swathes of wheat spread out towards the red ball of the setting sun.

"It's still freakin' hot, isn't it?" she said. *Pathetic.* Surely she could do better than the weather. "So, if I'm allowed to ask, where are you from, Solo?"

"Sydney."

"Sydney." She couldn't help a surprised glance. "How did you end up in Western Australia?"

"I rode over."

"Oh, yeah? Where's your faithful steed?"

"Parked out the front. The red Ducati."

An image of those thighs draped around a big shiny bike made her mouth dry up again. She feigned interest in the sunset. "Yeah? How long did that take?"

"Two weeks. I camped on the road."

"One more day and you'll be there, then."

"Yep, decided to go luxury for my last night. Only to realise I was gatecrashing a wedding. I was surprised the hotel had a room spare."

"Most people are staying at the bride's place. Her dad owns a zillion hectares of wheat out here."

He leaned his hip against the wall, studying her. "And you?"

"What about me?"

"Are you staying at their property?"

Polly kept her eyes on the sun as it slid lower. "Um, no."

"Why not?"

"I—um..."

"Too awkward, maybe?"

5

God the guy was astute.

"No, not at all." There was no need to explain how her long-term *friends with benefits* arrangement had ended abruptly six months ago when she'd introduced Jake to Lou. And that while she was ecstatically happy for them, she wasn't staying in the same building while they got on with their wedding night bonk.

"Here you are, I've been looking everywhere-—they're about to cut the cake."

Polly suppressed a huff, not sure whether to be annoyed or relieved at her friend Judith's appearance.

Judith beckoned. "Come on, quick."

Polly started to back away; realised she had a ninny grin on her face and gave herself a mental slap. "Mustn't miss the cake being cut. Nice to meet you, Solo."

"Likewise." Did his gaze darken, or was that just the fading light? "Catch you later, maybe."

Polly's heart did a little rap, the kind with really inappropriate lyrics. "Maybe." And with that she almost scampered after Judith.

"He is *gorgeous*. Who is he?" Judith said as they headed into the reception.

"Some random."

"Oh, really? You seemed to be having a very cosy chat. I wondered if he might be your new love interest."

"You know I don't do love, Jude."

Spotting a waiter nearby, Polly made a dive for his tray of drinks.

"You may not." Judith grinned, following her. "But there's a battle-field of Polly Fletcher slain hearts out there."

"And here's to the one that got away," Polly said, raising her glass as Lou and Jake's hands joined over the knife to slice the cake.

"You didn't want Jake that way," Judith hissed in her ear over the cheers. "And you know it."

Polly sculled her champagne. True enough, she supposed. All she'd ever asked of Jake was a warm, cuddly friendship with some pretty good benefits tagged on the end. But... it was just, well... where was she going to get regular sex with no strings attached, now that Jake was off in married-la-la land?

A pair of beautiful silver eyes danced into her head, along with a sensual mouth that she'd bet was capable of getting up to all sorts of wickedness.

Polly placed her glass back on a passing tray and smiled sweetly at the waiter as she grabbed another.

How, she wondered, did you find out the room number of another guest without looking like some sex-starved stalker?

CHAPTER 2

*S*olomon Jakoby—Solo to just about everyone who knew him —pulled up the rusty bolt of the French doors to his room and kicked them open with the heel of his boot. A quick glance revealed that the wood was rotting beneath peeled paint. This place was seriously falling apart.

He needed another cigarette. On Fridays and Saturdays he allowed himself three after 5 p.m. He wasn't stupid enough to let it go further; he knew he could probably become a chain smoker if he let himself.

Blame it on a shit year. And now, it was time for his luck to change. Except he didn't believe in luck, other than the kind you made for yourself. And wasn't that exactly why he was here? To force his luck to change?

He walked out onto the wide veranda of the hotel. Weird old place. Compared with the east coast, Western Australia was so vast, so empty. He liked the spacious skies, the red dirt and roads that went seemingly forever. And so far, the women—or at least one of them—were hellish cute.

He slid the cigarette from behind his ear. It was a habit he'd learned from his pop, and a way of keeping the packet out of reach. Fishing the lighter out of his jeans pocket, he leaned on the wooden balustrade, hoping it wasn't as rotten as the door. He tapped the cigarette like Pop used to, put it to his lips and flicked the lighter, once, twice, then dragged until the nicotine hit the back of his throat.

Somewhere out in the shadowy bush an owl hooted morosely. Solo blew out a smoke ring and thought—yet again—about his encounter with the woman called Polly. He'd never have placed her as a social worker. Way too... sexual. Christ, what would her young clients do with themselves when she walked in? His mouth twisted into a rueful smirk. Didn't bear thinking about.

She'd hit him between the eyes as soon as she burst out onto the patio. 1950s film star curves: real hips, serious cleavage, small waist, all squeezed into a silky red dress. A head full of black curls that bobbed and bounced and then, when he'd interrupted her strange mutterings, those vivid green eyes appraising him had started a throb in his groin that hadn't happened for too damn long.

He wouldn't have said she was his type, but clearly his body had other ideas.

Fuck.

Oh, yes. She made him want to. No words, no foreplay, just a wildly primitive, let's-get-down-and-dirty urge. With full permission, of course. And Polly sure looked like someone who would give it.

The thought surprised him; he'd never realised he could be such a Neanderthal. He grinned almost sheepishly into the dark. His wild little fantasy was hardly hurting anyone, was it?

And at least it gave him hope that his libido hadn't completely shrivelled and died.

He took another long drag and stared at the moon rising behind a row of straggly eucalypts. Apart from that darned owl, the quiet out here was eerie.

Until a loud banging started up from the room next door.

The next moment a curvy silhouette catapulted onto the veranda. Adrenaline spiked through Solo's veins. There was something serendipitous about this.

"Stupid door," muttered the shadow.

Holy cow, she mustn't catch him smoking again. Solo whipped the cigarette out of his mouth and hid it behind his back. He'd put it out, but it was the last one of the day and he was buggered if he'd let it go to waste.

"Hi again."

His voice sounded way too enthusiastic.

"You!" Her head jerked round.

"No need to sound so pleased."

He heard her sniff. "I can smell smoke."

"Bloody hell, you're a beagle. Have you thought of applying for a job at Customs?"

"Oh, you're such a wit."

He tapped ash and hoped it wouldn't fall through the slats. At least there were tiles below. "I try." He smirked.

"If I'd known you were next door…"

"What?"

"I'd ask to be moved."

"Yeah?"

"Yeah. You're a safety risk, probably set your bed alight with one of those cancer sticks hanging out of your mouth."

A little demon took hold. Solo brought his hand around and puffed, deliberately. Exhaled slowly. Smoke spiralled upwards in the arc of light thrown from his room.

They eyeballed each other.

"Quite possible," he said.

For all her protestations, she was shifting slowly along the balustrade towards him, head tilted, thick curls tumbling around her shoulders. He let his eyes quickly pan down and realised she was wearing PJs with the shortest little shorts. Her thighs were pale, temptingly luscious, not slender, but shapely. Capable of wrapping around him and holding on tight for the ride…

Shut it down, idiot. A hard-on was not what he needed right now. Solo shifted his bulging crotch against the balustrade.

Still she shimmied along the rail and, as she got closer, he could see she was smiling, her lips like juicy summer fruit; ripe and ready to sink his teeth into.

He swallowed.

"Put it out," she murmured as she got up close. Her perfume carried on the warmth of her skin.

"Make me."

Laughter rolled soft and husky off her tongue and he had to work hard to keep his gaze from straying to those perfect breasts. Suddenly she reached out and grabbed his arm. Surprised, he pulled back and she lost her footing and stumbled into him. The soft fullness of her breasts pressed into his chest, and he arced his arm back to ensure he didn't give her a cigarette burn. Her fingers latched on tighter, and now her hips and naked thighs were in full contact.

Solo stifled a groan. Polly's eyebrows arched up.

She'd felt it. His cock, muscling in on the action. Her smile broadened into an evil grin. God, she was all-round gorgeous!

Their cheeks were almost touching, her breath sending shivers down his spine.

"I would. But I don't like smoker's breath."

Holding his breath, he told his cock to back right down. Christ, it reminded him of when he was seventeen, getting it on with Jenny Bailey in the back row of the movies on his first ever date. He was thirty-two years old; surely he could control his libido by now? Even so, he couldn't stop his words from following where every eager cell in his body was leading.

"Are you implying that if I go clean my teeth—"

"Or I go find my breath freshener—"

"We could come to some agreement—?"

"—That would be mutually satisfying. Maybe."

"Hmm, that sounds... interesting."

Those fingers still circled his arm, one stroking excruciatingly sensual circles on the skin just above his wrist. Solo tried not to pant. Her curls were tickling his neck, her lips so close he could just shift an inch to taste them.

"Breathe," she said, ever so softly against his ear.

"No way," punched out of closed lips.

"Come on, breathe on me."

Did she have any idea how turned-on he was right now? Yes, he decided, she sure as hell did.

All of a sudden she released him and he watched, perplexed, as she flounced off in the other direction. She had the most amazing arse. His palms itched to fold around those beautiful butt cheeks and hear the sounds she would make as he pulled her close.

When she disappeared into her room, Solo fidgeted from one foot to the other, pinched the end of his cigarette out with his fingers, then slammed the butt onto the rail and stabbed at it hard several times.

No risk of fire now.

Not that kind, anyway.

Seconds later she was back, brandishing a small spray can.

"Hope that's not mace?" He laughed somewhat nervously as she sashayed towards him.

"You'd have to be *very* badly behaved for me to do that," she purred, coming so close he could see even in the dim light a dusting of freckles on her nose. "Now, open wide."

He opened his mouth like a baby cuckoo and the cold tingle of menthol and mint hit his tongue, coated the back of his throat.

He snapped his mouth shut.

"Oh no, you don't get away that easily." Ebony curls shook vigorously. "One more."

He opened again. Another shot of iciness.

A giggle escaped her as he pulled a face, then she turned the can, parted her lips and gave a quick spray.

"Why only one for you?" he demanded.

"Alcohol is nowhere near as yucky as smoker's breath."

"Want to bet?"

"We'll see after a taste-test, shall we?" She'd popped the can into a tiny pocket in those tiny shorts and her fingers started an itsy-bitsy spider walk along his forearm and up his bicep.

"Nice—hard—muscles," she murmured softly and glanced up from under her lashes.

When her splayed hand smoothed over his pecs, a guttural sound escaped him; the sort of sound a starving man would likely make as he was presented with a three-course feast.

She let out another giggle as their noses bumped.

"You haven't felt anything yet." He heard his words, husky and full of lust and confidence, two emotions that hadn't been in his repertoire for a very long time. "Now stop laughing and kiss me."

~

SOMETIME LATER, Solo rolled onto his back and tried to catch his breath.

"Wow!" he managed finally.

He heard Polly's throaty chuckle next to him. "Did that meet with your approval, Mr Motorbike Man?"

"You could say I've been right-royally fucked stupid, yes. And you?"

Deftly he removed and knotted the condom, then shifted onto his side, hooking his head onto a cupped hand. He let his eyes follow the outline of a shapely shoulder, dipping down to the hollow of her waist and the swell of her hip, pale as marble in an arc of moonlight from the window.

They'd ended up on her bed after a few minutes of frenziedly throwing each other against the wonky railings, accompanied by thrusting tongues and incoherent words of mutual appreciation. When Solo had worried out loud that there might be dry rot and they'd both end up on the veranda below, him with his jeans round his thighs and Polly with nothing much left on at all, they'd made the decision to stumble into her room. He'd been so turned on he wasn't sure what to focus on first, but clearly the gorgeous Polly was pretty experienced, presenting him with a condom from God-only-knew-where before wrapping her legs around him and urging him to thrust hard as she straddled him. Moments later one of her hands had taken hold of his and sneaked it between her legs, guiding his movements. In no time it seemed she'd helped herself to a very lyrical orgasm, which brought his own on with such intensity it nearly knocked his head clean off his shoulders.

Solo couldn't think of the last time he'd had such mind-blowing sex.

And with such an amazing woman, who was now saying sweetly, "Oh, yes, Mr-I-fly-solo, this time you took someone with you, right to the ver-ry end."

"Happy ending, huh?" He couldn't help feeling smug, even though he wasn't sure how much of it he could actually claim credit for.

"Oh, yes."

Here was a woman who revelled in her sexuality.

And, hell, he had no problem with that.

No problem at all.

He reached out and toyed with a curl that had fallen across her face, pulling it straight between his finger. "Real corkscrews." He smiled.

"Took hours at the hairdressers."

"Really?"

"Nooo! Why would I? Hate the damn things. Forgot to bring my straightener."

"You wouldn't want to get rid of them, they're classic."

"I don't very often; it depends on my mood."

"Tonight's was bouncy, huh?"

He leaned in, about to kiss her gently on the lips, then thought better of it. Just because they'd had great sex, he didn't need to get sentimental. This was neither the time nor place. Something inside him gripped hard and twisted, threatening to jam the air out of his lungs.

He sank back against the pillows, letting go of the curl, which promptly sprang back into shape.

"Hey, don't go all weird on me." She sounded slightly irritated. Obviously she'd read the sudden shift in his mood. "I get enough of that in my work. Don't need it spoiling my play time."

Solo sucked in a breath. *Play time*—of course. This girl was out for a good time, that was all. Perhaps his first surmising was right. She was on the rebound.

He cleared his throat. "How do you know the groom?"

Her chin retracted slightly as if surprised. "What made you ask that?"

"No reason."

"You sure have odd no reasons."

14

"Is he your ex?" *Solo, crap, mate, you sound like a jealous lover. Shut the frig up.*

"That's not for you to know, Mr Motorbike Man."

Solo shifted his gaze. He deserved that.

"Anyway, what's it to you if he was?"

"Nothing." He shrugged lightly. He really didn't like that this woman had just taken him to heaven, only to knock him right off the nice little cloud he'd been floating on.

She was a one-night adventure. He needed to get that clear in his head.

He sat up abruptly and looked around for his clothes.

She sat up too, folding her arms around bent knees, and even in the semi-dark he caught sight of her lovely breasts squashing against her thighs. Something stirred and pleaded; *one more for the road.*

"You're leaving, then?" Her voice was matter-of-fact but there was ice behind the words. Did she think this was the sum of him? That this was how he behaved with women? When there hadn't been a woman within coo-ee of his cock for nine months. In all honesty, he owed her the biggest bow for bringing his libido back to life with a bang. Literally.

He found his boxers and jeans in a crumpled heap by the bed. Shoved them on, stood, hitched them up and belted his jeans on the tightest hole he could.

"That was amazing. You were amazing," he said.

"And there's a but in there, right?"

"But... I have an early start. I've got to be in Perth first thing."

"It's Sunday tomorrow," Polly pointed out. He guessed this was her social worker voice. Very calm, very smooth.

"Yeah, it's the only day the boss could see me to show me the ropes and do the paperwork. I start *bam*, first light Monday on-site."

Polly bounced to the other side of the bed and snapped on the bedside light. He winced at the onslaught on his retinas and then blinked at the glory of her all lit up. Those breasts had felt amazing, but they looked even more amazing... large dark areolae on perfect creamy orbs, the rounded undulation of her belly, the tiny little Brazilian thing of dark hair between her legs, and—his gaze snagged on a little serpent

15

tattoo on her inner thigh. Oh god, he was salivating... and then she tugged the sheet up to her chin and narrowed her eyes.

He gulped. Dived for his T-shirt and flung it over his head, tucking it fiercely into his jeans with sharp thrusts of his hands.

"Hmm," she said, her lips shaping into a slow smile. "You really do fly solo, don't you?"

He just stared at her. He was the world's most complicated book right now, but she didn't need to know about any of that. Where would he even begin? And then there was the irony of her profession... and his.

Hell, what were the odds of them ever meeting again? Unlikely. Perth was a big enough city for the two of them to rattle around without their paths crossing.

Deliberately, he walked around the side of the bed until he was standing above her. She scooted up the mattress and rested her back against the bedhead, eyeing him warily. He bent down and, knowing he would be a goner if he kissed her mouth, touched his lips gently to the tip of her nose.

As he stepped back, those green eyes flew wide and she blinked as if trying to find words.

"Thank you," he said quietly into the gap. "You'll never know quite how much I appreciated tonight."

As he turned and strode through the French doors, around the veranda and into his own room, Solo could feel her energy snaking after him, though he was unable to make out whether she was angry, surprised, amused or all three. He shoved his feet into his boots, his arms into his jacket, swept all his belongings into his rucksack, grabbed his bike helmet and keys, and exited the room.

Yeah, he knew what he had to do.

He had to ride through the night to forget a certain woman called Polly.

And his demons from back home.

CHAPTER 3

 olly hurried along the hospital corridor, KeepCup clasped tightly in one hand and her bulky work bag flip-flopping over her shoulder.

As usual, she was late for a ward meeting and now her phone was trilling.

Spying an empty seat, she carefully placed her coffee down—you couldn't afford to spill a drop this early on a Monday morning—and located her phone in the depths of her bag just as it switched to message bank.

But not before she'd seen the name "Joe" flash up on the screen.

Guilt jabbed at her gut. She'd been only an hour away from home on the weekend. She could have made a detour and seen her older brother and his wife, said a quick hi to Dad and Mim.

But after Solo had jumped out of her bed like he'd been attacked by a swarm of angry bees, she'd been too pissed off to do anything on Sunday morning other than hop in her little Toyota and speed back to Perth with *Queen's* greatest hits belting out at full decibels.

So no, she hadn't gone home and she hadn't seen Dad, and yes, she should have.

Polly sighed, glanced at the time on the top of the screen, quickly texted, "in meeting call you later" and then, with a couple of gulps of coffee, headed towards Echidna Ward.

When she sidled into her seat at the table, she realised Dr Death (Dr Jonathon Pritchard, head psychiatrist to everyone other than Polly and a few other staff she'd initiated into his alternative title) was nowhere to be seen.

She let out a sigh of relief, opened her bag and removed her notepad and a pen.

There were bound to be new patients after the weekend, and with the way her brain was feeling right now, it would be good to have a few minutes to reset.

Smoothing down her hair to ensure all the crinkles were safely caught in the up-do she'd scraped onto her head this morning, she smiled at Judith across the table.

Judith winked. "All right?" she mouthed, then leaned forward. "How'd the rest of your weekend shape up?"

Polly stifled the tingle of a blush. Judith had stayed at the bride's parents' place, no way would she know anything.

She jabbed a thumb in the air. "Great."

True—until the fizzle of a finale. Amazing, actually. Better sex than she'd had with anyone in recorded history—so natural and easy and, yes, more downright playful than all her short-lived dates and even the six years of falling happily into bed with her dear old fuck-buddy, Jake. She'd reeled through the scenes shamelessly all yesterday: those long, lean limbs and his amazing six pack. And, holy shit, that mouth—hot and demanding, tongue sliding and coaxing, a perfect fit with hers and... and... that totally steamy look on his face as he thrust deep into her...

Oh, no, stop! Shut it down. Now.

Polly crossed her legs under the table and squeezed her clit into silence.

What a bastard, just upping and leaving before she'd had time to order from the dessert menu. No suggestion of "let's exchange phone numbers, meet up again". But why the hell was she bothered about that? She had Tinder, didn't she?

Focusing, she realised she'd doodled phallic shapes all over her nice clean page.

What the hell was her problem?

The nose kiss. Just before he scarpered. That was the problem. It did something weird to her insides, and then there was the sad look in his eyes as he thanked her, like she'd saved his soul from hell demons or something.

Stop fantasising, she ordered herself fiercely as she made hmm-hah noises to Leon, the ward's senior nurse, who was telling her that they'd had four new admissions over the weekend. Oh yes, and that Bernie Bullman had gone AWOL again and been found at the pub holding court over whisky chasers with the Western Dingos rugby team.

Good old Bernie. Made Jack Nicholson look like an amateur.

She'd just turned to a fresh page and was writing the date when she caught the sound of Dr Death's low drone. But when she heard a deeper, smoother, and disturbingly familiar voice in answer, her body turned into static electricity. Polly's head kicked up, her gaze locking onto Dr Death's familiar bald head in the doorway, his beady eyes peering over the top of his glasses at the assembled staff.

And behind him... Christ... oh God, no. *Him.*

Polly's stomach rode into her mouth.

Silver-eyed, piping-hot motorbike man with the perfect bod and stupid smoking habit was standing behind Dr Death, a head and shoulders taller—if you counted the spikes of his short dark hair—amazing pecs concealed under a crisp white shirt, suit jacket stretched over shoulders she'd bitten, yes, actually *bitten,* as she rode her orgasm. Daring to stand there, all neat and tidy, with those hands that had been everywhere on her body clasped neatly in front of him. All serious and *soo fuck-ing* professional.

Bastard.

And then he lifted his head and stared straight at her.

Polly's mind seemed intent on vacating her body. She ground the heels of her pumps into the floor to tether her butt cheeks to the seat. Great waves of heat pulsed up her neck and radiated into her face. She stared back down at her pad and squeezed her pen until the tips of her fingers turned white, then fixed her eyes back on Dr Death's wizened little face as if she'd never seen anything more lovely.

Totally oblivious to her state of inner pandemonium, Dr Death poked his glasses up his nose and turned, first to *him*, the sex *fraudster*, and then back to the assembled team.

"Sorry we're late getting started. I was showing our new psychiatrist around the ward. This is the locum senior registrar I told you would be starting this week. Let me introduce Dr Solomon Jakoby."

~

SOLO ALREADY KNEW she'd be here.

He'd checked.

When he arrived in Perth at 4 a.m. on Sunday morning he'd ridden down to the Swan River, then did what he only ever allowed himself to do in extreme circumstances: smoked two more cigarettes from his stash, one after the other.

Afterwards he'd got out his phone and scrolled through the website of Western State hospital.

Echidna Ward staff, he read.

Psychologist Ben Tan.

Head Nurse, Leon Novac.

Occupational Therapist, Judith Davenport. The photo looked familiar; the pleasant girl-next-door smile and long blonde hair—oh yeah, she'd interrupted them on the hotel patio.

Which likely meant… Yep, sure enough.

Senior Social Worker, Polly Fletcher.

Solo inhaled, let a stream of smoke out the side of his mouth and stroked his thumb over the image. It was the typical mug shot you had taken for passports or work ID, and it certainly didn't present her at her best. Without make-up her complexion was pale and her curls had been harnessed into a tight ponytail, giving her face a round, bland appearance. But those wide green eyes, the full definition of her lovely mouth…

His groin sprang alarmingly to life. Because he knew what those lips were capable of, the way her eyes turned vivid at his touch.

He got up and paced, took another drag, threw the half-smoked butt on the ground and drilled his heel into it.

What were the chances?

He'd lied to her. She'd sure find that out soon enough, wouldn't she? Solo Jakoby, manual labourer turned psychiatrist—slightly different job description. When she'd said she was a social worker he'd freaked out and said the first thing that entered his head. Perth wasn't as big as Sydney when it came to their line of work.

It was supposed to be a one-off. They weren't supposed to ever meet again.

Christ! He'd run away from complications over east, straight into the arms—literally, it seemed—of another one.

So here he was, and here she was. Solo could feel a trickle of sweat running down the back of his collar as he tried to keep his face expressionless.

As their eyes met, colour erupted like hives from her neck up to her cheeks, her mouth forming a momentary O before she snapped her gaze away.

Solo braced his shoulders and made polite noises as Pritchard went laboriously through the introductions.

Judith the occupational therapist gave him a quizzical smile. He smiled blandly back and wondered if his skin was going to shed.

"And," Pritchard was bumbling on in his peculiar toneless voice, "last but not least, Polly Fletcher, our very experienced social worker. Polly can help you out with any practical issues."

An explosion threatened at the back of Solo's throat. He swallowed and almost gagged.

Polly's eyes drilled into him for a second before sliding past his shoulder.

"Hi," she said woodenly to the air.

"Hi," Solo replied. He managed to stop himself tugging at his collar and sat down quickly in the seat next to Pritchard's.

He wasn't quite sure how he survived the meeting, except it involved absolutely not letting his gaze stray in Polly Fletcher's direction. Even when she spoke, her tone firm and confident about finding a patient some temporary accommodation or getting their welfare payments sorted, he managed to studiously keep writing notes, ignoring the buzz in his gut—or was it lower? The fact was, this Polly woman messed with his head, and apparently a number of other parts of his body, too.

Later, when everyone had scattered to get on with the day's work and he'd seen Polly's modest black slacks and pale lilac blouse heading at speed down the corridor, Solo finally found himself in the nursing station in front of a screen full of patient lists.

"Hey there. Good to have you on board." A guy Solo recognised as Ben, the team psychologist, sauntered up.

"Thanks, good to be here."

"Are you interested in group therapy?" Ben said.

Solo gave a grin. "Having some or giving some?"

"Ha, sorry—bad phrasing, I meant, have you ever led therapy groups? Some of the psychiatrists we've had on rotation tend to be more medication-focused and others enjoy getting involved in the talking side of things."

Solo shrugged. He had done his fair bit of psychotherapy in training. "I'm not into psychoanalysis, but I think cognitive therapy combined with medication shows pretty good efficacy."

Under the scrutiny of the guy's earnest dark eyes he felt uncomfortably like he was being analysed.

A moment later Ben's face relaxed into an easy smile and Solo decided maybe he'd misjudged him. At the teaching hospital in Sydney he'd just left, the professional jealousies had got a bit out of control, but maybe here in the west everyone was on friendlier terms. He cocked an eyebrow. "Why do you ask?"

"Oh, just that I'm heading off to Europe for four weeks and that leaves the PTSD group with only one therapist. We prefer for that not to happen. Thought you might like to take on co-leading while I'm away."

Post-traumatic stress disorder. Solo consciously relaxed his spine, breathed in and released it slowly, letting the breath pinch out of his lungs in three measured exhalations. It helped.

"Yeah, sure, if Pritchard doesn't have too many other things lined up, and it doesn't overlap with any ward meetings."

"Oh no, it definitely won't, it's an evening group. That's probably why I'm having trouble getting someone to take it on, if I'm honest, but thought, you know, with..."

"Me being new to Perth and having no social life, you mean?"

Ben gave a polite laugh. "No, not at all. Anyway, happy to talk you through it. Besides, you'd be working alongside another very experienced member of the team."

The hairs on the back of Solo's neck stood to attention. "Oh, right."

"Yeah, Polly, the social worker you met this morning. She's brilliant. The group was her brainchild and basically she holds it all together. Just let her take the lead and you'll get the hang of the dynamics real fast."

What bad joke was the universe playing on him? A momentary image of Polly flipping him onto his back and shaking her curls in his face as he palmed her amazing breasts, nearly erased Solo's last morsel of self-composure. It took a moment before he could trust himself to speak.

"I'll give it some thought and let you know," he muttered and stared back at the computer screen.

CHAPTER 4

*P*olly had barricaded herself in the toilets.

Sooner or later she was going to have to come out and face this frigging mess but, right now, letting her butt cool on the seat seemed like a viable alternative.

There was oodles of work to do. Mondays were like that; patients to interview, paperwork and forms to fill out, the usual disasters of homelessness and government benefits being cut—and here she was, sitting on the loo, wondering what the hell to do next.

Elbows on knees, she let her head sink into her hands on a silent groan. One small curl wiggled out of its restraints and fell over her eye. She flipped at it angrily.

How the hell was she going to deal with this fiasco? She never mixed work with pleasure. It was her golden rule. There was *night-time* Polly: figure-hugging dresses a la the good old days in Hollywood and her collection of heels—Alexander Wang, Louis Vuitton, Jimmy Choo (all purchased second-hand on eBay)—plus her itsy-bitsy Victoria's Secret undies and a trusted pack of ribbed multi-colour condoms in her clutch.

And then there was *work* Polly: sensible slacks and shirts, no make-up, not a single curl allowed to escape. And flat pumps. Designer brands not important. Functionality paramount.

And ne'er the two would meet.

Until now.

The external door to the women's toilet banged open.

"Polly, you in here?"

Urkkk, Judith in stalking mode.

Polly hunkered down and played possum.

"I actually know you're here. I saw you come in ten minutes ago." Long pause. "Poll. Are you okay?"

She'd have to say something or Judith would be scaling the cubicle.

"Sure. Never better."

"That's him, isn't it? The spunky guy from the hotel? I mean, what were the odds of that happening? Like, we were out in the middle of the bush." Judith was in the cubicle next to her, rustling down her knickers.

Polly reeled out reems of toilet paper. "Mmm. Bit weird."

"Did he tell you on Saturday that he was coming to work here?"

"No, of course not. We were just having a casual chat."

"Didn't look that casual to me." Judith giggled on a tinkle.

Polly stood and pulled her knickers up her thighs, chucking the paper into the toilet.

"You blushed, by the way," Judith chirped.

"Did I?"

"Yes, when Death introduced him. You went all blotchy."

Polly would have described her blush more accurately as a bag of melted pink and white marshmallows; an annoying habit her skin broke into every time she got even slightly embarrassed. She blamed it on her rag-tag mix of Irish and English genes that had homogenised somewhere back in the early nineteenth century before being packed onto a boat to Botany Bay for stealing a loaf of bread.

Somehow she'd have to brave this one out.

"It was a surprise, that's all. One of those weird coincidences."

"Are you sure nothing, *you know*, happened?"

"Jude, will you please stop? Okay, I admit, he's cute. But we had a five-minute conversation. That's it."

If lies sent you to hell then there was a little demon stoking up the fires right now, and getting a pitchfork primed with Polly Fletcher's name inscribed on it.

Reluctantly, she unlocked her cubicle and came out to survey the damage in the mirror.

Judith glanced at her as they both washed their hands. Polly got a paper towel and dabbed cold water on the V of still-mottled flesh above the top button of her blouse.

"I think they've turned the heating up. Either that or I'm in premature menopause," she grumbled.

"You're twenty-eight," Judith pointed out.

"It can happen."

"Not to you. You're too fecund. Don't you think fecund is a lovely word?" Judith mused. "I wish I were more fecund. Maybe Mark would propose if I were fecund like you. Do you want some of my foundation? Our skin tones are about the same."

Polly hesitated. Her strict no make-up policy ensured that if she bumped into an ex-patient on one of her after-dark forays, the possibility of recognition would be remote.

Except now, it seemed, the situation was much, much worse. Her new doctor colleague had intimately examined her and she was going to have to play all professional, sit next to him in meetings and patient assessments, maybe even, heaven forbid, be in a group therapy situation together. Worse, she'd have to resist morning cake in the staffroom while those silver eyes surveyed her every move across the table.

At least this would make her new diet a complete breeze. With those eyes on her lips, her salivary glands would dry up. No need to start the lemon diet she'd been researching. The sudden image of Solo's gorgeous mouth sinking into a cream doughnut, his tongue licking those long fingers, had the blotchiness threatening to re-emerge with a vengeance.

She grabbed the foundation from Judith and plastered a layer around her neck and dabbed two blobs onto her cheeks. Countering was her best bet, she decided.

"So, how are you and Mark?"

"Oh, you know, much the same. Chugging along." Mark was Judith's childhood sweetheart. He worked as the manager of a packaging company and was terminally boring. Honestly, Judith with her coltish legs, truly lovely smile and seriously warm heart could do better than a guy whose idea of being a bit daring was watching two episodes of *Orange is the New Black* in the same evening.

Give me a chance, sweet Judith, thought Polly. *I'd do for you what I did for Alice. Find you your Mr Perfect.* She was so darn good at matchmaking. Strictly reserved for *other* people, of course.

With a last look in the mirror, Polly hitched back her shoulders and gave her now-evened-up complexion a final pat.

There. Utterly professional, cool, calm, and collected. *And that, Dr Solo Jakoby, is all you are ever going to see of Polly Fletcher from now on*, she told herself as she marched out with her head held high.

So why, as she followed Judith, trying not to let her eyes flick wildly around the ward for a sighting of hunky suited shoulders and thick cropped dark hair, did a small part of her want to throw a holy fucking tantrum?

Fecundity. That's what it did to you. All those freakin' hormones.

But when she walked into the nurses' station a few minutes later, Polly's professional façade almost crumbled. Her breath hitched at the sight of Solo, his head on one side, brows pensive, deep in conversation with Ben Tan. Brooding and sexy. Freakin' forget the psychiatrist's couch. He was the kind of shrink whose lap you'd jump right into.

As for Ben, he had the look he got when he was buttering someone up: pleasant, eager, interested. The perfect psychologist putting you at ease, bum hitched on the edge of the desk, one leg swinging casually.

Oh yes, he was up to something for sure.

Polly watched Solo's silver eyes narrow in response. He looked less than enthusiastic about whatever Ben was suggesting

As Solo gave a final nod and turned away, Ben stood up and spotted her. His face lit up. "Here she is!" He grinned. "Polly, I think I've found our fill-in therapist for while I'm on leave."

Shite. The PTSD group.

Ben. Europe.

Double shite.

Not Solo.

Not her co-facilitator.

Oh, *no way.*

~

SOLO'S HEART revved like his faithful Ducati when he went full throttle on the accelerator. Polly looked so prim and proper, which made her almost hotter than when he was ripping off her silky little pyjama shorts. Something about knowing what she was really capable of made him jittery as all hell as she eyed him with cool professionalism. Before he knew it, the words were flying out of his mouth, the backdrop to a story he'd prefer not to share.

"PTSD is an interest of mine, I guess. I worked with quite a few ex-military back from Afghanistan, so I was quite intrigued when Ben suggested it. Hadn't exactly agreed yet, but—"

"And I haven't accepted," Polly cut in smoothly. "We don't know if our facilitation styles are compatible." Her chin tilted and her eyes gleamed. "Can I ask, do you prefer group therapy to working on construction sites, Dr Jakoby?"

Ben was watching them with a puzzled frown. "You—um, know each other from somewhere?"

"Nooo," they both chorused in unison.

Fucking get me out of here.

"We bumped into each other before work. This morning, that is," Polly filled in.

Her eyes stared him down, china-doll wide and innocent, but issuing some wordless challenge. Then she draped herself behind a nearby desk and logged onto the hospital network.

"Right," Ben said. "Perhaps we could all have lunch together and discuss it."

"Can't. I'm way too busy today." Polly pulled a face at the screen. "Shit; I forgot Mavis Clegg's husband and daughter are coming in at nine for family counselling. Gotta go. Why don't you two have lunch and you can tell *Dr Jakoby* all about the PTSD group." Her shoulders moved in a shrug. "Guess I can't be choosy who I co-lead with. It's not like anyone else has offered to give up their Wednesday evenings."

Solo watched with a sense of helplessness as she swung out of the chair and practically flounced out of the room, the sway of her butt in those neat slacks sending inappropriate messages to his groin even now. A curl popped out of the top of her bun and bounced as she closed the door behind her.

"Ok-*aaay*." Ben raised his hands in the air. "She's a bit grumpy this morning. Guess we'll be discussing it without Polly. I'll see you at 12. Hospital canteen. Level 5. Food is edible, mostly. Avoid the rissoles at all costs." He picked up his laptop. "Sorry about my colleague. She must have got out of bed on the wrong side."

Solo was trying to form an answer when Leon walked in and saved him. "Have you had a chance to review Bernie's notes? I need you to talk to him about actually taking his meds, not flushing them down the toilet."

"Sure." Solo jumped up, glad to focus on having a job to do. Clearly, he'd have to find a way to cope with this snitchy professional Polly—hopefully her barbed tongue would be enough to get his libido under control over the coming weeks.

Right now, with the way his body was behaving, that seemed like no easy task.

Luckily the day went quickly, one patient interview after another. A lunchtime catch-up with Ben clarified that the PTSD group happened on Wednesday evenings between 7 and 9 and was for outpatients who were working but struggling with their symptoms.

Confidence started to return.

Yep, he could do this.

He caught sight of Polly twice: once as he was about to enter a patient interview room with Bernie, as she chatted to a nurse. And again when she was talking to a young woman who was curled up and rocking in her chair. From the safe distance of the nurses' station, he watched as Polly squatted down next to the woman, clearly reassuring her. She placed a hand gently on the woman's arm and handed her a tissue box.

This was a very different Polly. An empathetic, gentle Polly. Suddenly Solo recalled the way she'd looked at him, wide-eyed, the momentary glint of vulnerability as he kissed the tip of her nose.

And for some weird reason his heart almost ground to a halt.

As Solo climbed onto his motorbike at the end of a long, tiring first day, he was aware of a figure close by, and then, holy shit, there she was beside him, one hip jutting, her big work bag over her shoulder, car keys jingling in her fingers.

"Good first day?" Her face was bland but her eyes sparkled dangerously.

"Great."

She flashed a too-bright smile. "Guess it beats huffing and puffing on a building site."

He sighed, looked down at his hands. "Sorry about that. I guess I thought—"

"We'd never have to cross paths again? Reasonable deduction. I would have thought so too. A quick shag out in the middle of the bush and on your bike. Literally, it would seem," she finished with a laugh. Not a particularly nice one.

He didn't answer. The silence stretched on for several hideously awkward moments.

"So, Dr Jakoby—"

"Solo."

"Solo-*man* Jakoby."

Jeesh, she was being Miss Bitch. Guess he couldn't really blame her. He eyed her warily.

Her head kicked back in a gesture that told him he was barely worth her breath. "Okay, *Solo*, I guess seeing as we have to work together, and it seems you may be running a therapy group with me, we had better clear the air." She stepped forward, dropped her voice. "Just for the record, I love sex. We met by chance and it seemed you quite liked sex too, so, we had sex—really nice sex, I have absolutely no complaints on that front. But I never, ever mix work with pleasure. So there's no risk of me coming on to you, again. I thought I should make that crystal clear to avoid any further misunderstandings."

"Very good policy."

She bared perfect teeth at him. "Fantastic, we're on the same page then." An exaggerated eye-roll. "So *good* to clear the air, it's been worrying away at me all day." Her foot, he noticed, was tap-tapping on the tarmac. "Just one thing I'd love to know before we put it all behind us. Why did you lie to me about your work?"

He shrugged. "Guess I thought it might spoil the fun. It can put people off, once they hear you're a shrink."

"By *people,* I presume you mean *women.*" She gave a shrug and her bulky bag slipped. "Must admit I'd never have placed you as one. Psychiatrist, I mean, not casual shagger. You're clearly great at the latter." She yanked the bag almost viciously back onto her shoulder. "Though something was a bit off about the construction work thing. I couldn't quite put my finger on it at the time, but of course... now it makes total sense."

She cocked her head, eyes too bright. "So, your official chat-up line is manual labourer? Rough and ready works, huh?"

Hell, no. He wasn't prepared to let her think he was like that. He didn't do casual sex the way she clearly did, and for some reason that fact stabbed him in the solar plexus.

He met her exaggerated innocent look steadily. "I've never said that to a woman before in my life."

A perfect eyebrow flicked up. "No?"

"No. Despite what you may think, I'm not in the habit of wild Saturday night *shags* in hotels. And yes, you're right, it was very nice sex. Don't worry, I won't make another move. Strictly professional from now on."

He shoved his helmet onto his head, flicked up the visor. "If you don't mind, I'll be on my way—it's been a long first day."

She nodded, lips curling. "Go home and have yourself a smoko, why don't you?"

He narrowed his eyes at her, shoved the key in the ignition, and revved the engine.

As he drove off, Solo made sure he did a couple of zigzags along the street, just in case Polly Fletcher thought for one moment that he actually cared about the possibility of never having sex with her again.

Very. Very. Nice. Sex.

CHAPTER 5

This was bad.

She'd been talking to herself most of the drive home, muttering and cursing out loud. When she'd finally navigated her car into a sardine-sized parking space in the narrow street, several houses up from hers, Polly's mood was in deep conversation with the soles of her shoes. Storming inside, she slammed the front door and threw her bag in a crumpled heap on the floor. She'd spent the last thirty minutes replaying her conversation with Solo, batting around in her head what she should have said, how much cooler and wittier she could have been.

Saturday night shag, he'd called it. By default, that meant her. She was a shag. A shag was a rather ugly sea bird with a big beak. Not a woman.

Nice to know.

Except a part of her, the small rational part that was no bigger than her pinkie right now, knew she'd started it. She'd used the shag word first, not Solo. She wanted to hate him, but it was actually herself she hated for completely losing her cool and behaving like a bitch in the first place, and that made it even worse. She stomped into the kitchen and yanked open the fridge to be met by a shrivelled carrot, two sticks of celery and a half-consumed pot of hummus.

Oh, and three lemons.

No way could she face starting the lemon diet today. She scanned the shelf for anything worth drinking. But she'd cleared out the alcohol in anticipation of the new eating plan and besides, she rarely let herself drink when she was alone. That was a slippery slope and she knew too well where it could lead. Nor, for that matter, would Rowena take kindly to her raiding her stash of fine reds.

Especially when Rowena was overseas visiting Alice and Aaron. By rights that should make Polly really happy, because pairing those two up had been her *piece de resistance*.

Except right now the house felt so damn lonely without them.

She grabbed a glass, held it under the tap and filled it to the top with water, before sinking down at the kitchen table. She wasn't one to fret, didn't allow herself bad moods. Life was too short. And even if her childhood had been less than happy, when Gran had bought her a thumbed copy of the kid's classic *Pollyanna* from the book exchange van that used to rotate around their wheat-belt towns, she'd just about inhaled the "be glad" philosophy. They shared the same name, more or less, so in her nine-year-old logic, they were almost the same person. Always see the bright side, find the silver lining in even the worst experience, right?

Except now.

Because now she didn't feel like being glad. She had prickly sensations behind her eyelids and her nose was oddly stuffy.

The guy seemed to have got to her. Which was unheard of. That didn't happen to her, did it?

So what was it about Solo Jakoby? *Doctor* Solo Jakoby. Sure, yeah, mind-blowing chemistry, fantastic sex, yadda, yadda, yadda, but there was something else, wasn't there? Something brooding and troubled about him, something that belied his super-sexy looks, the Jack Sparrow swagger and repartee of the other night.

It hooked her in, intrigued her. Pissed her off.

Gah! A few days of proximity and she'd start to notice all those jerky annoying things that always put her off guys. He'd develop a nervous tic in one eye, or keep saying some annoying word, like *seriously*, or *joy*, or he'd eat pickled onions straight out of the jar for lunch and talk with his mouth full. Besides, she reminded herself, she had the sticking power of a Teflon pan when it came to dating, so she'd be over the whole thing in the blink of an eye.

Straightening up, Polly opened the freezer, feeling relieved when she found one Weight Watchers' chicken korma staring back at her. The lemon diet could start tomorrow. Lemon juice for breakfast. Lemon and rice soup for lunch. Shit, did she even have any rice?

About to forage through the pantry, she heard her phone ring and had to sprint down the passage to her bag. When she managed to grapple it out, Joe's name flashed to message bank. Again. Damn, she'd meant to call him on her way home but all her obsessing had pushed it out of her mind.

She rang back and her brother picked up immediately.

"Poll, finally. Did you listen to my voice message?"

"Um, no, sorry, super-busy day at work. Is everything okay?"

"Yeah, I was calling about Dad's seventieth."

"Oh, of course." Guilt did a 180-degree twist in her gut. She kept trying to forget the fact that Dad was turning seventy in a month and a party was planned up at the farm.

"You are coming, aren't you?" Joe's voice held an edge of worry. Her older brother was in charge of holding the farm together, overriding the bad times, putting money aside during the good times while Dad swung from frenziedly working 24/7 to drinking binges that saw him disappear for days on end.

Polly sighed and tugged her hair out of its confines—she could almost hear her curls sigh with relief. "Of course, what do you want me to do?"

"Mim's making up a list."

"Right. Are Dad and Mim in a good space?" She tried to keep the cynicism out of her voice.

"Yeah, they've actually been getting on well recently."

"None of Dad's dark nights of the soul then?"

Joe laughed like a man guarding enemy lines. "Not for a while now.

Fingers crossed." He paused and Polly knew what was coming next. "Call him, Poll, he'd love to hear from you."

"Sure," she said lightly. "I messaged him last week. He didn't reply."

"You know Dad doesn't check his mobile. He's completely old school. Ring on the landline."

"Tomorrow. Promise," she said quickly.

"Good girl. And how are you? Missing Alice?"

Polly traced a pattern in the dust on the hall console with her finger. Time she did some cleaning. She missed her best friend more than she'd imagined. Alice's quirky smile, her big brown eyes behind her glasses, nose buried in a book at the kitchen table. Herbal tea in a mug beside her.

But hey, she didn't regret a thing, did she? Helping Aaron realise he was madly in love with Alice had to be one of the finest things Polly had achieved in recent years.

The words "always the bridesmaid, never the bride" popped into her head as she answered, "It's fine. Great to have the place to myself. Organising wild orgies and smashing Rowena's antique glasses—beats washing up."

Rowena, Alice's mum, ran the best second-hand bookshop in Perth: The Book Genie. Polly had worked for her when she arrived in Perth from the bush and desperately needed a job. A couple of years back when her rent had escalated beyond affordable on a social worker's salary, Rowena had offered her a room. And here they'd been ever since: Polly, Rowena and Alice, a happy trio of oddball women who adored each other. Until Alice finally got her happy ever after. And found her long-lost father and went to visit him in England.

Joe was chuckling. "Rowena would kill you if you broke her best crockery."

"Okay, then, lighting fires with her first-edition classics."

"Liar. How's work?"

"Work's… fine."

"Do I detect a note of hesitation?"

Joe knew her too well. Being six years her senior, he'd always looked out for her when things weren't good with Dad and Mum. Gran and he had helped her to choose happiness instead of continually chewing on the proverbial shit sandwich.

"Oh, just busy, you know how it is with mental health."

"We could sure do with your skills up here; can't get social workers for love or money in the wheatbelt."

"I'm used to being in the city now, Joe. Not sure I could take living in a small country town again. But you? How are you and Kate?"

He paused. "Funny you should ask. We're expecting."

Polly squealed and nearly dropped the phone. "OMG, when?"

"We're just past the three months' phase. You know, with the miscarriages, we wanted to keep this one quiet from everyone, which is why I didn't say last time we spoke."

Polly bounced on the balls of her feet. "I'm going to be an auntie."

"Yep—the scan looks pretty much like the little fella's stuck in for keeps. Not that you can tell for sure, but Kate's been sick as a dog, which is always a good sign, apparently."

"Does *little fella* mean a boy?"

"We're choosing not to find out, but it's a hunch, I guess... or wishful thinking maybe..."

"I'm so, so happy for you." Polly's eyes were prickling again, this time with joy. Joe and Kate had been trying for a baby for three years now, with several heartbreaking miscarriages. It was the best of news, and maybe it would give Dad reason to shape up once and for all.

They chatted a bit more after Polly had finally calmed down, mainly about the party arrangements. When she placed her phone down, she let out a big sigh. Tomorrow she would phone Dad. Not now. Staying happy meant having as little contact with the past as possible, and too much of the past surfaced at the sound of Dad's voice.

She stopped still for a second, breath hitching in her throat. She hated remembering the shitty times. The skin of her forehead was a painful band as she hurried back into the kitchen, ripped the lid off the container and shoved the curry in the microwave.

Wallowing in the past never helped anyone. Look at Dad: blaming Mum for leaving. Blaming his time in Vietnam for his drinking problem. Blame, blame, blame.

She'd vowed she would never, ever do that.

No, she chose to help people improve their lives. Because that was what worked. Understand your past but live in the *now*; make the changes you can and leave the rest behind.

Oh yes, she knew how to handle personal pain. Rely on yourself. The thought made her feel a tad more like her usual optimistic self again. She opened the microwave, jabbed a fork into the chicken and gave it a vigorous stir.

And when she'd lost these extra ten kilos, heck, there'd be no stopping her, would there?

Polly Fletcher versus the world. Tight butt cheeks, slender thighs and all.

She looked at the little square of steaming plastic and her glass of water, and something inside her rebelled. Joe and Kate were having a baby. Surely this called for a celebration?

"Oh, fuck it," she said, then grabbed her mobile and rang Judith.

When Judith picked up, Polly barely allowed her a "hi" before rushing in. "Fancy joining me for a glass of bubbly at the pub? I'm going to be an auntie!"

SOLO GUESSED this was what was meant by the expression not enough room to swing a cat. In this case, even a very small cat with a very short tail. The walls of his new room were barely the span of his straightened arms. It was one of those modern townhouses that should really only be described as a shoebox, in a suburb inhabited mostly by young professionals. He'd barely met the guy he was renting from since he moved in. All he knew was that he was an extremely tall dude with a terrible haircut who worked as an accountant and needed help paying the mortgage.

His name was Carter, but, he'd told Solo with a grin that lit up his otherwise rather unremarkable face, "Everyone calls me Carts."

Apart from that, all Solo had deduced about Carts so far was that he wasn't into crockery or cutlery, because there seemed to be very little of it around. Apparently it saved on the washing up, but when he decided to rent out a room, maybe he could have thought about buying a few more plates and an extra knife and fork?

Solo sighed, placed his bike helmet on the bed and peeled off his leather jacket. He needed to unpack the contents of his rucksack, still sitting in the corner of the room from when he got here yesterday. He'd literally brought just what he could carry on his back. One suit, two work shirts, two pairs of jeans and two T-shirts. He'd have to go shopping at some stage but for now he'd make do.

Guess this was what happened when you decided to duck and run.

The last text message had made the decision for him.

He'd erased it straight away, but it was grafted onto his eyeballs.

I'm better off dead.

Fuck you for fucking that up.

Now U R dead to me.

He'd known the best thing was to leave for a while. Get out of Sydney, let everything calm down. Allow the treatment to start to take effect.

Hopefully after a few months…

He closed his eyes for a second and another image, of a gorgeous woman eyeing him with a serious degree of animosity a mere half hour ago, jumped into his head. He ruffled a hand through his hair. God, they needed to clear the air. Otherwise working with Polly was going to be hell.

And he'd taken this locum position to get away from hell, hadn't he?

Right now, he didn't want to think. What he wanted was a drink. There must be a bar or a pub close by somewhere. He bounded down the stairs to find Carts coming through the front door, swinging a briefcase in one bony hand.

"Just the guy I was hoping to see," Solo managed with false cheer. "Where's the best pub round here?"

Carts, who had the look of a man bowed down from a day dealing with bad-tempered small business owners, noticeably brightened. "Hell, yeah, I could do with a drink. Shit of a day. Let me go change and I'll take you to the best Irish pub in Perth."

"Cool," Solo agreed, almost salivating at the thought of an icy cold draft beer.

"Yep, imaginatively named the Shamrock. Been going there for years. It's a fifteen-minute walk. We can grab a bite to eat, too."

At least they wouldn't have to fight over the one knife, fork and spoon, Solo decided as he watched Carts' long legs leaping up the stairs two at a time. Maybe after a couple of pints and some comfort food like beef and Guinness pie—didn't all Irish pubs serve beef and Guinness pie?—he'd feel better about his move to Perth.

Feel better about a certain curvaceous, insanely sexy and totally off-limits someone.

Maybe even feel better about himself.

CHAPTER 6

"*T*his is nice." Judith sat bolt-upright on a stool in the corner of the Shamrock sipping elegantly at her prosecco. "I don't normally do this on a Monday."

Polly grinned, hooking her feet on the rungs of her own stool. "You don't normally do this on any day of the week. You need to come out with the girls more often."

Judith's face fell. "Mark likes me home with him. He's not mad on me socialising. Mind you, I have to say he doesn't mind spending hours at his computer gaming and drinking with his mates when it suits."

"That's plain wrong."

"I guess it's been a gradual thing."

"How long now?"

Judith frowned. "What do you mean?"

"How long have you been waiting around, cooking for him, cleaning up after him, living in hope that he'll finally get around to popping the question?"

"Oh, I'm not. That comment in the toilet about him proposing was a joke. We're absolutely fine just living together."

Jude's lie was so well-rehearsed her nose had given up growing.

"Nonsense!" Polly huffed indignantly. "You're the marrying and baby

41

kind. You knit baby clothes in your spare time, you crochet, you do macramé..."

"I'm an occupational therapist, that's what everyone expects of us, so why disappoint?" Judith laughed, swiping a good-natured hand at Polly's arm and missing. "Anyway, I knit them for my friends' babies. It's a nice thing to do."

That was hardly surprising, considering Judith was officially in the top ten list of the world's nicest people. Which was probably why she'd put up with Mark for so long. Polly didn't get how you could lie down, spray paint the word *"welcome"* onto yourself, and let a man wipe his feet all over you. When she lay down for a man it was a completely different welcome on offer... and a very short-lived one at that.

Say g'day, play, and move right along.

And then the memory of Solo's hands cupping her breasts and his warm lips coaxing her nipples into hungry peaks sent such a throb to her sex, she almost winced. Okay, so she'd had fun, but if ever there was a reason to move right along, it was the fact that she'd be working with the guy. Quickly, she reverted to Judith's love life. "Remind me how long you two have been together?"

Judith hid behind the curtain of her long blonde hair. "Twelve years," the answer came in a very small voice.

"So you were...?"

"Seventeen."

"Right. That's a hell of a long time. How often do you do it these days?"

Judith blushed to the roots of her hair. "God, do you—is that what I think you mean?" She cast Polly a horrified look. "Yes, you really do—honestly, Polly, I'll never get used to how direct you are about these things."

Polly popped her eyes. "What are *'these things'*? Ball-bearings, egg cups, garden gnomes? Just say it, Jude. Sex. S.E.X. It's perfectly natural and normal."

Judith gulped down a large mouthful of prosecco, her eyes watering as she lowered her glass. "For you, yes, Polly Fletcher, the sexologist. Not for me."

Polly laughed. "What's wrong with discussing your sex life with a friend?"

"It's embarrassing."

"Only if you let it be. Besides, I tell you stuff." Apart from the last adventure; that particular little interlude she would take to her grave.

"That's different."

"Why?"

Judith giggled. "You actually have something worth telling. Besides, no-one ever mentioned the word 'sex' when I was growing up. If it ever got to a kissing scene in a movie, Dad would say, 'Time for a cup of tea, Marg', and Mum would fuss off to make one with a lot of harrumphing and Dad would stomp around and pick up his newspaper and rustle through it, and if you were hoping to immerse yourself in how lovely it was to see Brad Pitt making out with Angelina Jolie you'd feel so awkward you'd have to suddenly take a pee break instead. Not exactly the recipe for feeling comfortable around S.E.X, is it?"

"At least you've got insight."

"Are you therapising me?"

Polly laughed. Maybe Jude was right, maybe she would look up sex therapy post-graduate training when she got home tonight. "Dare you to 'fess up."

Judith's blush intensified as she stared into her glass. "Once a month, on average."

"Who initiates?"

"Oh, c'mon, I'm not going into the finer details." Judith's eyes rolled. "You've squeezed enough out of me already."

Polly smirked. "So *you* do, right?"

Judith's shoulders bunched into a sort of shrug. "Maybe."

"Oooo—kay."

Judith had begun to fiddle with the ends of her hair, which Polly guessed was her cue to back off a bit. Two glasses of prosecco on a very empty stomach set off her tendency towards increased candour—okay, *bluntness*. And, sure, she was pushy in a playful way, but she never meant it *unkindly*. To give Judith time to regroup, she swung to face the bar and beckoned to Paddy, the Shamrock's beefy, adorable barman, who came sauntering over.

"Poll. What can I do for you?" He cracked his knuckles and flexed inked biceps as if in anticipation.

"Don't flirt, I know you're taken."

"Sad but true." Paddy pulled a face that said happy but true. Paddy was the picture of devotion. All brawn and ink and shaved head, still madly in love with the woman who'd tempted him to leave his beloved Ireland for Australia fifteen years earlier.

"What brings you here so early in the week, Poll?"

Polly raised her chin proudly. "I'm celebrating—just heard I'm going to be an auntie."

"Congratulations." Paddy's grin cut a swathe across his face. "You want some practice changing nappies? I've got three you can skill up on."

Paddy had six kids at last count. His wife Shereen had squeezed out twin girls eleven months ago, barely a year after little Adam appeared on the scene.

"Think I'll pass on that," Polly replied swiftly. "I'm going to be a hands-off auntie in the poop department. Strictly cuddles only."

"Coward."

"Some of us aren't built for dealing with the icky bits. Ask Judith, she'll do it, she loves everything about babies. She secretly sniffs baby's heads when no-one's looking."

"I do not!" Judith squealed indignantly.

Paddy's grin swung to Judith. "I'm with you on that; I'm thinking of bottling my 'Baby Head Blend'. Reckon it'd make a me a fortune."

Judith managed a weak laugh.

"Jude and I work together. Apart from baby-head sniffing, she's our team occupational therapist at the hospital."

Paddy's face lit up. "Craft? Even better. If you want a career change, we could do with a nanny."

Judith's mouth turned down. "Why is it as soon as someone mentions I'm an OT people just think of basket weaving and stuffing toy rabbits?"

Paddy's eyebrows waggled. "Sounds fun."

"Fun? Can we join in?"

Polly wasn't expecting the addition of another voice. She knew that rumbly tone—Carts.

Her foot slipped from the stool rung as she swivelled, tipping her headlong into a very firm, hard wall of muscle. Definitely *not* Carts. A waft of clean male, and something subtler and *intimately* familiar hit her nostrils. At the same time her fingers splayed against firm pecs, and a hand steadied her shoulder. Something about that touch sent a shiver along her spine. Her eyes flew up, and oh *fuck*, here she was again, just about drowning in a pair of sinful silver eyes.

Abruptly, she righted herself as Solo drew his hand away. Cheeks flaming, Polly turned quickly to the familiar giant next to him.

"Carts, what are you doing here?" she heard herself say, a good few notes higher than her normal speaking voice. *And what's he doing with you?* a voice screamed at a thousand decibels inside her brain.

"I just about live here," Carts said with a grin. "You should know that."

"It's Monday." Which was kind of illogical, because she and Judith were here, weren't they?

"So? Mondays are good; nice and quiet, and you get served quicker, eh, Pad?" Carts grinned, then his hound-dog eyes slid onto Judith and widened. "Hello there, I'm Carts."

Judith turned a faint shade of pink. "Hi, I'm Judith, I work with Polly."

Polly couldn't help but see the way Carts' eyes lingered. Even in her heightened state of arousal—no, wrong word choice—abject horror, she managed to file that little piece of information away.

"This is my new housemate," Carts continued, half turning towards Solo while still ogling Judith. "Solo Jakoby."

Polly kept staring hard at Carts, who was staring harder at Judith, who was almost bouncing on her seat with glee staring at Solo. "Hello again," Judith said, eyes popping. "Wow, these coincidences just keep cropping up, don't they?" She turned to Carts. "Solo has just started working with us at the hospital as our new psychiatrist."

"Really? Classic." Carts looked at Judith like she had just spouted a pearl of ancient wisdom.

Polly cringed. Any second she'd have to acknowledge Solo... *Okay, large sinkhole. Open. Swallow. Now, please...*

Her heart bounced painfully against her ribs as she snuck a glance and caught Solo's mouth twisting in that laconic sideways smile that she would totally wallow in if there was no history to it.

"Seems we're doomed to keep meeting," he observed drily.

"Yeah, *Groundhog Day.*" Inwardly she cringed. He'd think she was a permanent bitch at this rate.

He didn't blink. "Or *50 First Dates.*"

"Oh, I love that movie sooo much," Judith threw in.

"That's the one where she loses her memory, right?" Carts' eyes beamed in on Judith's glowing face.

Carts, you are so blatantly trying to impress, one part of Polly's brain thought abstractly as a more primitive part tried to deal with the steady thrum in her vulva. This was utterly crazy. It had to stop, but the more she tried to control it, the more her body seemed to want to hurl itself at Solo's chest, sneak her fingers around his neck, sucker her mouth shamelessly onto his. And he was wearing another black T-shirt, just like the one she'd wriggled up his torso and ripped over his head only two—*two*—crazy nights ago.

If only it was *50 First Dates* and she could forget and start all over again.

And keep on doing it.

She flailed an arm behind her to grab her glass, missed and knocked it over, sending bubbly liquid gushing down the front of her jeans.

Oh, flying fucks. Paddy threw over a bar towel. Solo caught it and handed it to her, straight-faced, but she knew that delectable cheek crease was hovering.

"Thanks."

"Pleasure." Somehow that one word zapped down the length of her spine and sent heat spinning into her abdomen.

Pushing back the blush that was about to joyride into her cheeks, she busied herself dabbing at her crotch. Carts ordered a couple of pints of draft beer and offered a drink to Judith, who primly refused, and another to Polly, who refused then changed her mind and asked for a gin and tonic, all the time painfully aware of every movement Solo made.

They sat and drank, both Solo and Polly remaining doggedly silent while Judith and Carts exchanged detailed rundowns of their favourite movies. Have you seen that new black comedy series on Netflix? What's it called... yeah, that one... You haven't seen it yet? God, you absolutely must watch it, you'd love it, can't remember the name but it's the one where she runs over the other woman's husband and... blah-de-blah-de-blah.

Polly glowered at their animated faces. Carts and Judith were obviously picking up on energy beaming out from some great big data cloud of attraction in a virtual sky. Meanwhile, back on Planet Embarrassment she and Solo were behaving like dark matter, both repelling and sucking each other closer at the same time.

Finally Judith's phone beeped and, glancing at her message, her face took on a slightly pinched look and she jumped up. Flicking her hair behind her ear, she bent and grabbed her bag off the floor. "That was Mark wondering where I've got to. Better dash. I've only had one and a half glasses, that should still mean I'm fine to drive, shouldn't it?"

Polly nodded. After two proseccos and a G&T, she was anything but fine to drive, which meant taking an Uber yet again. And picking her car up after work tomorrow, damn it. Her fun evening seemed to have disintegrated, leaving nothing to show for it but an embarrassing damp patch between her legs.

Carts sprang up too. "I'll walk you to your car."

"Oh, no, really," Judith protested.

"No, no, I insist, it's late. Polly will vouch for me. I'm not a mad axe murderer."

"He's not a mad axe murderer," Polly said. *"Here's Johnny!"*

Carts delivered a hurt look and Judith patted his arm solicitously. "Don't worry, she's just as mean to me. That's really sweet of you, thanks."

As she watched them depart, Polly's heart sank, rose, then sank again, like a bobbing cork.

After an awkward moment Solo said, "Fancy a game of pool?"

Polly cast him a squinty look from under one eyebrow. "Is this like when parents suggest kids help with the washing up so they don't have to look at each other during awkward conversations?"

He shrugged. "Were you planning on having an awkward conversation?"

"You tell me."

Solo banged down his glass on the bar. "Jesus, are you always this infuriating?"

Polly tried to look innocent. "Probably."

"Okay." He held his hands up. "Please yourself, I'll go and finish my pint down the other end of the bar."

"Fine. You do that."

Abruptly he got up, but as he made to push past her she found her hand had connected with his forearm. The muscle flexed, his skin warm under her touch. She didn't even know what she was going to say but as his eyes met hers, there was a cloud of hurt there and something caught in her throat. She muttered, "Forget I said that—sure, let's play a game of pool."

For a split second she was certain Solo was going to shake her off, his face hard and tight, then his expression softened and, oh god, that glorious little smile tugged at the corner of his lips. Little creases shunted at the skin around his eyes, adding contours to a face that was already way too enticing.

"Okay, then," he said. "You're on."

Dark matter, thought Polly as she followed the sway of Solo's lean hips towards the pool table. *We are totally dark matter.*

Capable of mutual annihilation.

CHAPTER 7

*N*ever had Solo wanted to light a cigarette quite as much as he did now.

Anger warred in his gut with an even stronger urge to grab the hand Polly had placed on his arm, drag her out of the bar into the warm night air, find a dark alley somewhere and kiss her senseless.

Abruptly, he picked up the pool cue, turned and passed it to Polly, making sure his gaze didn't fix anywhere in particular, because every part of her seemed to turn him on. He wouldn't be surprised if her big toe turned him on... he flicked a glance down to see glittery silver nails on toes encased in strappy sandals, and had to turn away as his jeans tightened.

He put the coin in the slot and balls tumbled out. When he turned back, Polly was standing with one hip kicked out, busily chalking the end of her cue with fast little strokes of her fingertips. His gaze dipped to the dark stain at the v of her thighs, and he wished his eyes hadn't been drawn there. Everything about this woman shouted sex, great sex, sex he wanted so much more of.

You're just lonely, mate.

Of course, that's why she was affecting him so much. He had no friends here; he'd buried his pop eight weeks ago and then there was the hideous mess with Drew.

He frowned fiercely at his pool balls as he scattered them on the table. Sydney was thousands of miles away, and right now he needed to focus on getting one up on Polly Fletcher. Whipping her ass at pool would do for starters.

"Who's going first?" she threw at him with a little upward flick of her eyebrows.

"I'll toss a coin." He pulled out his wallet from his back pocket, winkled out a dollar coin and threw the coin in the air, catching it.

"What's your call?"

"Heads."

He drew his hand away, took a glance. "Tails. I start."

"*Pphhht.*"

When she pouted like that it conjured up… oh fuck, never mind. He grinned to hide the fact that his brain had just migrated way down south. God, this girl hated to lose at anything. Feisty. A wildcat, in bed and out. Not like anyone he'd ever met before. Not at all like Emma…

Solo pulled himself up short. He was going to enjoy the moment, not let the past spoil it. He bent down, ordered his brain to be rational, and putted his balls with careful precision. Three scattered into separate corners, two netted. He cast Polly a glance over his shoulder and had the satisfaction of seeing her eyes flick quickly from his butt. She bit her lip and flounced past him.

She flunked, hitting so hard that one ball actually bounced off the felt liner. She swore under her breath. Solo smiled.

The game seemed to see-saw infuriatingly. One ball to him, one to Polly. He got distracted every time she bent down and her full butt cheeks wiggled in his face. And then, worse still, she started to ask questions.

"Okay, Dr Jakoby, since we have no choice, we might as well get to know each other, *professionally.*" She emphasised the word as she waltzed past with a little jab of her elbow into his ribs.

He leant on his cue and eyed her with the expression he used with patients whose moods were at risk of escalating. Calm, appraising. No emotion that could raise the stakes. Inside, his heart was hammering. "Sure."

"How about we take it in turns?"

"Sure." *No, not fucking sure at all.*

"Okay." Polly thrust her cue with deadly precision and a ball went into the net. "My turn. What made you train to be a psychiatrist?"

"You're clearly wanting a one-word answer?"

She cast him a dark look, suddenly realised he was joking and grinned. "Don't be a tool."

"Thanks. My parents were both doctors, so—"

"Were?" God, she sure latched onto small details. "Have they retired?"

Solo hesitated. Already things were going down a path he didn't want them to.

"No. They're dead."

"Oh, right. Sorry."

"Don't be. I was only seven when it happened. Plane crash."

She straightened up and appraised him. Then he saw it sink in and her eyes flew wide. "Shit, that's heavy. What happened?"

Something about the forthrightness of her gaze made him feel like he could open up. "They were ophthalmologists. They'd gone on a medical vacation to Papua New Guinea to perform eye surgery in the remote villages when their aircraft crashed in the mountains."

"Oh, Christ. That's, just... shit."

"Yep. You could say that."

"Who brought you up, then?"

"My nan and pop. Nan died three years ago; Pop died just over two months ago."

"Heck. Are you trying to make me feel sorry for you so I lose?"

Solo blinked. Somehow her irreverent comment loosened the tightness that blanketed his heart. He threw back his head and laughed. "Yes, that's the master plan."

She bent down. He couldn't help his eyes sliding to her butt again, the almost heart-shaped gap at the juncture of her thighs. Such a perfect spot to nuzzle his hand.

Death and sex. Freud would have a field day.

"So why psychiatry? Why not ophthalmology?" Polly asked, after putting a ball into the net.

"Guess I wanted to stay alive."

"That's black. Seriously, why psychiatry?"

He took his turn. Struck at the balls. Missed spectacularly. "I feel faint at the sight of blood."

She frowned. "Are you joking?"

"That's the honest-to-god truth."

Her nose wrinkled and a sudden memory of kissing the tip of it lurched through him.

"Don't be ridiculous," she said. "How would you have got through your medical training if you're blood phobic?

"It had its moments. I had to see someone for desensitisation training and the guy happened to be a psychiatrist. He was an amazing man, Dr Brian Crayshaw, wise, compassionate, funny. I guess knowing I was a med student, he told me a fair bit about his work, about the human mind, suffering... despair... I started to delve into the *DSM-5* after that."

Polly nodded, clearly aware of the psychiatrist's diagnostic bible. "Right. A bit of light bed-time reading."

"I got hooked. I realised how complex the mind is, all the things that can go wrong, and how psychiatry can help put that right, and I knew I'd found my vocation."

Polly studied him, her eyes suddenly serious. "So, Dr Jakoby, tell me, do you believe Freud when he said we are all done and dusted by the time we are seven years old?"

"To some extent I do. Not lock stock and barrel, obviously."

"How about his theory of hysteria? All those repressed nineteenth-century women who collapsed onto his couch. Supposedly fixed by a good shagging."

He grinned. "Now *that* I certainly agree with."

Polly straightened and glided along the pool table towards him. His breathing was suddenly fast and shallow, every nerve on high alert. But this time she stopped just before she reached him and he didn't know whether to sigh with relief or beg her to keep right on coming.

"I'll tell you a secret." Her head was within whisper distance, *kissing* distance. "Freud knew fuck all about women."

He fought off the desire to nuzzle into her neck. "What makes you say that?"

"He thought we envied men their penises."

"Don't you?"

"Why would we? A clitoris is so much prettier." She smiled up at him sweetly. "Don't you agree?"

He lost his cool. Spluttered.

"Ha, by that look you obviously do." Eyebrows kicked up over dancing green eyes. "It's your turn."

He shifted forward, holding back the tide of questions, the urge to crack her open, find what made this woman tick. Suddenly, out of nowhere, Carts appeared. Solo bit his lip, gripped his cue and forced a smile as disappointment roiled in his belly.

"Who's winning?" Carts had a dreamy smile on his face. Walking Judith to her car had obviously met with his approval.

"Moi, of course. Back already? Carts, you are such a gentleman." Polly was leaning lightly on her pool cue, rubbing her hand up and down it. Solo really wished she wouldn't. He thought of her at work, handing the tissue box to the young girl curled up in her chair with such a sweet solicitous expression on her face, and it occurred to him that she was one hell of a complex woman.

"You're only saying that to make me feel better about my abject lack of dating prowess," Carts grumbled. "Same old story. Already taken or whipped out from under my nose."

Polly gave him a motherly pat on the arm. "I promise the right woman is out there. It would never have worked with you and Alice. Neither of you would have made it past hand-holding. Besides, the height discrepancy was unacceptable."

"That's a discriminatory statement," Carts muttered, to which Polly gave a wicked giggle.

"Who's Alice?" Solo asked.

"My best friend," Polly replied. "Long story."

"*My* supposed best mate decided to fall in love with her just as I was about to ask her out," Carts grunted. "And it's all *her* fault." He jabbed a finger into the flesh at the top of Polly's arm. In return, she swiped him playfully on the butt with her cue.

"So how do you two know each other?" Solo asked. He guessed this was one way to get a bit more info about Polly without looking like he was nigh on drooling.

"We vaguely knew each other at uni and then saw more of each other through mutual friends over the years. That's Perth for you. Six degrees of separation," Polly said. "We'll no doubt find out we know more people in common, even though you're from Sydney."

"Hope not."

Solo hadn't meant it to come out so sharply, and she cast him a funny look.

"Why? Are you on the run from something?"

His forehead tightened. "No. Time for a change, that's all." He turned abruptly back to the pool table and potted a hole in one.

End of conversation.

The three of them played a few more rounds, making light, meaningless banter, and the muscles down Solo's spine slowly unlaced. This was what he needed right now. Fun. Pure, unadulterated, uncomplicated fun.

And heck, if he didn't look at her *that* way, he would get used to being around Polly Fletcher, wouldn't he? Desensitise himself just the way he had to the sight of blood as a medical student. He had to simply think of her looking neat and professional in her lilac blouse and slacks, hair pulled back, no make-up, talking in a calm voice to her patients. Yeah, he could do this. They were colleagues now.

Just colleagues.

When they all decided some while later that no-one was sober enough to drive, the three of them stood out on the street and waited for an Uber.

In the back seat, Polly was pushed unnervingly up against him because they were ride-sharing and someone was already in the front, which meant Carts had to fold himself like a human tripod on the other side of Solo with his knees practically jammed around his ears. Solo's thigh was pressed along the length of Polly's, and he was consumed with the warmth of her seeping through his jeans and her perfume tumbling him right back to a hotel bed with bad springs.

In the space of a nano-second, Solo found he had to clasp his hands over his throbbing erection and hope to god she didn't have X-ray vision.

But knowing what he did of Polly so far, she probably did.

~

SQUISHED UP NEXT TO SOLO, Polly was trying not to respond to the steady thrum between her legs.

Out the corner of her eye she could see Solo's hands clasped in his lap; hands that were tan and strong and those long, blunt-tipped fingers that looked like they belonged to a guy who rode motorcycles and worked on building sites, not a psychiatrist. Hands that had smoothed and stroked all over her body, bringing every inch of her skin into delicious focus...

And now... the heat of his leg against hers, his hands shifting and... and was he covering his crotch because... because...?

Polly wriggled, but the wriggle brought her thigh into more contact with Solo's and she registered the immediate reflexive twitch in his quads, as if he wanted to come closer and shift away all at once; except there really was nowhere else to go with Carts jammed on the other side of him.

Her body screamed its response, heat flooding and pooling low in the crotch of jeans that had only just dried out from the prosecco incident.

Head averted, she stared at the city bars and restaurants gradually turning into houses. Told herself to focus on anything but his body. Instead, she homed in on Carts' conversation with the guy in the front seat, who happened to be an accountant at a firm that Carts had tried to get a job in. She hadn't a clue how they had got onto that, but that was Perth for you. Big enough to lose yourself in, small enough to know someone who knew someone.

Always.

Which was how people's secrets eventually came to light. Because Solo Jakoby sure as hell had one. Was he running from a relationship break-up? She recalled the way he'd looked at her just before he left the hotel room on Saturday night, the sorrow in the depths of his eyes, darkening them to the colour of storm clouds.

Yes. She was certain of it. He was running from something. Or someone.

Outside Carts' place, Carts wrestled his arms and legs out of the door with difficulty. As Solo scooted across the seat with a quick "see you at work", his warmth and scent disappearing was almost a physical wrench. It would look wrong not to wave goodbye, so Polly gave a cheery little flap through the passenger door. All she caught of Solo was his hands dug deep into his jeans pockets and the crotch of his jeans and oh, *shit-on-a-stick*, the sooner he was gone the better.

As the car drove away, Polly let out a huge sigh and spread herself out on the seat. Her hand caught on something bulky and cool. A leather wallet. Holding it up to the light from a passing streetlamp, she opened it gingerly and peered at the driver's licence. Her heart pattered against her ribs. Of course. Solomon Jakoby. Who else?

She was just about to close it and tell the driver to turn around when her eye caught on a photograph set into the clear plastic inner sleeve. Two kids, boys around the age of nine or ten, she guessed, and an old guy with a cigarette hanging out of his mouth and an arm flung loosely around both their shoulders. As she peered, she could detect Solo's grin in the smaller boy, that unmistakable hitch to his lips that was so appealing. The other boy looked about the same age but blonde. A handsome, wholesome-looking kid, with a bigger build than Solo.

Polly chewed at her lower lip, thinking. Was the old guy Solo's pop? She guessed so. But who was the other kid? Solo hadn't mentioned a brother. Maybe it was a cousin? Or a friend? And what was the significance of this photo? Why save this one?

And somehow, in amongst all this, she just couldn't bring herself to get the Uber driver to turn around. It was wrong, so wrong. She wasn't a snoop, she didn't go through people's belongings, but the little she'd learned about Solo Jakoby intrigued her beyond reason.

Glancing around as if there were some invisible special agent in the back seat with her, Polly popped the wallet into her bag.

She'd text him when she got home, tell him she'd found it and then give it back to him at work first thing tomorrow.

And of course, she'd leave it in her bag. She wouldn't dream of rifling through it.

Absolutely wouldn't dream of doing such a thing.

CHAPTER 8

Solo eyed the two overcooked eggs and limp piece of fatty bacon on his plate, and his stomach rose to meet his mouth. He had no idea why he'd ordered it except the brekky feast was the easiest thing to ask for from the grumpy woman behind the counter.

In truth, all he could focus on right now was meeting Polly at 8 a.m. and the fact that she had his god-damned wallet. He'd been trying to remember if there was anything in there she could have sussed about him. No. The emergency numbers were on his phone. There was only the photo in his wallet and there were none of Emma. He'd shredded them, but that one of him and Drew and Pop, that had been good times —great times, in fact. He couldn't bring himself to get rid of that one, even when everything he could ever claim as friendship between them had blown apart.

He sighed, raked a hand through his hair, picked up his knife and fork and looked up to see Polly marching towards him.

A part of him wanted to laugh. He could imagine her as a little girl, pugnacious and determined, curls framing a Shirley Temple face. Probably into everybody's business even then. Precocious. The sort of kid you loved and hated at the same time.

Like now. The totally confusing urge to take her in his arms and kiss her, or put her over his knee and... *back up the truck,* all sexual fantasies must be kept right out of the picture from now on. With the effect she had on his body, and her being privy to the contents of his wallet, his sleep had been fitful. He'd had to take a very cold shower to get rid of his morning glory.

Enough was enough.

"Hi." She bounced her bag onto the table, drew out his wallet and almost threw it at him. "Money's all gone. Credit cards too."

He gave her a sideways smirk, said "thanks", and shoved it deep into the inner pocket of his jacket.

She leaned over, both palms on the table, and peered onto his plate. "Euwie. Not nice. Should have warned you to avoid the brekky feast. And never, ever eat the rissoles."

"Yes, Ben told me."

"Hmmm, I'm gonna get a coffee. Back in a sec."

Trying not to let his eyes follow her as she flounced off to the counter, he cut off a tiny rectangle of bacon and put it in his mouth. A film of lukewarm grease coated his tongue. He followed it with a mouthful of cardboard toast, which got stuck in his throat as he tried to swallow.

In no time Polly was back with her coffee. "Guess we could have gone to The Healthy Bite café, but I'm a bit off it at the moment."

"Oh, why?"

"No reason." A pause, followed by a little quirk of the lips. "Okay, I'll fess up. I used to have a long-term fuck-buddy thing going with the guy there and, unfortunately his new wife works in the café with him so, you know, I don't want to look like I'm stalking."

"Are you?" He kept his tone light.

She was edging her fingers around her coffee cup. "No, of course not. But I guess it gets awkward once there's another person who could misunderstand things."

"That was their wedding on Saturday, right?"

"Yep. Sort of changed the dynamic. And they're not going on a honeymoon yet, so I thought I'd keep my distance."

Solo nodded. Why was there this strange contraction behind his ribs? Was it the wistful look on her face that kept jabbing him sharply in the region of his chest, or something from further back? Past and present blurred. Hurt about the past, yeah sure, he could be pretty clear what that was about, but hurt right here and now? Shit. Was he actually jealous? *For God's sake, man, grow up!* One night and he was Mr Moonie Teenager.

He picked up his coffee cup, ready to hide behind it. "You guys were serious?"

She cast him a quick glance. "No, never actually. But we were good mates for years, and I miss that—quite a lot, to be honest. There, now you have it, Polly Fletcher factoid number one. I have a heart, after all."

Solo took a gulp of coffee, a warm wave of something like relief softening his belly before a hit of bad coffee made it tense up again. "Urgh. Maybe you could get over it for the sake of decent coffee."

Polly gave him a dazzling smile. "Well, Dr Jakoby, I'm sure in a few days I will. One thing you'll learn about me, I never pine for a man."

"Great philosophy." Solo forced a grin. This time the knot in his stomach had nothing to do with the coffee.

He put his knife and fork down. He couldn't actually eat with that disconcerting gaze surveying him over the top of her cup.

"Guess we should discuss this group we're going to be running together," he said.

Polly put her cup down. "How much group facilitation have you done in the past?"

He shrugged. "Some. Mainly while I was in psychiatry training. Once you're fully qualified you get too bogged down in sorting out medication reactions and keeping people from self-harming. Lots of crisis work."

"Yeah, much the same for social workers. You said yesterday you had experience working with PTSD?"

Solo willed his spine to relax, then flexed his fingers and noticed her eyes went to his hands. "Yes, a reasonable amount."

"I mean counselling, not just doling out the medications?"

"I've counselled people with PTSD, yes."

"In what context?"

A muscle ticked in his jaw, as it always did when he clenched his teeth. He glanced at her face as she took another sip of her coffee, her lashes sweeping her cheeks. Had she read the newspaper articles? Would she suddenly put it all together? The photo in his wallet was burning its way through his chest.

Solo cleared his throat. "Like I said, the hospital I worked at had a contract with Veterans' Affairs, so there were a few soldiers from Afghanistan, some older guys who'd been through Vietnam, plus a few police officers. Then there was a wave of people who'd been through the bushfires and lost everything. Yeah, I guess I've done my share."

Polly relaxed back in her chair. Solo breathed again. Why the hell would she make the connection anyway? It's not like they'd named him. He was just Doctor X. The cameras had caught the back of his head. It was Drew they were interested in, not him.

"In the first session, just take your lead from me," Polly said. "I've been running this group for the past two years, it's sort of my brain-child. It's a space for participants to talk, to discuss coping strategies, but just as importantly to gain support from one another. We try to keep off the topic of medications. That's for them to discuss with their doctors. Oh, and we take it in turns to bring cake."

"Cake!"

"Yeah, cake. The participants don't, we bring it. Ben and I take it in turns. Sometimes I bake. Not right now because I'm dieting."

"You're dieting?"

"Yep, the lemon diet."

Solo raised an amused eyebrow. "Just lemons?"

"Until midday, and then lemon and rice soup alternating with a kale and lemon smoothie for two weeks."

"What the hell for?"

He realised he'd fixed her too hard with his gaze, genuinely surprised that she could want to change a single glorious curve, and he noticed the base of her neck flush, then mottle. Her hand flew up and pulled the edges of her collar tighter, and her eyes did a totally un-Polly-like skitter around the busy canteen. "Oh, um, bum fat. Hard to shift. You know, and the thigh thing…"

Solo grinned, his own neck suddenly hot, and he flicked a look at his untouched food and then back at her. "I had no complaints," he said, and his voice sounded deeper, husky, as something twanged and hummed below his waist.

Really, it took nothing, nothing at all for his thoughts to turn into a haze of Polly-induced lust.

A certain part of him felt smug as the cloud of pink and white warred for attention on Polly's cheeks. "Um—okay. Subject change in order." But she wriggled her butt on her chair and he was as certain as he could be that her thoughts were going the same way as his.

Maybe, for all her bravado, she hadn't quite moved on from Saturday night either. Which made him feel much happier than it should.

He picked up his coffee, took a swig and made a face. "Okay then, what made you decide to do social work?"

She looked slightly startled. Hesitated. "I wasn't clever enough to be a doctor."

"Oh, come on… I bet you were."

"I guess in my family you didn't consider it. Three generations of farmers. Social work was branching out into unknown territory. Though my gran was a nurse before she married Gramps, which is about as far as we got in the world in terms of professions. I'd probably have made a pretty good nurse; I love pulling bits of glass out of body parts, but I'm not very good at taking orders, particularly from doctors."

Solo couldn't help a smirk. "You don't say?"

She smiled, a tiny bit sheepish, her lips softer without lipstick, in some ways even more sensual. He remembered how they'd moulded to his, the way her tongue had explored his mouth, and another spear of lust hit his groin.

Proximity clearly wasn't desensitising him. He wanted her like crazy.

"Seriously, why did you choose social work?" he said, pulling his dick-brain into order.

She looked suddenly uncomfortable, like he'd poked a glass shard into her own personal wound. "My childhood wasn't so great."

Something about the matter-of-fact admission surprised him.

"There was a lot of fighting between my dad and mum. I was the peacekeeper. Guess it seemed natural to continue that when I got older."

Solo blinked. *This*, he had *not* expected.

"Oh, right," was all he managed, struggling to find something suitable to say.

Her lips quirked. "Hard to imagine me as a peacekeeper?"

"No, that wasn't what I was thinking at all."

She twirled both hands in the air, swayed her shoulders. "I was the singing, dancing baby of the family who came in and made everyone laugh, defused the tension, helped Gran clean up the breakages, bathed Mum's fat lip."

"That bad, eh?"

A rogue curl jiggled out of its confines and he watched as she pulled out a hair pin and shoved it back into place. He almost felt sorry for it.

"Occasionally. Outright blows between them only happened a handful of times. I made sure I gave award-winning performances before it got to that."

"Sounds pretty shitty."

"Not as bad as losing your parents in a plane crash."

"At least my early memories of Mum and Dad were happy. My parents never had fights, as far as I can remember."

She stared into her coffee cup. "I'm really not sure why I'm telling you all this, Dr J."

"Shortened to Dr J now, am I? Next it'll just be '*hoi you!*'"

She kept her head down, but he could see a little smile playing on her lips. "You got it."

An awkward silence ensued, Polly stroking the handle of her coffee cup with one finger, him tearing a piece of crust off his toast and toying with it.

A sudden smack on his shoulder made him jump and he looked up to see Leon's big frame. "Mind if I join you?"

"Sure, why not."

Polly flung herself back in her chair. The button of her blouse strained and he caught a tiny show of white lacy bra and looked away quickly. "We're discussing the PTSD group."

"Oh yeah, I forgot, when's Ben off on his break?"

"Today's his last day for four weeks, lucky bugger," Polly said. "Singapore to see his parents, then France, Italy, Croatia."

Leon grinned. "Nice to know my country is a tourist destination. From war-torn to tourist-ravaged."

"I've heard it's beautiful," Solo said politely.

"It is. Went back last year. You'd never know, unless you scratched the surface. Bosnia, Iraq, Afghanistan. What do we have all these bloody wars for?" Leon's expression took a downturn. "Now we have truckloads of traumatised people trying to put their lives back together and the repercussions for their families go on and on and bloody on."

Polly made a face. "Off your soapbox, Leon."

To Solo's surprise, Leon's craggy face turned up in a disarming grin. Polly seemed to have a unique way of insulting people into taking themselves less seriously. "Do you want one of my wife's apple strudels for the PTSD group this week?"

Polly beamed. "Are you trying to let Solo off his initiation ceremony?"

"It seems a bit unfair to pitch him into baking straight off. I don't think Ben's ever forgiven you."

Solo squared his jaw. There was no way he was going to look like a complete dud in the cake-making stakes. "I don't need any favours, thanks, Leon."

The corner of Polly's lips kicked higher. "You're prepared to bake a cake for Wednesday night? Do I have your word on that?"

Solo fortified his shoulders. Pushed his chair back and picked up his almost-untouched plate. "My solemn word." And with that he turned and stalked off, with the combined chuckles of Polly and Leon in his ears.

Gran's chocolate cake.

He'd probably be able to remember the recipe.

And if not, heck, he'd improvise.

No way was Polly Fletcher going to have him on his knees over a cake.

CHAPTER 9

*T*ugging wasn't working.

Fuck-a-doodle, this served her right for buying size twelve leggings, because, of course, she'd reasoned she *would* be a size twelve after a month on the lemon diet.

But she freakin' wasn't *now*, was she?

One last heave and a firm suck of her stomach and the lycra rippled reluctantly over her hips. She stared in disgust at the white muffin top that surged over the band.

Why wasn't she born with the skinny gene? Like Judith. Super tall, long-legged Judith. Or Alice, petitely packaged with just enough curves in all the right places?

Polly's heart tugged painfully in her chest at the thought of Alice. And without Rowena here too, the little weatherboard house was quiet and empty. She'd luxuriated in the space for a few days after dropping Rowena at the airport and being nearly suffocated by hugs. When she got home, she'd walked around completely starkers and promised herself that now she had the perfect opportunity for sex without stuffing her hand in her mouth at the moment of O to stop the sound reverberating around the paper-thin walls.

Except, apart from her one night with Solo, there hadn't been any sex for a while, had there?

Maybe that was why she couldn't get him out of her head? And right now, it was either a run or a rendezvous with her vibrator. She wasn't sure which burned more calories, but she'd hazard a guess it was the run.

So a run it had better be.

Followed by a bowl of lemon and rice soup. Fantastico.

She was about to fling open the front door and head out into the warm summer evening when her phone screen lit up.

A message from Mim.

I've emailed you the list for your dad's birthday party. Can you let me know what jobs you will do asap?

Polly grimaced. Only three weeks to go and Dad would be seventy. Her stomach contracted with that familiar queasy feeling. Over the past ten years he'd tried, he really had. Whenever he'd come to Perth to buy equipment for the farm, he had done his best to play at being the interested father over an awkward meal. Would they ever be able to put the hurt behind them? She wasn't sure. Even at Mum's funeral, when his big shoulders shook with sobs, she just couldn't bring herself to say she forgave him.

She was about to fling her phone onto the hall console when it lit up again with the words "Alice" and "FaceTime". Polly's heart soared; exercise could wait.

"Munchkin!" she squealed as Alice's face bobbed onto the screen. She was wearing a big floppy hat and the sun was glinting off her glasses. She looked so darned blissed out.

"Poll!" Alice's voice was full of excitement. "Guess what? We've got some news!"

"Don't tell me, you've brought the beast to his knees?"

"Watch out, I can hear you." Aaron's blond head bobbed into view over Alice's shoulder with a seriously silly hat on his head.

"What the fuck are you wearing?"

Aaron pushed out his lower lip in a mock pout. "A straw boater. We're punting."

"Aaron's just proposed!" Alice flashed up a hand, the massive diamond clearly visible on her finger. "And guess what? I said yes!"

The same jab she'd experienced at Jake's wedding, just where her ribs met above her heart, stabbed Polly hard. Oh no, no, no, not the green-eyed monster, not when she was so happy her best friend had found happiness with her man.

Wrong, all wrong.

What a bitch she was.

"I'm so, so happy for you," she said swiftly and meant it; she really did. A sudden vision of Solo down on one bended knee, with a look of total adoration on his face, flashed in front of her eyes and she gulped it down so hard she nearly choked. Clearly, she'd gone raving loopy. Maybe it was too much lemon juice turning her brain cells to acid. "When's the big day? I need to gear myself up."

"Oh, gosh, no date yet. But you had to be the first to know. After all, Poll, if it hadn't been for you…"

"Yeah, yeah, I know. I'm the fairy godmother. Can I be godmother to the first baby, too?"

Alice bit her lower lip and giggled. Aaron flung an arm around her shoulder and kissed the top of her head. "I'm not sure I'll have you leading my firstborn astray."

"Huh, trust a reformed womaniser to fling moral shit."

"We do it best," Aaron mocked, "like reformed smokers."

"Don't choke on your virtue, your holiness." Polly grinned, trying not to think of a certain someone with the smoking vice.

Alice shoved Aaron out the way and took up the screen. "What are you up to, Poll?"

Polly skimmed the phone down her body. "You may be surprised but I'm about to go for a run."

A frown pulled Alice's brows down. "Really? That's not like you. Are you okay? When we spoke on Sunday, you sounded a bit—"

"Bit what?"

"I don't know, a bit flat, I guess."

Polly painted a bright smile on her face. "All good. Totally fine."

"You aren't feeling bad about Jake being off-limits?"

"Nope. The wedding was fantastic. Has Rowena arrived yet?"

"Next week. She's still swanning around Bangkok indulging in green curry and daily massages." Alice laughed.

Which somehow led to a conversation about strawberries and cream at Wimbledon, and how Bath buns differed from Chelsea buns, which only made Polly's mouth water. When they said their farewells, Polly chucked her phone down, did a little warm-up jog on the spot, then took a big breath to prepare herself and flung open the front door. And let out a surprised yelp.

A tall spectre lurked in the shadows of the porch.

Polly's hand flew up and clutched at the front of her Lululemon T-shirt. "Jesus, Carts! You scared the crap out of me. What are you doing here?"

"I need some advice." Carts shifted from foot to foot.

Polly sighed and looked down at her thighs, quite sure they were mocking her. It was getting dark, it had been a long day at work, and frankly she was weak from hunger. Her resolve wavered.

Carts presented a bottle of wine from behind his back.

Her resolve vanished.

"Pressie. Wine in exchange for dating advice."

Polly groaned. "This better not be about who I think it is."

Carts' face took on its stricken sheepdog look. "Pleeease, Poll. I just want a bit of background info."

She stared at the wine. Her tongue tip licked her bottom lip and her stomach growled loudly. She thought of the pallid, porridgy soup congealing in the fridge.

"Pizza." It was out of her mouth before she could halt it. "Get a pizza delivered and I'm all yours."

Carts' face morphed into almost handsome as his grin widened. "Now you're talking."

"Not literally, you understand. You and me, Carts. Not a good combo."

He laughed, pulled out his phone and handed her the bottle of wine.

Running and nasty tasteless lemon rice soup could go take a hike... at least until tomorrow.

~

NEVER HAD pepperoni and mushrooms tasted quite so delicious. Polly gulped and tried to slow the onslaught of teeth meeting pizza crust. She was behaving like a pig at the trough, having already devoured one more slice than Carts. He was nibbling almost gracefully at his piece, and observing her with the expectant look of someone about to hear some startling revelation. When all she had for him was bad news.

"Carts, Judith's in a long-term relationship."

He picked another piece of mushroom off and added it to the pile on his plate. Why hadn't he said he didn't like mushroom when she chose the pizza? And would it be really crass if she reached over and grabbed them? She loved, loved, *loved* mushrooms.

"We had a connection," he said, a sullen little frown settling across his forehead.

"Probably because she's met someone significantly taller than her for once."

"She's so petite," he commented wistfully.

Polly rolled her eyes. "She's six foot one, Carts."

"That's five inches shorter than me. What about him. Her man? Is he tall?"

"Mark?" Polly put down her crust. She wouldn't eat it, even though it looked so crunchy and yummy. That, at least, would cut out some carbs. "He's a tiny bit shorter than her, I think. Yes, definitely, because she grumbled that she always has to wear flats around him."

Carts punched the air. "Yesssss."

Polly's heart went out to him. He was really the sweetest guy. Kind, considerate, cute when he grinned. But he needed a confidence boost, and clothes that didn't make him look like a scarecrow. He also needed to get the hems of his pants let down. She should give him a makeover.

Immediately she shot that idea down in flames. It was high time she stopped this matchmaking fetish. She was damn good at it, but lately it was losing its appeal. What was this feeling she kept getting in the pit of her stomach? *Left out,* her mind supplied.

Hell no. It must be just a hormonal surge happening as she slid towards thirty. It would pass.

She returned her focus to the tasks at hand: letting Carts down gently and not eating another slice of pizza. Her stomach begged. She homed in on the splurgy feeling of her butt cheeks on the chair, fisted her hands and placed her chin on them to stop her fingers sneaking towards the pizza box.

"Judith and Mark have been together since they were seventeen. She's very happy. She wants to settle down and have babies."

"Who says I don't?" He eyeballed her defiantly. "And don't look at me like that. Why can't a guy say he's keen to get married and have kids without people thinking he's got a testosterone deficiency and a mummy complex?"

Polly chuckled. "Oh, you are the best. I think it's lovely you feel that way, but I have a question for you. Ever thought you might be falling for unavailable women to get away from the fact that you like being unattached?"

Carts sent her yet another hurt look and took a large gulp of wine. "Lucy and I were together for over a year. Not my fault the day I proposed she said she preferred her personal trainer." He stared dolefully into his glass.

"At least you got the money back on the ring," Polly said, then kicked herself as Carts said gloomily, "And that's supposed to make me feel better?"

She had the urge to get up and hug him. Except she wouldn't know where to start, there was too much of him, too many sharp angles. Come to think of it, Judith and he would fit perfectly together. Mr and Mrs Tall and their tiny talls.

Maybe there was something in that, after all. What with Judith's admission of her abhorrent lack of a sex life. Maybe...

"At least give me some background, just in case she dumps the guy," Carts said. "Likes and dislikes. A kind of Judith starter kit."

How could she not, with that pleading look on his face?

"Okay. She's twenty-nine, she's into craft, she'd probably knit you a sweater before thinking to let you kiss her. She adores her mum and dad and her brother and sister. All tall, just like your tribe. They've had specially adapted bench tops in the kitchen. She likes cats. Crochet. Baking. She makes the best chocolate brownies in the entire universe. I don't think she's ever said a really negative word about anyone or anything. Is that enough to be going on with?"

"My dream woman."

Polly rolled her eyes and took a sip of wine. After a week of lemon juice, it tasted divine.

They talked a bit more about Judith and her home-making skills and her sunny disposition and finally, against her better judgement, Polly promised that if she ever heard Judith was a free woman, Carts would be the first to know. She really didn't want Carts getting his hopes up. It had taken a few months for him to get over the fact that Aaron had—in his books, at least—snatched Alice from under his nose. The fact that Alice had loved Aaron for five years before he finally saw the light and returned her feelings hadn't figured in Carts' reasoning.

At the door, Polly stood on tippy toes and gave Carts a peck on the cheek.

Before she could stop herself, she asked, "How's your new house-mate settling in?"

Carts didn't seem to register the higher note in her voice that screamed *tell me everything you know*. Thank goodness being male and an accountant made him a less emotionally observant species.

"Okay, I guess."

"Mmmm?" she said hopefully.

"Weird how it turns out he works with you," he offered with a little brow pucker.

Now it was Polly's turn to feel like a dog waiting for her owner to deliver a treat. "Yep, sure is. Has he said much to you about his life in Sydney?"

"Not really. Just that his pop died and he wanted to take a break between contracts and try a new city." He paused and stared down the street for a second. "He keeps getting strange messages on his phone."

"What kind of messages?"

"I guess I shouldn't have snooped, but he gets lots of messages, I mean, *loads*, and the other day he was in the shower and his phone just kept pinging, like every few seconds, so I thought maybe it was urgent, the hospital or something, and took a quick look. You should have seen the string of vitriol."

It felt like someone had shoved ice cubes down the back of her T-shirt. "What kind of vitriol?"

"Like seriously abusive. Fuck you this and fucking hate you that. That sort of shit. Like one after the other, ping, ping, ping."

"That's heavy." So was her breathing right now. Her hunch was right, then? Solo was running from some kind of trouble. "Did you tell him you'd seen them?"

"Nah, of course not. Like, what would be the point? He came in and grabbed his phone and I could tell he knew exactly what was going down. Then he just went to his room. No way, after seeing that look on his face, was I going to say a word."

"What did he look like?"

"Completely gutted."

CHAPTER 10

*A*s he grabbed the cake tin out of the oven, the tea towel slipped and heat raged through his fingertips. He managed to thrust the tin onto the stovetop, where it teetered, flipped sideways and fell onto the kitchen floor with an ominous thud.

"Fucking hell," Solo shouted.

When he'd got in from work an hour ago he'd flung the ingredients he'd bought onto the kitchen bench top, plus the bowl, scales and cake tin he'd purchased, because there was no way in the world Carts would have any, and mixed and stirred and hoped to God he'd remembered Nan's recipe correctly.

And now the thing was literally a hot mess on the floor.

He looked around desperately for something else to pick it up with; salvaging it was definitely going to require both hands. Nope. Nothing. Carts' kitchen was like an operating theatre; one where all the equipment had been removed for sterilisation. Carefully doubling up the tea towel, he tried to twist the tin upright, using his other hand to prod the cake back in place. It broke, half remaining in the tin, the other half ending up on the floor tiles. He'd let it overcook and now it was clearly going to crumble to buggery.

With a quick flick of his wrist and the heat of the cake burning his other hand, Solo managed to get it onto the kitchen counter and finally breathed a huge sigh of relief. It was more or less intact. And the four-second rule with regard to floor contact applied. Besides, hadn't they'd proved a few germs were good for you? Though looking at Carts' kitchen floor, you could probably eat off those shiny tiles with no risk to your health.

Solo gathered his scattered wits.

Now for the topping. Grabbing the icing sugar, butter and cocoa, he threw it all together in the bowl and started beating with grim determination. A glance at his watch told him he had twenty minutes before he had to leave if he was going to get there in time.

Solo cursed liberally under his breath. Why hadn't he just bought a stupid cake? Or used a packet mix? What the hell was he trying to prove?

For the last couple of days, he and Polly had studiously ignored each other on the ward—apart from one encounter they'd had no say in. Dr Death had insisted they do a joint interview with Bernie because, after twelve weeks on the ward, he needed his medications stabilised and to be gently encouraged to move into hostel accommodation. The psychiatrist and the social worker were the obvious choice to raise the issue. They'd sat in the doctor's office awkwardly waiting for Bernie to be located, Solo trying not to get side-tracked by the fact that Polly was wearing a skirt that showed off a tiny slice of tantalising thigh as she crossed her legs.

He was at risk of turning into a letch. For Christ's sake.

So he'd mentioned how humid the weather was and that there must be a storm brewing.

Double Christ's sake.

And then her lips had quirked and that eyebrow raised like she could see right through his neat suit and into his heart...

Heart?

No way. She wasn't affecting him that much. It was just that she fascinated him. That was all. He really wasn't sure what drew him to her in a way that was more than that initial crazy physical attraction; why the odd urge to confide in her, spill out all the misery of the past year.

Or, for that matter, why he had such an urge to find out more about her. That tantalising glimpse into her childhood had intrigued him because it wasn't what he'd imagined. He would have guessed Polly had a loving, rough-and-tumble, rag-tag family who teased each other and hugged a lot.

From her brief account, he'd clearly got that all wrong.

And as for the sex thing—truly he couldn't get his head around it, he'd never been that turned on by curvy women before. Emma was waif-like. He'd got used to the way her body fitted so neatly into his hands, how he could smooth his palms over her hip bones, trace his fingers up her ribs one by one and cup her almost non-existent breasts. Nothing about Polly's body fitted neatly; it overflowed, it enveloped, it drowned him in all sorts of delicious possibilities.

Having located the one dessert spoon in the cutlery drawer, he used it to smash icing onto the cake, then stared helplessly as it dripped down the sides. Goddamn it, the cake was still too hot. And there wasn't time to let it cool down properly…

Rifling a hand through the short spikes of his hair, Solo debated messaging Polly and telling her he'd just got a bad bout of food poisoning. But, hell, he wasn't that much of a coward, surely?

He shoved the cake into the freezer, leaving a trail of icing blobbing across the kitchen floor, and went upstairs to take a lightning-fast shower.

Twenty minutes later the cake container was in the box on the back of his Ducati. He'd have to ride carefully so as not to dislodge the precarious icing.

The desire to go to his dressing table and find his cigarette packet before he left was almost overwhelming.

That would be a good look, turning up smelling of smoke.

Yeah, he'd really be setting a great example.

When he arrived at the centre, Polly was already setting up the room. He stood for a second in the doorway, helmet in one hand, the container with the apology of a cake in the other, watching the play of her arms, strong and capable as she lifted chairs and arranged them in a neat circle. She'd looped her hair into a loose ponytail—maybe it was an evening concession—and a few curls had wiggled their way out of the sides, glinting in the rather harsh lighting of the community centre meeting room.

She must have sensed him there, because she turned and looked over her shoulder and her mouth spread into a glorious smile.

Her beauty smacked him right between the eyes, took his breath away.

"Hey there, Dr J." She straightened and faced him. Tonight she had on a more casual T-shirt-style top in candy pink and grey stripes, and he had to be careful not to let his eyes stray to the way those stripes spread across her full breasts. Feet planted wide, she splayed her hands on her hips and cocked her head.

Heat shimmied around his groin and his only option was to move. Fast.

Striding over to the trestle table in the corner, which was covered with cups and an urn of boiling water, he plonked down the container. Within seconds she was next to him, so close he could smell her sweetly familiar perfume, and he wanted to turn and bury his face in the curve of her neck; tangle his fingers in that mass of curls and smother her mouth with his.

"What have you got in there?"

"Cake."

"Did you make it?"

"Yes, and it's a complete disaster."

She let out a cross between a snort and a giggle and the sound was so infectious he couldn't resist an answering tug at the corner of his mouth.

"Okay, let's take a look," she ordered.

Reluctantly, he opened the container. The cake made him think of a guy desperately trying to disguise a bald patch, icing sagging off to one side and a big patch of emptiness in the middle that he'd tried to rectify with some hundreds and thousands. Botched, completely and utterly botched.

"Full marks for effort, Dr J. It probably tastes delicious."

He looked sideways at her and she caught his eye and bit her lip.

Something zapped, tangible and electric, between them. More heat arrowed most inconsiderately to his cock and he had to step away.

He ripped off his leather jacket and laid it around the back of a chair.

"So, when does everyone arrive? Arghh, no don't touch it." He saw her trying to lift the broken cake out of the container and dived forward. "It has to stay in the box."

She pouted as he wrestled it away from her.

"It will be easier to cut if it's out of the container."

"I promise it won't be."

"Okay, defender of the cake, I'll take your word for it." She was squinting at it through narrowed eyes. "Looks a bit crumbly."

"It's supposed to, it's called chocolate *crumble* cake." He tried for serious but she just made him want to laugh and, in all honesty, laughing was something he hadn't done enough of for months.

"Don't tell me; an old Jakoby family recipe."

"Absolutely. Passed through the generations from grandmother to grandson."

"Impressive. Can't wait to taste it."

"Hi."

They both swivelled to see a big guy about their age, hovering in the doorway.

Polly swung into action. "Grant, I'm so glad you're here, we missed you last week."

"Yeah, bad few days to be honest."

Solo observed him carefully. He was strong and well-built, but his face was blank, his tone flat.

"I was a bit worried. I tried to call you the day after the group." Polly said, ushering him into the room.

"Yes, thanks, I saw that." The young man stood stiff and awkward, avoiding eye-contact. "I messaged Ben to say I was okay; you got that, right?" He flicked a glance at Solo and Polly launched into introductions.

"Grant, this is Dr Solomon Jakoby, he'll be co-facilitating with me for the next four weeks while Ben's on holiday."

Solo knew better than to hold out his hand. Polly had briefed him on the participants and he guessed this was Grant Lewis. Ex army. Afghanistan. Grant gave him a smile that didn't touch the depths of his blue eyes and a tiny shudder passed up and down Solo's spine.

He knew that look.

He steeled himself. "Hi, good to meet you."

"You too." Grant's gaze shifted quickly from his face. The flatness of his expression was starkly at odds with his super-fit physique. Solo could almost recite the guy's story for him. Grant Lewis had no doubt been strong and confident once, ready to face whatever life threw at him, except somewhere in war-torn Afghanistan, life had thrown him hell and the devil, and now the haunting just wouldn't stop.

Yep, Solo knew the story off by heart.

As Grant meandered over to the table to grab a cup of tea, a few more people filtered in, all with the posture of having been defeated by life. It was something about their shoulders, like the weight of the world was bearing down on them. They stood talking in low voices, or simply sat down, cupping their mugs between their hands and staring into space.

Finally, Polly looked at her watch, gave her hands a quick clap and raised her voice a little over the murmurs. "Looks like this is it, guys. Shall we get started?"

There were six participants. Some weeks, Polly had told him, there were up to ten, but rarely did everyone attend at once. Six was manageable for starters. At least he wouldn't have too many names to remember.

"Okay, before we share how your week's been, I just wanted to introduce our new psychiatrist, Dr Solo Jakoby, who will be co-facilitating with me for the next four weeks while Ben is away."

All eyes shifted to Solo. "Maybe you'd like to say a few words." Polly flashed him her best professional smile.

"Sure." Solo nodded. Why did he feel so nervous? Was it Polly and her unwavering scrutiny, or was it once again being around so many sufferers of PTSD?

All of them potent reminders of Drew.

He cleared his throat. "Hi, everyone. Good to meet you. I guess you'd like to know a little about me? I've been qualified as a psychiatrist for six years, previously working in Sydney and now here in Perth as a three-month locum." A wave of near-panic dragged over him like a physical weight, threatening for a second to pull him under. He forced his spine back into the chair, cleared his throat. "PTSD has been a special interest area of mine for a while now."

All eyes were on him, one pair in particular, green and curious, and he swallowed hard. "So, it will be good to be joining you for the next few weeks. And if you have any questions, particularly about medications, I'm your man."

He cast a quick look at Polly to see a frown pleating her eyebrows. She smiled tightly. "Thank you, Dr Jakoby," she clipped out.

Solo returned an equally tight smile. "Please, feel free to call me Solo." He cast his gaze around the assembled group. "I don't tend to stand on formalities."

Polly's smile was now like a shot of saccharine. Why did it feel they were in some kind of battle of wills here? It was subtle but the energy was definitely there, pulling against him, like a rip tide.

"Let's start with sharing how everyone's week has been," Polly said, snapping her gaze away from his face, her voice bright, as she fingered a curl behind one ear. "Would anyone like to go first?"

Solo leaned back and put on his best listening face.

Deathly silence. Six heads bent, eyes cast downward, staring at their laps.

Oh God, this was set to be a long hour and a half. Group therapy situations like this were like pulling teeth. Every mental health professional dreaded them.

Finally, Grant cleared his throat and hunkered his elbows onto his knees. "I've had a bit of a rough time. Sleep's been crap. I think my medications have stopped working." He looked at Solo from under pinned-down brows. "So, doc, any advice would be greatly appreciated."

Another woman, stockily built with a short buzz cut muttered, "Yeah, same here. Shit dreams. Really vivid, takes me back to the incident. I'm a police officer. Actually, retrenched, as I haven't been able to get back even on a rehab plan. My GP's not much good with this stuff and it's another six weeks before I see my psychiatrist again, so it would be good to have an idea of what to ask the GP for when I see him."

Relief surged through Solo at being able to do something tangible. "That's entirely understandable, and getting better sleep is a big part of handling PTSD symptoms. Working with your doctors to get the medication right is paramount. I'm not your treating doctor, of course, so I can't give individualised advice, but would you guys like an update of the medications currently used to treat PTSD?"

"You bet, doc. I have no idea about my meds, or what the side-effects might be," an older guy called David said. "But my doctor keeps wanting to increase the dose. I'd like to try something different, to be honest."

A universal yes came from the group. Except for one black cloud that seemed to be hovering over the curly head of his co-facilitator.

"Sure, I can give a quick run-down," Solo said.

"Perhaps we should just remind ourselves that this is a *support group*, and we are here to share *coping* strategies," Polly said crisply.

"Medications are part of my coping strategies," Grant replied, his chin suddenly jutting a little. "I'd like to hear from Doc Solo here."

"Yeah, so would I," David chipped in.

"Perhaps we should ask the rest of the group," Polly responded. "What does everyone else want?"

"I'd like to hear what Doc Solo has to say."

"Yes, me too."

"I'm sick of trying to do that relaxation exercise Ben gave us, I need some other ideas."

Polly sat back and folded her arms, then quickly unfolded them and ran her palms down her thighs. Solo wished she wouldn't do that just now.

"Right," she said. Her fingertips tapped her knees. "It seems, Dr Solo, that you have the green light."

Solo cast her a glance and registered the challenge in her eyes. Clearly he'd taken the group somewhere Polly didn't want it to go. But then he looked at the other six faces turned in his direction, full of hope that maybe there were some answers out there that didn't involve sitting and talking. And heck, medication for PTSD was something he knew a fair bit about, wasn't it?

He stood and went to the whiteboard. These guys clearly wanted his knowledge, and this time, he wasn't going to let Polly Fletcher put him off his stride.

CHAPTER 11

Sweeping a pile of plates and cups into her arms, Polly stomped over to the small kitchen and dumped them by the side of the sink. She twisted the tap until hot water gushed out, then squeezed the bottle of detergent like she wanted to strangle the life out of it.

Out in the therapy room, she could hear the buzz of voices and Solo's laugh, warm and mellow.

The PTSD group had wound up formally ten minutes ago, but Solo was still answering questions from participants who'd hung around. No-one seemed in a hurry to go home.

She grabbed the washing-up sponge and scrubbed bits of chocolate cake off plates like she was performing an exorcism. After this, she'd make sure she went and scrubbed off all the names of medications that Solo had written up on the whiteboard.

Sertraline and Propranolol and Minipress and Zoloft.

Polly ground her molars together.

As soon as you made it about the medication, that was it, people stopped trying other things.

Just like Dad.

After every trip to his psychiatrist, Dad would come back with a new script. There'd be a week or so of peace, Dad telling Mum he thought these meds were actually working, and they'd all collectively sigh with relief. Then it would rain and flatten the wheat, or it wouldn't rain enough to help the green stalks push through the dry dirt. Or the tractor would need a new part Dad couldn't afford. And he'd disappear to his shed in the back paddock and lock the door.

Joe would have to go and break the lock and drag him out two days later, and then it would be back to hospital for another detox.

What had Dad ever learned from a script pad? Just tell her that.

Polly swiped a curl off her cheek with the back of a damp hand and noticed Grant was hovering in the doorway. He was actually smiling. She hadn't seen him smile since he started attending the group.

"Can I give you a hand?" he asked.

"No, I'm good." Her voice sounded brittle and harsh. "No, thank you, Grant," she added more gently. "You go home. It's our job to clear up and lock up. Legal responsibility and all, but you could give Dr Jakoby a nudge to help, if you want."

"He's talking," Grant said.

"I know, I can hear him." She waved the washing up brush at Grant in a way she hoped would be construed as light-hearted. "Not just women's work, you know."

Grant did a little uncomfortable foot shift. "I'll go and grab the rest of the cups."

Polly pulled herself into line. She was at risk of being unprofessional. "Okay, thank you. One load only, then you go home."

Grant appeared seconds later with some cups and put them down next to the sink. "Great group tonight, thanks. That new doc's a great guy."

Polly hitched her chin in the air and narrowly avoided a disdainful sniff. "Make the most of him, he won't be here for long."

"Really?"

"Only until Ben comes back from holidays."

"Shame."

"Don't tell Ben that."

"Oh, I don't mean it that way. It's just good to get some medical input."

Polly stapled a smile to her lips. "Sure."

"He's really approachable; it's easy to forget he's a psychiatrist."

Polly smoothed honey into her voice. "That's why we decided to ask him to co-lead the group."

"It was a good choice," Grant said.

Polly had to admit he looked like someone had lifted a weight off his shoulders.

"I don't know, it's weird," Grant mused, "but I feel like he really gets this PTSD stuff better than any other health professional I've talked to."

Polly had to force her fingers to let go of the squeegee. Okay, she'd concede her reaction was probably about her own baggage. She was big enough to recognise it. "I'm pleased. Glad the session was worthwhile."

Grant nodded. "Thanks, Polly. I'll be off, then—if you're sure you don't want any more help?"

"Absolutely." She gave him a mock frown. "Now go home."

After Grant left, Polly grabbed the tea towel and wiped up the crockery, her ears still focused on the farewells drifting through the door. Finally, there was quiet.

Where was he?

She crept over to the kitchen door and peered out.

Solo was pensively rubbing words off the whiteboard.

Something about the angle of his head, the bunching around his shoulders, made her heart do a strange little turn in her chest.

For fuck's sake, she didn't need to start feeling sorry for him.

Irrationally irritated, she went back to her washing up. If he wanted to stand there cutting some brooding tragic figure, let him. Like, what was his problem? Half an hour ago he'd been firing on all cylinders, standing up there at the front of the group. And grudgingly, yeah, she'd concede he had conveyed just the right mix of authoritative and approachable. She'd had to stop herself from staring at his firm butt cheeks as he turned to scribble on the whiteboard. Had to stop her insides unfurling like one of those sped-up YouTube clips of budding flowers every time he ruffled a hand through his hair or looped it loosely on his hips. That really nice way he had of listening, head tilted to one side, small encouraging nods as group members voiced their concerns.

There was a sudden clatter as her crockery stack collapsed and Polly dived to grab the pieces flying off the draining board.

Too late. A plate and two mugs smashed onto the kitchen tiles.

Hell, this was what Solo was doing to her—completely messing with her ability to organise a simple clean-up.

"Everything okay?"

Crouched down, Polly glanced up to see black-jean-clad legs in the doorway.

"What does it look like?"

In a flash, Solo had squatted down next to her and was picking up pieces. "A plate-throwing contest?"

"Ha, ha."

"Where's the dustpan?"

"Under the sink."

She averted her eyes from the strong V of his thighs before he sprang lithely up and returned a moment later. As he started to brush up the shards, Polly got up and threw the broken bits in the bin. The kitchen suddenly felt too small.

"So," Solo said as he shook the remains of the dustpan into the bin. "How did my medication spiel go?"

"It was fine," she said. Then, unable to stop herself, she added, "If a bit long-winded."

When she glanced up a sudden darkening in those silver eyes made her swallow. That wasn't true, not for a second. His knowledge was textbook accurate, and somehow he'd made it fascinating.

She just didn't want to admit it.

"I see," he said.

"It was good to do an update." Polly leaned her butt against the bench, her hands gripping the edge behind her until her knuckles hurt. "But focusing too much on medications shouldn't override our program's goals."

"Meaning?"

Polly flicked her head. "We're here to help participants develop strategies to combat their symptoms."

"So getting their medications right doesn't count as a strategy?"

"I—phht, yes, and no."

Solo's eyes held hers with a certain steeliness. "What does that mean?"

"It means there's an appropriate time and place to discuss their meds. Like when they visit their psychiatrist."

"You heard what Jenny said, they often have to wait weeks to see their psychiatrist."

"Sure." Why was she feeling so flustered? "And this is a safe space to air their frustrations about the health system. But in here our focus is on self-empowerment, not disempowerment."

"Are you implying that educating them about their medication options is disempowering?"

"That's not what I said."

He was propped against the doorframe, one leg crossed nonchalantly over the other, which made her feel on the back foot. In fact, she almost wanted to stamp her foot. He had no idea how much thought and care Ben and she had put into this program. No way was he pulling rank over her just because he had more letters after his frigging name.

She purred in her best therapist voice, "Look, of course medication has its place. But you have to understand, the group is about developing coping skills."

Solo crossed his arms over his chest. "Building resilience, sure, I get it."

"Exactly."

"All the more important we provide the facts. Making informed choices helps people build resilience, right?"

Smug bastard doctor, Polly thought as she met the triumphant twinkle in those silver eyes with a frosty smile. "When Ben and I put this together, we were clear we didn't want the program to be medicalised."

"Maybe you shouldn't have asked me to fill in, then. Considering I'm a doctor."

"If you recall, I wasn't the one who asked you." Polly pushed off the bench, aware her annoyance was doing nothing to lessen the pheromones in the air. Right this minute, she wasn't sure if she wanted to slap the supercilious smile off his face or lick it off.

She flounced past him into the therapy room and started busying herself with clearing the last bits and pieces off the table. He followed her, and they both stood staring at the remains of the cake.

"What do you want to do with it?" Polly finally asked.

"Bin it."

"You don't want to take it home to Carts?"

"He does look like he needs a bit of fattening up but... no."

She sensed him grinning and the atmosphere softened between them. A shift of an inch or two and their arms and hips would bump. It was like a giant invisible magnet, dragging her towards him.

He said ruefully, "Maybe I should buy a cake next time."

She couldn't help a snicker at that. "I always do."

His head jerked around with a look of exaggerated outrage. "You do?"

"Tim Tams, mostly."

"Hell, why didn't you say so?"

"It's a rite of passage. You had to prove yourself."

"Jesus Christ. Do you know how stressed I got? It would have made The Great Australian Bake-Off look like a stroll in the park."

"Now you've earned your stripes, we can relax the rules."

"So next time I can swing by IGA?"

"Sure."

Solo rifled a hand over his hair and a little stab of pure want shot through her, knowing how soft those short spikes would feel under her fingertips.

"I can't believe you and Ben stitched me up like this." He was shaking his head now. "And that I subjected those poor guys to eating it."

"It tasted marginally better than it looked."

They exchanged glances, the undercurrent unmistakable, funnelling heat into her sex. The urge to reach up and actually run her fingers over his hair, pull his face down and kiss him was so overwhelming Polly had to bound into remedial action.

"You dump the cake; I'll stack the chairs." She almost sprinted around the room, grabbing chairs, feeling Solo's gaze on her, before he turned and cleared the rest of the debris off the table.

They finished and Solo went to get his helmet and the empty container. Polly grabbed her bag and coat and they exited.

After she'd locked the doors, they stood together in awkward silence.

"We'll need to do a de-brief of the group at some time," she said, to fill the gap.

"Now?" he suggested.

A sudden spasm pulled her belly into a tight knot. If she spent a moment more in Solo's company, it was practically a given that she'd drag him into bed. It would get messy, and she'd seen enough mess to last her a lifetime.

There were guys you got down and dirty with, and guys you worked with. It was rather like enemy lines. You never crossed them.

Polly shook her head. "No, I'm pooped."

Did his shoulders stiffen under the leather of his jacket?

"I'll be writing up the group first thing in the morning." She tried to sound casual. "We could discuss it then."

"No problem." He swung his helmet under one arm and turned to go, then turned back. "Look, I'm sorry."

Her breath hitched. "For what?"

"For hijacking the group. I realise you probably had an agenda for the session and I—let's just say I... should have worked with you on that. So I apologise."

A warm feeling spiralled around her chest. The guy was big enough to apologise. She blinked at the unbidden memory of warm hands cupping her face; the tip of her nose tingled, and instinctively she wrinkled it to try and dislodge the sensation of his lips just there.

Solo cocked an eyebrow. "What was that look for?"

"What look?"

"Like I hit a nerve or something?"

"No need for the psychoanalysis, thanks very much."

He'd hit a nerve all right. Every nerve in her body, to be precise. Sure, he turned her on, that was a given, but this... this other pull, like she wanted to bury her head into his chest, feel his arms circling her tight. Christ, she barely knew this guy.

The fact was, being around Solo Jakoby made her feel vulnerable as all hell. And that was an emotion she'd promised herself years ago that she'd never let herself feel again.

Solo gave a harsh bark of laughter. "Seems I'm good at firing wide of the mark with you. Catch you tomorrow."

She glanced at his features to see them drawn tight, and silenced the soft corner of her heart that yearned to say something, anything, to make it better between them. Instead, she watched as those long legs reached his bike and he slammed on his helmet, the actions followed by the throaty roar of the Ducati's engine starting up.

Swallowing a weird lump in her throat, Polly located her car keys and stamped on the ridiculous urge to follow him home.

STEPPING OUT OF THE SHOWER, Solo towelled himself dry and stared at his features in the mirror. He smoothed a hand over the light stubble on his jaw. He was deadbeat, as the shadows under his eyes bore testament to.

He rubbed at the furrow between his brows, as though he could scrub it off if he tried hard enough.

Why was it that everything he did or said around Polly Fletcher seemed to go wrong? Was it him or her?

Apart from in bed, but he could forget about that right this minute.

Shit. He didn't want—didn't *need*—to be so attracted to her, but the fact was, he couldn't seem to keep her from invading his brain. The way she shook her head so her curls bounced, that habit she had of crossing her knee over her other thigh and holding on to her ankle, that little wiggle of her butt in her seat just before she said something.

There had been a fair few wiggles as she'd tried to get a word in this evening.

Solo groaned. He shouldn't have taken over the session like that, but the thing was that maybe, just maybe, if someone had made sure Drew got the right advice straight after he'd returned from Afghanistan, and the right medications, things would never have gone so pear-shaped.

Seeing the hollowness in his reflected eyes, Solo thrust himself away from the mirror. Thinking about all that wouldn't undo the whole goddamn train smash of the last few months. But at least Drew was in hospital, safe for the time being. He couldn't harm himself. Or Emma.

Or Solo, for that matter.

The vitriolic spew of those text messages was hard to take, each new one like a punch to his gut. Even so, he couldn't bring himself to erase Drew's number. That would be like severing a limb. And he knew, once they got the combination of treatments right, things would change. Most likely Drew wouldn't even remember these episodes once he was well again.

Right now, the guy was lost in a living hell. And Solo was trained to understand that. His shoulders were broad enough, surely?

Solo clamped down on the direction his thoughts had gone, padded into his tiny room and stared glumly around.

What a clusterfuck. He hadn't brought much with him, but he hadn't been doing much to keep it tidy either. Frankly, it was hard to see a space on the bed to crawl into. He started to sort the pile of clothes so he could at least get into bed. Picked up his wallet and threw it onto the bedside table. It flipped open, and there, staring back at him, was the photo of him and Drew with Pop

He smiled grimly, feeling the bittersweet tug of happier times.

He'd never imagined, when Pops and Nan fostered a boy one year older than him, that they would become as close as brothers. That Drew would be the magic human bullet that would drag Solo out of his shell.

The Huckleberry Finn to his Tom Sawyer.

Drew, with his wild adventurous spirit and his fearlessness, had changed Solo irrevocably. For the better. He owed Drew for instilling in him the courage to follow his dreams. To make the world a better place.

The fact that Drew's dreams had turned to dust wasn't Solo's fault, though, was it? Not his responsibility. What was he thinking? That by carrying this photo around he could turn back the clock, make everything right for Drew?

The familiar tightness pounded around the base of his skull. He'd done enough, put up with enough... even the whole messy business with Emma.

He'd never whispered a word of recrimination or blame to either of them.

Maybe he needed to give himself a break from the guilt trip. To not have to be confronted by Drew's toothy ten-year old grin every time he went to grab his credit card or his driver's licence.

Slowly he drew out the yellowed photo, eyes narrowing as he studied it. His own smile was reticent, uncertain. Drew's was like sunshine radiating out of a clear blue sky. Ready for whatever life threw at him. Daring it to test him.

And then there was Pop, the glue that held them both together.

Except, when Pop died, everything came unstuck.

Solo went to the cupboard and dragged out his rucksack. He opened the front pocket and got out a small album of photos, and leafed through it until he found a transparent sheath and slotted the photo into it. Then he closed it and put it carefully back into his rucksack.

One day, when Drew was well, Solo would be able to look at that photo without feeling like he'd been put through a shredder.

He had to believe that would happen.

CHAPTER 12

"*N*o, not like that." Judith laughed. "It's knit one, purl one, not knit for the whole row."

Polly looked down at the knitting in her hand. "I thought you meant knit a row, then purl a row."

She was only here as an extra pair of hands; knitting squares to make blankets for the homeless wasn't exactly her thing. She preferred ringing around hostels until she actually found someone a home. She hated craft, but Judith was down a staff member and frankly, with a quiet afternoon ahead, it stopped her antennae trying to locate Solo.

It was Friday, and other than a quick, stilted discussion about the PTSD group, they'd managed to avoid each other for the past two days. There had been a lot of unwell people admitted, and Solo had also been on call to ED, so their paths had rarely crossed.

Trouble was, that antsy feeling inside her didn't seem to be abating. Which was just not like her at all.

It was a great big blessing, Polly told herself, as she frowned at the offending bit of knitting, that Solo had been a scarce commodity on the ward.

Fuck it. How could it take this long to knit three rows?

From across the table Esme Yates let out a loud chortle. "Go, girl," she hollered. "At this rate you'll be finished by Christmas." Esme was on the upward swing, which was better than having her shuffle around the ward gently sobbing.

Polly gave her a thumbs-up. "You know me, Esme, a whizz at this stuff."

After Judith had "tinked" Polly's row, and informed everyone that tink was knit spelled backwards—frankly, the only fact about knitting that could be construed as even vaguely interesting—Judith went to help Jenny Blaine with her felt teddy bear. Jenny had over-stuffed the poor thing until its button eyes had taken on a look of abject horror.

Polly tucked the knitting needle under her arm and smiled brightly at her table of three.

"So, who's going home this weekend?"

"Me!" Esme said with glee.

"Not me." Clarke looked at her balefully over the top of his painting.

"Oh, why not?" Polly asked.

"I went AWOL last night."

Polly raised an eyebrow. "For how long?"

Clarke looked sheepish. "Got back at 6 a.m. Trouble is, freakin' Leon spotted me climbing in the bathroom window, didn't he?"

Polly smothered a smile. Clarke was nineteen, in for the second time after another drug-induced psychosis. He was a great kid from a messed-up background. Often enough, she wondered what her own fate would have been if she hadn't landed the job at The Book Genie when she ran away from home at sixteen. If Rowena hadn't become like a second mum to her, and Alice her best friend, would she have fared any better than Clarke?

"The rules are the rules, Clarke." She had a real soft spot for the young ones who found themselves in here. "I'm sure Judith will let you use the craft room to do some painting over the weekend."

No-one, least of all Clarke, had realised his artistic talent, until he'd started to use the art room on his previous admission. His colourful canvases were now hung around the ward, something he was rightly proud of. And this, at least, was legal, unlike his spray-paintings splashed on shops and hoardings.

"I've got a leave pass for a weekend at home," Celine Taggert said quietly, head bent over her tapestry. "Trent's picking me up at five o'clock." Her face had taken on a worried frown. Celine had three small children at home, and with this last bout of post-natal depression was in here with her baby. But today she looked fresher and a bit brighter than she had for the past week. Her hair was washed and she'd put on a new outfit.

"It's just a trial, Celine," Judith said as she moved around to check everyone's projects. Celine gave her a wobbly smile and Judith plopped down on the seat next to her. "Drop the perfect mum story you're telling yourself," Judith said kindly. "The kids and Trent will just be happy to have you home. Remember the daily plan we wrote up? Stick to that and it won't feel so overwhelming."

Judith squeezed Celine's arm. Watching her, Polly knew she could never match Judith's saintliness, or creativity, for that matter. She sighed and turned back to her task. If Judith wanted her to be a role model for crafting, she was going to be sadly disappointed. At least her effort would make everyone in the room feel like they were doing fantastically. If it improved anyone's self-esteem, Polly guessed she could cope with another thirty minutes of knitting hell.

Until, that was, she looked up to see Solo strolling through the door of the room.

The knitting needle fell out of her grasp, the stitches sliding off and landing in a spaghetti heap of wool in her lap.

Clarke laughed, Esme cackled loudly, even Celine giggled.

"Bat shit hell," Polly muttered under her breath.

"Hi Solo, what are you doing here?" Judith sprang up with a great big welcoming smile.

Solo's eyes held amusement as they met Polly's, then dropped to the pile of wool on her lap. "The ward's pretty empty, I thought I might find a few people in here."

"Where else would they be on a Friday afternoon?" Judith chirped.

An eyebrow jagged up. "Didn't know you were such an accomplished knitter, Polly." His lips twitched.

Polly put on her best scowl. Did he have to look so edible? His white shirt casually undone at the collar, cuffs rolled up to his elbows and eyes so luminous it was as if they'd been backlit.

All the other women in the room seemed to notice it, too.

The thing was, Solo didn't. He appeared oblivious to his appeal, unlike so many men she'd met. And somehow that only served to make him sexier.

Oh god, he was actually strolling over. Polly ducked her head. He went around the room, smiling and commenting on everyone's master-pieces. He picked up Jenny's teddy bear and agreed that it was just about the right cuddliness for her granddaughter. He said all the goddamn right things in just the right way. All the patients looked up at him adoringly.

Polly stifled the urge to shout, *"He's not a demi-god, you know!"*

Finally he reached her table and complimented Celine on her tapestry. Clarke was looking at him warily; he would have had the hard word from Solo this morning about his escape from the ward, but Solo grinned and complimented his painting in a way that had the kid grin-ning like he'd just won the Archibald Prize.

Polly focused on ramming the stitches back on her needle.

Too late, his shadow loomed over her. "Let's have a look at *your* project, Polly."

She tried to cover it with her hands.

"Go on," Esme crowed. "Show him what a pig's ear you've made of it."

"Thanks, Esme," Polly gritted darkly.

With all eyes on her there was nothing to do but plonk it on the table. Only three stitches remained, hanging onto the needle like they were clinging to a precipice.

"I acknowledge it's a disaster," she remarked airily. All eyes around the room peered over. She added, "For the record, the social worker on Echidna Ward can't knit for toffee."

Quick-smart, Solo's hand shot out and grabbed the needle and spaghetti of blue wool. Then he pulled up a chair and sat down next to her.

She gaped in amazement as he reached over, grabbed the other knitting needle off the table and wielded them both in his long fingers like chopsticks.

Silver eyes glittered. "Let's put this right, shall we?"

Polly's mouth went slack.

Swiftly, he cast on the stitches. "How many?" he directed at Judith, who was smiling at him like she'd gone a bit daft.

"Oh, um, forty."

He nodded, lips tight with concentration. Polly leaned back in her chair, crossed her arms over her chest and tried not to notice the way the muscles of his forearms stood out as he worked the needles. How could a guy knitting be this *hot*?

A frown etched his brows as he counted stitches, then started to knit rows, his movements fast and fluid.

As he got the third row done, the place she had finally lost control, Solo held it up.

The room burst into applause. Esme put her fingers between her lips and whistled like she was barracking for her favourite footie team.

Polly gave a shrug, muttered, "Where did you learn to knit?"

"My nan taught me."

"You took it in better than her baking tips, obviously."

Apart from the quirk of those gorgeous lips, he ignored the obvious jibe. "I enjoy it. I knit scarves, the odd beanie for friends."

"We'll get you in here to run the group, if you're not careful," Judith threatened.

Esme chortled. "Never gonna look at you the same way again, doc."

Solo winked, and Esme's round face went pink with pleasure.

As Solo handed Polly her knitting, their fingers skimmed. A sizzle of heat licked at her core. As he rose from the chair, she caught the scent of him, washing powder, and warm, clean maleness. A particular smell that was all his, and suddenly she was transported back to tangled sheets and a vision of his features contorted with pleasure.

Twang.

This was so not the place, but she knew it was mutual as their eyes locked.

"I'll leave you to get on with it," he said, his voice husky-edged. "I've got to write up some discharge summaries."

There was a general buzz of "don't go, Doc Solo. Stay and teach us how to knit beanies", to which Solo raised his hands and backed, laughing, out of the room.

"Don't spread this around," he said. "It might cost me my job."

Then he was gone, leaving Polly staring at her knitting, aware that Judith was staring at *her*.

WALKING off the ward at the end of the day, Solo had trouble keeping the grin off his face. Polly's gobsmacked expression had been classic; he wished he'd been able to catch a snap on his phone. For the first time since their amazing, explosive night together, he was pretty sure he'd done something right.

Yep, he was proud to admit it, he was good at knitting. Nan had taught him. Perfecting cables and trying out new and intricate patterns had become a form of stress release since then. It had taken him a few years to walk into knitting shops with his head held high, but he'd got to the stage now where he went in to feel the wool under his fingers, the colours and textures, and had become comfortable discussing patterns with the sales staff.

He'd even knitted Emma a sweater. Back in the day.

He was just having a fantasy of what colour wool he'd choose for Polly when a footfall, light and swift, made him turn.

Wild curls tumbled out of her up-do, making her look dangerously cute, cheeks flushed as she bounded towards him. She must have literally run to catch up with him, and the realisation made him stand that bit taller.

"Hi," she gasped as she came level.

"Hi."

"That was some stunt you pulled earlier."

He gave a little snort. "No stunt. Just clearing up the mess you'd got yourself into."

Now it was Polly's turn to snort. "I wasn't in a mess."

"No? You enjoy torturing balls of wool in your spare time, do you?"

"It just so happens"—she tilted her head at him, and he found his eyes dwelling on the creamy skin at the hollow of her neck—"some of us have better things to do with our spare time than knit."

They'd reached his bike and he put his helmet on the seat and stared straight at her.

Polly shoved her hands into her pant pockets.

"Like what?"

Her brows creased and she nibbled on her lower lip. *She wants to ask you on a date.* The thought sent a zing of electricity along his spine. If that was the case, he wasn't going to refuse. Professionalism be damned. He planted his legs wide and let his gaze drill into her. He was rewarded with a wave of colour shifting across her cheeks.

Her green gaze zoned in and sparked with his. "Like partying," she said, chin kicking up. "And when I party, I party hard."

"Yeah?"

"Yeah."

He propped his hip on the saddle. "You think I couldn't keep up?"

She popped her eyes at him "Is that a challenge?"

"Could be."

"Phhttt, you haven't seen my moves on the dance floor."

He cocked an eyebrow. "Maybe not on the dance floor." He let the ending hang between them.

He watched her throat move as she swallowed. Her feet did a little shimmy, like she wanted to rub her thighs together.

His fly obligingly tightened.

An image of their bodies grinding and bumping and covered in sweat in a nightclub had him even more uncomfortable.

He squinted into the lowering sun behind her shoulder. Tried to sound casual. "Maybe you should show me some of the hot spots around Perth sometime."

He should have let her make the first move, but frankly, with Polly, you never knew which move she was going to make next. So what the hell if he hung himself with the tiny piece of rope she'd thrown him.

He saw her draw in a breath, the swell of her breasts under her plain blouse making his brain flash to the memory of her beautiful dark nipples. Was he hallucinating or was that the outline of them against the material of her shirt?

He flicked his eyes back to her face, only to see her lick her lips, leaving a gleam of residual moisture. What she could do with those lips... he stifled a groan.

The silence stretched loud between them. Was she ever going to answer? She pushed the hair off her face and said suddenly, "Tomorrow night."

"Tomorrow?"

"So, do you want to or not?"

Solo blinked and picked up his helmet, started playing with the catch. Shit, if she glanced below his waist it was embarrassingly clear he wanted to. He tried to sound super-casual. "Sure, I think I'm free."

She threw back her head and laughed at that. "Oh yeah, I know what Carts will have planned for you. A night at the Shamrock with Dan and a curry, then on to the casino."

Solo smirked. That had already happened, last week. And while Dan was a great guy, he had a one-track mind—that track being rugby. Carts, he was warming to by the day, except that he talked non-stop and wore seriously strange exercise gear. Solo was learning to zone out to the constant patter.

However, that did not make a night out on the town with the two of them more attractive than bumping hips with Polly on the dance floor.

"Okay, where? And what time?"

She tapped at her lip and rolled her eyes heavenward as if thinking hard. He drank her in. The line of her cheeks, the softness of her pale skin, the tiny little dusting of barely-there freckles on her nose.

She met his gaze squarely, her lips curving up at the edges.

"Meet me at the Ark. It's a bar on the main drag in Fremantle. Then we'll go on to the Fly by Night club."

"Sweet," he said, and then thought that was probably more the type of thing an adolescent would say. "Cool." Frig, that was even worse. "What time?"

"Eight o'clock."

He swung his leg over his bike and hid a little smirk of satisfaction as he saw those green eyes fix briefly on the v of his thighs over the shiny metal chassis. "I'll be there."

Solo flicked the key and the engine roared into life. Polly stepped back, but she was smiling the sort of smile that women wore when they were secretly impressed.

He worked the throttle, let the engine rev. Shoved on his gloves.

"See you tomorrow, 8 p.m. at the Ark." He grinned, and she grinned back, and then he slammed down his visor and left in a shit-shower of fumes.

They were in a power struggle. He knew it, and for once he was looking forward to seeing who came out on top.

CHAPTER 13

Swiping the mascara wand over her lashes, Polly propped Alice against the mirror.

Or, to be more accurate, her phone, with Alice on FaceTime.

Alice's face bobbed in and out of view.

"What are you doing?" Polly asked, then frowned as the screen went dark for a moment.

"Digging the veggie patch in Dad's garden."

There was a blur of a pink nose, whiskers and two wide staring yellow eyes and then the sound of Alice complaining in the background. "Get away, Beelzebub."

Polly's eyebrows flew up. "Beelzebub?"

"Dad's cat. He's a devil of a mouser, that's how he got the name."

"Could you tell him to scoot? Two's company, three's a crowd, kind of thing?" She'd never been much of a cat person; they always had this look like they knew best.

"Be gone, Beelzebub," Alice ordered. The flash of a bushy tail, then some liberty-print gardening gloves took brief centre screen before Alice's smile flashed back into view. "So, tell me everything about this guy."

Polly poked the mascara wand in her eye and blinked madly. "There's nothing to tell."

"Oh, come on, you've been as coy as a vestal virgin lately."

"Me? Virginal?" Polly placed her mascara down and debated on her lipstick shade. Possibly Crimson Seduction was a little too obvious.

A backdrop of weeping willows and puffy clouds framed Alice's head. "Beelzebub's gone. I'm all ears." Alice peered eagerly over her glasses.

Honestly, what harm would it do to tell Alice? For one thing, she was 12,000 miles away in Cambridge. And it wasn't like Polly hadn't dissected plenty of dates with her best friend in the past. Trouble was, this feeling like someone had shaken and then uncorked a bottle of champagne inside her wasn't something she was used to. Nor was the way her breath hitched at the memory of those metallic eyes, as if they could strip her naked with a glance.

"Okay, he's probably just over six foot, dark, good-looking in an unconventional way, seriously nice pecs..."

Alice's face cracked a big grin. "So far so good."

Oh god, she was actually blushing, she could feel it doing its slow creep. This was crazy. She did her best to firm up her voice, but the words still came out all breathy. "He's not macho, not my usual hunk style at all, to be honest. More lean, mean muscle, I guess. Not big... urm, he's actually quite big... in certain places."

"I see!"

There was nothing for it but to fill Alice in on the night of Jake's wedding, the shock of finding out Solo was her colleague. It took a few minutes to finish the story.

Alice's glasses took up most of the screen. "You like him, don't you?"

"I have a case of the screaming hots, if that's what you mean."

"I think it's more than that."

Polly held up two lipsticks to her phone "Which one, Munchkin?"

Alice stabbed a finger. "The one on the left, or is it your right and my left?"

"Helpful."

"Go on."

"He intrigues me, that's all," Polly said, unfurling the bright-red tip of the imaginatively named Rosebud Red. "There's some mystery around why he left his job in Sydney." Should she mention the photo? The strange text messages Carts had told her about? But there didn't seem enough to build a substantial case on, and she didn't want Alice to think she'd gone weird and romantic like one of the Brontë novels her friend adored.

"Oooh, tell me more."

"Oh, look, there's nothing really. He's just been a bit evasive about why he's over here, that's all. Anyway, he's a locum for three months, so I can have fun and then send him on his bike back to Sydney."

"What if you're still hot for him in three months?"

"You know I'll be bored by then."

So why did the idea of Solo getting on that big beast and riding off into the sunset suddenly make her stomach bottom out?

Alice chirped even more unhelpfully, "What if your biological clock suddenly starts ticking?"

"It can tickity-tock right along without me," Polly clipped back. "I'm never going to be in the game for babies. Being an auntie will be enough, thank you."

Alice sighed heavily, clearly defeated. "Anyway, you look beautiful, you'll knock the poor guy's socks off like you always do."

Polly fluffed out her hair. "Should I straighten these babies out?"

"No, they're who you are."

A memory of Solo coiling one of her curls over his finger as they lay in bed together cemented the decision to leave her tongs in the cupboard. Polly grabbed her Diorissimo and sprayed liberally. "Everything okay in the city of golden spires?"

"That's Oxford, I'm in Cambridge."

"Almost the same, all the buildings look like Hogwarts. How's Aaron?"

"Perfect, we're pretty much blissed out as usual." The phone wobbled and Polly got a view of Alice's jeans-clad knees. Then a bunch of radishes appeared. "It's like Peter Rabbit's garden here. Want some?"

"No, I think I'll pass."

"From Mrs Tiggywinkle, loads of hugs. Have fun with Sigmund Freud."

Polly ignored the last comment. "Love to Aaron. Bye."

When she'd put down her phone, she got up from the dressing table and admired her reflection in the mirror. A figure-hugging 1950s-style black sateen dress she'd got for a song on eBay accentuated her curves. She'd gone to town on her outfit. But hell, she'd promised to show Solo a good time, and that meant pulling out all the stops. That was the only reason, she told herself firmly as she did a quick boob hitch. The only disappointment was that since Solo had turned up, her lemon diet had fizzled. There had been too many nights she'd needed chocolate these past two weeks. Which meant that while her butt hadn't shrunk, her breasts were looking magnificent. Why could you never get the balance right? Small butt and your boobs sagged like a half-empty sack of potatoes. Big butt, and—*boobalicious.*

If it was good enough for the Kardashians, it was good enough for her!

Another quick slick of Rosebud Red, a brush of blusher high on her cheekbones and she would have to do.

She was about to toe on her red stilettos when the doorbell rang.

She stilled.

It came again, more urgently. Barefoot, she tiptoed along the hallway and put her eye up to the peephole in the front door.

There stood Judith, her nose huge in a distortedly tiny head.

What the heck? From Judith's usual description of a weekend, on a Saturday night she and Mark would be chomping on Cadbury's Fruit and Nut and binge-watching Stan.

As Polly flung open the front door, Judith catapulted over the threshold and promptly burst into tears. Concern mixed with a dull *thunk* in the pit of Polly's stomach as her night with Solo receded like the Starship Enterprise on a mission to another galaxy.

"Jude, what's happened?" Her arms came around and hugged her friend. They didn't normally have that much of a touchy-feely friendship, but this was clearly way out of the ordinary. Jude was not the kind of person who fell apart; she was always on an even keel.

"Mark's... dum—ped... me."

Polly's eyes widened in disbelief. Mark of the terminal incapacity to do anything that didn't comply with routine. How on earth had he gone so far out of his comfort zone as to dump the kindest, most giving woman in the world?

"Come in here." She locked her arm around a sobbing Judith and marched her—gently—into the kitchen, sat her down at the kitchen table and drew up a chair.

Leaning forward, Polly probed gently, "Tell me what happened."

Judith peered out from between her fingers. "Have you got a—a tissue?"

"Of course." Polly jumped up and found the tissue box on top of the fridge. She couldn't help a surreptitious glance at the clock. 7.45. There was no way she would make Fremantle by eight, even without Judith's arrival.

She could wave goodbye to her night of rampant sex.

A gaping hole threatened to open up inside her but she stepped right over it.

"What happened?" She handed over the box and Judith ripped out a bunch of tissues, stuffed them against her eyes and then blew her nose noisily.

"We were planning next year's holiday—correction, *I* was—Mark never does a thing towards holidays. I've been trying to discuss if for weeks, and Mark just keeps being evasive. So tonight I had the two websites up and I said, 'okay, it's either Scotland or Greece'. And you know what he said?"

Polly shook her head.

"He said *'neither'.*" Judith's voice escalated, finishing on a wail as her eyes squeezed tight and tears shot out in all directions.

"Oh hon, maybe that just meant he didn't like the options."

"I asked him that, *obviously*," Judith came back almost vehemently as she swiped at her eyes. Probably best to back off and let her just get it off her chest, Polly decided. "I said, 'Mark sweetheart, if you don't like my choices, then I'm happy for you to choose a destination, but you know you haven't exactly shown a whole heap of enthusiasm.' He wouldn't look me in the eye, but his face went this kind of grey colour and I got this horrible sense of dread in my stomach."

Polly sat very still.

"I had to dig it out of him." Judith hiccupped. "I asked, 'What's wrong, sweetheart?' about a thousand times. He just sat there like he'd lost his voice. And then finally he said... he said... 'I just don't want us to go on holiday'. So, you know, I said, 'Okay, we won't go.' And then he said, 'Full stop.' He even said *full stop*, like *who even says that?*"

"Does he want to go away on his own, maybe?"

Judith balled the tissues in her hands. "I asked that too. I said, 'okay then, we can take separate holidays for a change', and after ages he said, 'no, I don't want to take a holiday on my own. I want to live on my own. I don't want to be with you, Judith'. I mean, he never calls me Judith, I'm always Smidge."

Polly tried not to look aghast. Smidge did not work on Judith.

They stayed silent for a long moment, while Polly digested and Judith snuffled.

"Is there anyone else?" It had to be asked.

Judith shook her head. "That's the problem. I almost wish there was, but I don't think so."

Admittedly, the idea of socially challenged Mark having someone on the side didn't add up. Unless it was one of his nerdy online gaming mates. Falling in love online. That happened all the time, though how you could start something without touching and tasting first was hard for Polly to fathom.

Judith glanced up out of puffy eyes. "We had a talk a little while ago, about... about ... you know..."

Polly gave an encouraging eyebrow waggle. "Sex?"

"Yep. After you asked me—you know—in the pub, I realised maybe it wasn't that good between us any more, so I went home and asked, and he—" she let out a strangled little cough— "he said, like, it's not that high on his agenda. He's too stressed or something, though what he'd be stressed about, god knows. Must be trying to win at those stupid computer games."

Polly found herself lost for words. How could a guy prefer gaming to spending time with Judith?

"He said he needs space to find himself, develop his own interests."

Polly's eyes sprang wide. "He actually said that?"

"Uh-huh." By now Judith had turned the clump of tissues into a papier mâché sculpture.

"He's only got two interests. Television and gaming."

"Perhaps that's the problem. Maybe he feels I've stunted his growth. That I've smothered him."

"Nonsense. You've given him so much space he practically lives in a parallel universe." Polly took Judith gently by the shoulder. "Look at me, Jude. You deserve so much more. You deserve to have someone worship the ground you walk on, to want to have crazy passionate sex with you every day and make oodles of babies with you."

Judith gave a grimace. "I don't know if I think that's possible."

"It is." Funny how powerful her belief in love was. For everyone except herself.

"I'm sure, in the end, it'll be for the best, it's just there's this great big hole that Mark has always filled. It may have been full of dry dirt but at least it was filled." Judith started to weep again. Quiet, copious tears that splashed down her cheeks and into her cupped hands.

Polly ripped out some more tissues from the box and handed them to her.

"Nothing grows in dry dirt, hon. You have to have rich soil, and it has to be well-watered." Judith gave a trembly smile at that. "And lots of sunshine, and bees to cross-pollinate... Okay, maybe I'm getting a bit carried away, but you get the gist. You can't spend your evenings crocheting while Mark sits on his computer and slams asteroids into virtual galaxies for hours on end with his hobbity mates."

Now Judith really laughed. "That's rather a mixed metaphor." Her nose was shiny and her eyes still swimming in water; she looked like she'd been attacked by a hailstorm, but at least she'd been able to share.

This, thought Polly, was so overdue that the recovery would likely be swift once they sorted out all the practical shit. "You don't have a dog, do you?"

Judith looked surprised. "No, why?"

"Custody can be a nightmare."

"Only a goldfish." Judith sighed. "And he's on his last fins."

"I think you'll navigate that problem okay."

Somewhere, from the depths of her room, Polly's mobile pinged an incoming message. She stiffened.

Judith looked at her properly for the first time, her eyes narrowing as she panned down Polly's black dress. "Oh my god, you were about to go out, weren't you?"

Shrugging away the arrows of disappointment, Polly said airily, "Nothing major." The lie hit her in the stomach like a wrecking ball. "I'll just go and let them know I can't make it."

As she rose, Judith reached out and touched her arm. "Seriously, I'll go home. It won't make any difference. He'll be on his computer, or in front of telly, and I'll go to my craft room and—"

Her lower lip wobbled and Polly's resolve hardened. She had to support her friend. She couldn't even imagine how it would feel to have twelve years of togetherness collapse in a heap, even if it was totally sub-standard togetherness.

"You're not going home. I'm going to get you a drink."

"A cup of tea would be nice," Judith said wistfully.

"I've got chamomile, peppermint or English breakfast. And you're going to stay over." Polly's smile was plastered on; the itch to go find her phone intensified. "You can start to sort out how you deal with all this in the cool light of day."

As Judith opened her mouth, Polly put her finger to her lips. "Hush. I wasn't even interested in going out tonight anyway."

With that she turned and went to find her phone. Her head might be held high, but the truth was, her body felt heavier with every step she took towards what she was sure was Solo's text asking where she was.

Hell, it was for the best, wasn't it? Imagining those long fingers and that wicked mouth exploring her body had required her to put her vibrator back on charge way too often this past week.

Best to let the batteries run down on this one before the damn guy burrowed into other places he had no right to be.

Like her heart.

~

SOLO INHALED. The nicotine hit his lungs and he dragged out the familiar hit for longer than normal, then pursed his lips and exhaled, the smoke spiralling up in the light from the streetlamp.

Heaviness cloaked him. It felt like someone had promised him a shiny cut diamond and instead delivered a bucket of dull pebbles.

When he'd messaged her earlier, he'd expected her to reply, "on my way," not the abrupt, "can't make it. Something's come up". It had made his gut contract with a slug of something more than annoyance, more than disappointment even.

Feeling completely deflated, he'd got on his bike and rode home, then paced around his room for half an hour, maybe longer. Tried to work out a suitable reply that looked like he couldn't give a fuck. Dialled down the overpowering urge to call her and demand to know what the hell was more important than their night out, more important than both of them ending up hot and sweaty, down and dirty between the sheets.

Oh, Christ, who was he kidding? He wasn't a down-and-dirty type of guy.

Except he had been, with her. He'd been spontaneous and testosterone-driven and full of beating-his-chest machismo.

But however much he tried to fool himself that it was only her sexy butt wiggle and the wicked light in those emerald eyes, if he was honest, their connection had got under his skin. He saw the shadow of past hurts peeping out from behind her bravado, sensed the pain behind her swagger.

Polly Fletcher could say all she liked, but she was running scared.

Yes, they damn well had a connection. No-one could tell him otherwise—he'd known it from the moment she swung around and their eyes had fused at that old outback hotel.

He almost wanted to punch the wall, which was way over the top. Stupidly, he'd dropped his guard, let himself feel happy, elated even, for the first time in months. He couldn't recall when he'd last felt this good, not even when he'd finally plucked up the courage to ask Emma out on a date.

He'd loved Emma, adored her for years.

But he'd never wanted to freakin' boogie with glee before a date with Emma. She'd never made him feel like doing a John Travolta in *Saturday Night Fever*, a Patrick Swayze in *Dirty Dancing*.

But Polly Fletcher, in just two weeks, had.

So after he'd sent an equally curt, "no worries, catch you Monday", he'd gone into the kitchen and rummaged around for something alcoholic. He'd just found a bottle of shiraz and scribbled an "I owe you one" note when Carts shot through the door in his yoga gear. He was wearing an OM-inscribed T-shirt, spidery legs encased in tight black shorts and a bandana wound round his head. His appearance would have lightened any normal mood, but tonight, no.

"I am deeply relaxed and sending peace to all sentient beings," Carts had said, bringing his palms together in response to Solo's confession that he'd stolen the wine. "Have it on me," he said as he threw his towel on the back of a chair and tugged off his headband. "Better still, instead of guzzling that on your own, why don't you join me and Dan at the Shamrock?"

Solo didn't want to, but he didn't want to be alone either. So he'd gone, shared a couple of Guinnesses, gritted his teeth through the rugby talk and then excused himself.

He couldn't stomach a vindaloo.

Back home, he'd sat and looked at his cigarette stash. And then lit one, smoked it down to the butt and lit another. And now here he was on the front porch, wondering whether he should try and find a locum position in some little town in the middle of nowhere and hide out for the next year.

Until his wounds had healed enough to…

To what? Return to Pop's farm, which he knew he'd likely have to sell, as the caretaker had only promised a year? Watch Drew piece his life back together from a distance, probably with Emma? Either way, nothing was ever going to be the same between the three of them again.

He took a last puff and turned to go inside when a shadow on the street caught his eye. The familiar tilt of a head was suddenly illuminated. Bobbing curls, that swift gliding step, and his heart lurched like someone had taken a turbo charger to it.

The click of the gate and then she was skimming up the path and his heart was suddenly doing the tango.

"You," was all he could get out gruffly as she drew to a standstill and tilted her chin at him.

Her eyes glittered like two bright jewels and her lips were full and parted, and so soft and inviting it took all his willpower not to dive in for a kiss, to remember he'd just put out his second cigarette and she'd probably find him disgusting.

"Yes. Me."

"What are you doing here?" He stalled for time as the light from the front door arced onto her features, lighting up her cute round cheeks, the dimples bracketing her perfect mouth.

A smile hitched at the corner of her lips. "Just hanging out. Like you. Had to cancel on a hot date."

"Really?"

"Yeah, shame, eh?"

"Shame."

"But I'd be prepared to settle for a nightcap. What've you got?" Reaching out, she gave his arm a mock punch, then her nostrils quivered. "Do I detect smoke?"

He grinned. "Terrible pollution problem this end of town."

"Really?" She shimmied closer and he caught her delectable heady perfume. "Breathe on me."

Anyone would have thought she'd said *go down on me,* the way his cock rose to immediate attention. Christ, look what this woman did to him. He went from 0 to 100 in a matter of seconds. Ferrari, eat your heart out.

Solo tightened his lips. She reached out and touched him there with a fingertip and, unable to stop himself, he sucked her finger into his mouth. With a little gasp she melted against him, and all he could register was her breasts against his pecs and a pair of hot, eager lips meeting his.

He gave up worrying about his breath.

They kissed ferociously as Polly backed him hard into the front door, her palms sending heat into his chest. In a flash, he swung them round and it was Polly's turn to be backed against the hard surface. He let his tongue explore her mouth with deliberate precision, and she moaned softly, her body all yielding curves, pressed against his rigid cock. And then... Jesusss *Christ*, when she reached a hand between them and palmed him over his jeans he nearly tipped over the edge. In answer his fingers ruched up the satin of her dress, relishing the slide of fabric, of skin meeting skin, as his palm found the top of her suspenders.

"Wicked thing," he muttered, hot against her mouth.

"What did you expect?" she panted.

"Nothing less from you." He tongued the rim of her lips.

Right now, all he wanted was to dive into her, bury in deep and happily never surface again.

When she wrapped her hand over his and moved his fingers higher, he almost forgot to breathe; no way was he going to stop her, even though they were still in full view of the street. She directed his hand under the drenched gusset of her panties to the slippery delight of her sex. Strumming the hard nub of her clit elicited little gasps and sighs as her head kicked back against the door.

Her body was melting into his touch but he had the presence of mind—just—to know that a crazy coupling against Carts' open front door maybe wasn't the best idea.

"Bedroom," he gritted out and she nodded wordlessly.

Somehow he'd managed to silence Polly Fletcher with a few deft strokes of his fingers. Sweet fucking victory.

Reluctantly, he removed his hand from between her legs, looped his arm around her waist, and tugged her through the door before slamming it with his heel and heading with her up the stairs.

It appeared Polly had no problem with a show of primitive male behaviour, if the light trip of her feet and that soft breathy giggle close to his ear was anything to go by.

Seconds later, Solo had slammed the bedroom door with the same finesse, and for a moment they stood gasping in the light cast from the street lamp outside; eyes eating into each other, before Polly's nimble fingers ripped at his shirt buttons.

"Nice." Her voice was thick like treacle as she admired his bare pecs.

"Nice? Is that the best you can do?"

She stepped back and shimmied out of her dress. Seeing her in just her lacy bra and undies, he felt a rumble of delight rising up his throat.

"Now you." She tossed black curls away from her shoulders.

He grinned. Slowly undid his belt.

"Take your bra off," he demanded, sliding his jeans lower over his hips, aware of his erection wanting to burst from the confines of his boxers. "Or I don't go another inch."

"Fighting talk," Polly murmured, but biting at her lower lip, she did as he'd asked.

Moments later her beautiful white breasts, big and full and heavy and just as amazing as he remembered, stood proud, her nipples dark against the luminosity of her skin.

Hot air whooshed from his nostrils. His mouth went dry. The buzz in his balls tightened to a deep ache.

In front of him her hands toyed with her breasts, a look of triumph curling her lips as she tweaked each nipple into a hard peak.

"Boxers. Off." Her voice was hoarse, and such a turn-on his cock bucked an immediate response.

Trying to pretend he wasn't desperate, Solo shucked down his jeans and boxers and his cock bounced free, ready for action. She licked her lips, gave a little sound, almost a battle cry, and as if of one mind they sprang at each other like two wild animals. In between wild, wet kisses her warm fingers were shafting him, his own exploring between her legs, working her as she moaned with pleasure. It felt to Solo like the boundaries of their bodies had merged.

Pulling back with super-human effort, he pressed her gently down onto the bed and propped himself on his arms above her. Polly flopped backwards with a husky moan.

He worked little kisses down her body, over the soft mound of her belly, until he reached the heart-shaped little patch of dark hair.

She spread her legs and arched her back.

Almost reverently, he kneeled between her splayed legs and, taking her gently by the thighs, slung one leg over each of his shoulders.

As she squirmed deliciously below him, he dipped his head... lower... lower...

"Oh-myyyy-god," she sang and her fingers weaved tight into his hair.

With a groan of pleasure, Solo buried his mouth deep and let his tongue work its magic.

CHAPTER 14

*W*as that really her?

At some level she knew those little mewls and gasps were coming out of her mouth, but with the mind-blowing tactics of Solo's tongue, she really was too... preoccupied to—ahhhhhh...

He'd just hit the sweet spot so perfectly that a string of fairy lights lit up behind her eyes. And when two warm hands sneaked up, cupping her breasts, his thumbs skimming over her taut nipples in perfect sync with his tongue and... oh, boy, this was her complete and utter denouement.

Polly's hips bucked wildly, at which Solo let out a low, sexy chuckle.

Maybe it was the total appreciation in that laugh, as if she was the most delicious thing he'd ever tasted, maybe it was the firm sweep of his tongue... backwards, forwards, deeper, firmer, combined with the blissful tweaking of her nipples, and... suddenly... everything was climbing fast and furious, coiling tighter and tighter into one bright, bunching seismic almighty...

"Ohmygodohmygodoh myyyyyyy—GOD!"

Polly's body was no longer hers to own, limbs jerking, back arching, complete nonsense flying out of her mouth and her fingers riveted to Solo's head as she clung on for the ride of her life.

A ride that kept on giving... and giving...

Who knew how long afterwards? Maybe minutes... maybe hours... she found herself lying limp and utterly sated on the rucked-up sheets of Solo's single bed.

Eyes wide, all she could do was stare into the darkness and gulp in great mouthfuls of air, like a fish dumped on the shore.

Finally, fingers stroking Solo's spiky soft hair, she managed an off-key, "That was intense."

As he grinned up at her, it struck Polly that he had the look of a hunter who'd emerged victorious with his prey.

Okay, okay, she'd concede.

He'd won. Hands—or rather, mouth—down.

After a long, long moment to regain her breath, she decided to do a little exploration with her foot between their bodies. Yep. There it was. A magnificent erection. Polly let her toes do a spidey massage up and down the length of him, which elicited a deep growl and a sudden catapulting of his body up the length of hers. He leaned on his elbows, looking down at her, and she held her breath at the sheer animal beauty of him. The silver of his eyes, slits of brilliant passion, his lips full and juicy from the wickedness they'd been up to, and his short hair standing up in little spikes around his head.

Oh god, he'd make a wonderful werewolf.

She kissed his mouth and it tasted musky and sweet as a drop of moisture fell on her thigh from his cock. As her fingers closed around the thickness of him, he pulled back.

"I don't have a condom." His look was so alarmed she had to laugh. She waved the hand that wasn't occupied at the floor.

"Over there."

"What?"

"I slipped one in my bra before I left home. It'll be on the floor somewhere."

Solo shot up so fast, and with such determination, Polly kept laughing. She watched him as he searched the floor. Slim, taut, beautifully put together, with the agility of an elite athlete.

"Do you run?" she asked.

"What?"

"You look like a marathon runner."

'Got it.' He dived to pick up the little foil package and landed back on the bed. "The only running I've done lately is chasing after you."

For some reason she felt insanely pleased by this.

When he loomed over her, his lips pursed, and a wicked glint in his eyes, she suddenly realised what he was up to. Oh god, he was going for her nose. With a squeal, Polly clapped a hand over her face. "Don't kiss my nose."

"Why not?"

"I don't like it. Here, give me that condom!"

"Do I trust you?"

"Never trust me." She went to bite his neck and they fell around laughing and kissing, until she managed to pull the condom pack from his hand. Finally, kneeling above her, his thighs scissoring her pelvis, Solo let her take over. His gaze burned into her as she concentrated on ripping the packet with her teeth. Swiftly, she rolled the condom down his erection, then cupped his balls, heavy and rock-hard. Just like his beautiful big cock.

When he sank between her legs, Polly opened to accommodate him with a sigh.

So what if it was missionary position? So what if it was good old orthodox vanilla-flavoured sex? It felt beyond amazing as Solo hovered, then thrust, then drew out and did it all over again. Lips tight, eyes like lightning streaks in his taut face, his beauty commanded her to watch. He bit his lip, the veins in his neck prominent as he focused. With each one of his deep thrusts, her pleasure escalated, needing him deeper, harder, needing... more... She pressed her palms into his buttocks, pulling him closer, and he slammed into her.

How could it be that her body was begging again for relief?

As if he read her, he whispered against her ear, 'Touch yourself.'

A guy had never instructed her to do it, but it seemed Solo knew instinctively what was needed.

"I want us to come together," he husked out and gently took her hand and placed it in between her legs. Her fingers grazed the rigid base of his cock, his balls nudging against her fingers as their bodies found purchase and rhythm.

He was close, she could tell by the swell of him inside her, but god, so was she, soooo sooo close... Her fingers moved faster.

Solo's vivid gaze held hers. "Come with me."

Their eyes locked.

To her infinite surprise the sheer intimacy of it catapulted Polly right over the edge. As she spasmed tight around him, she felt him release deep inside her.

Heard her name rung out of his lips.

And all the time those silver eyes held hers in thrall.

Finally, he slumped heavy against her, breathing hard and she wrapped her arms around his sweat-slicked body. Letting her hands shimmy around his back, up his neck and into his damp hair, Polly gulped down the tightness in her throat and blinked away the watery feeling in her eyes.

No big deal.

It was just a case of multiple orgasms messing with her brain chemistry.

Nothing more.

～

SOLO LAY PANTING, loving the feel of her fingers smoothing through his hair. He had to withdraw. Take the damned galoshes off his cock. But all he wanted was to hold her close.

His release had been so mind-blowing, so powerful, he actually wasn't sure what he'd shouted.

He just knew he'd yelled a hell of a lot and the word "Polly" had featured high on the list. Christ, he wouldn't have had a clue if Carts had come home in the middle of it, but with the amount of "Oh my god, Polly" he'd shouted, he'd probably left the whole street in no doubt as to who he was fucking.

He rolled over and she made an appreciative sound that made him feel like he was exiting the podium after scoring gold in the Olympics.

He removed the condom and knotted it, and chucked it with expert precision at the bin. Then he rolled back to face her.

To his absolute delight, she snuggled into him, pushing damp curls off her face and eyeing him out of bright perky eyes. She was so beautiful his breath caught; swollen lips, pink cheeks and an orgasm flush between her breasts. He loved how easily they enjoyed each other physically. There seemed to be no barriers when the clothes were off. Maybe they should stay naked in bed for a week, a la John Lennon and Yoko Ono.

Stroking her cheek gently, he said, "You look gorgeous when you come."

Her mouth quirked, "Glad my O face met with your approval."

He kissed her forehead. She snuggled into him and her curls tickled his nose. It was tempting to tease her that a mere week and a half ago she'd warned him she didn't fraternise with work colleagues, but he wasn't going to test his luck. If it were up to him, this would be only the beginning...

He frowned. The beginning of what?

He didn't know, except he didn't want to think of an end point...

As if she sensed his body tighten, Polly cast a glance up. One eye peeped out from behind a waterfall of curls.

"You okay?"

"Never better."

"Are you the kind of guy who smokes after sex?"

He mockingly cast a glance down at his cock and it dared to stir with renewed interest. "Not that I've noticed."

Polly gave him a playful slap on the arm. "Dag."

She was stroking her hands across his chest in slow sweeps. "So, where did you learn to pleasure a girl so perfectly?"

A bubble of pride swelled his chest. "Don't all guys?"

She gave a startled burst of laughter. "Are you kidding me? No, they do not."

"And you're an expert, right?"

"I might have slept with a few men, yes." Her lip curled. "So what?"

"So, nothing. I'm not judging." Not judging, no, but he could feel the shadow of jealousy lurking somewhere inside him. The sharp jab in his solar plexus was not welcome. He didn't need to risk any more wounds right now.

"That's good." She pushed away from him, and it felt like someone had opened a door next to his heart and let in a draft of cold air. "Because I have no time for all that double-standard bullshit you men think you can pull."

"'You men?' What makes you think you can shove me into the sexist jerk basket?"

"I didn't."

"You got close."

She stuck out the tip of a pink tongue. "Tetchy."

"Yeah, dead right. I'm not judging you, so don't pull that on me." His tone was sharper than he'd meant, and for a split second she looked confused and suddenly child-like. He longed to ask more questions, to connect, dig deeper, but right now he sensed he should tread carefully.

Placating, he murmured, "So what made you change your mind?" Stroking her neck, he was pleased she didn't pull away; she was more inclined, it seemed, to nudge against him like a kitten about to purr.

"Mmm?" she queried, eyes darkening as his fingers moved to the swell of her breast.

He phrased it differently. "Why'd you decide not to stand me up?"

She was watching his fingers, and so was he, the way her nipple peaked as he lightly pinched it. "I—" She lay back against the pillows and frowned; that was his cue to stop. Probably a good thing, since they'd used up the one and only condom.

"Keep it quiet, but Judith's long-term partner has just called it off."

Relief flooded him, and then he felt bad that his gain was Judith's loss. "So that's why you pulled the pin earlier?"

She nodded, playing with one of her longer curls, pulling it out, staring at it so her eyes nearly crossed, then letting it ping back into a tight coil. Solo swallowed a smile. He'd bet she'd done that since she was a kid.

"Yes, she turned up just as I was about to leave. She was a complete mess, poor darling. She's well rid of him—he's about as inspiring as a wet dishcloth—but she doesn't see it that way, obviously."

"Poor Judith." He knew what unquestioning devotion felt like when it got slammed into a brick wall without notice.

"I couldn't really explain in a text."

"A bit more info might have helped."

"Yeah, sorry about that."

"Better for my health, too."

She cocked an eyebrow. "Meaning?"

"Meaning it might have saved me smoking a full month's ration of ciggies."

"Wow! I affect you that much!" It was a tease, but a little glimmer of something else shone out of her eyes. Hope flared in his chest but he forced his face into casual lines. "Friends always come first," she finished, breaking eye contact.

Doof. That put him in his place. "Is she okay?"

"As okay as you'd expect. She's a trooper. She was going to stay at my place overnight, but then decided to go to her mum and dad's. So I, um —made the split decision to pop over and see"—she turned on her side again, supporting her head under her cupped hand, and looked up at him out of lazy emerald eyes—"whether you were still interested..." Her finger traced a line down his shoulder, over his bicep and along his forearm.

"And found I was," he croaked.

Not smiling, she placed his hand back on her breast and let out a husky little sound as he took the invitation seriously and squeezed her nipple between finger and thumb.

"Jes-us," he groaned. "Why did you only bring one condom?"

"An oversight." She sat up now, looking like a kid in a candy store, starting to skim kisses across his chest, over his stomach, down the line of fine hairs that thickened towards his groin. He had no say over what was happening below his waist and she knew it. Warm fingers closed around his suddenly throbbing length.

She grinned, like she'd landed the best lollipop in the whole wide world. "But we have other ways and means..."

With another groan, Solo threw himself back on the bed and let her have her wicked, wicked way.

~

POLLY WOKE WITH A START.

Solo's arm was heavy across her waist. After another very satisfying and creative bout of sex, they'd both fallen into a deep slumber.

But now her bladder was full to bursting point.

She shifted Solo's arm and he grunted. "Whatsh up, babe?"

Babe. The way he said it made her go mushy inside for a second, before the nerve endings in her bladder made her shoot out of bed.

"I need a pee," she hissed. "Do you think Carts is home?"

"Dunno. Does it matter?" He rolled over, and even in her state of desperation she could appreciate the play of his pecs and biceps, his long legs, and the hand flung across his eyes. She cast an eye around for something to cover her nakedness, spied his T-shirt on the floor and flung it over her head.

She tiptoed to the door and opened it a crack. The house was dark. Good sign. Nobody home.

Solo's sleepy voice came from the bed. "Missing you already."

Something in her chest tugged at the sweetness of that comment, but she shooed it away as she made her way into the bathroom.

Sitting on the toilet, she tried to think this through. Logically. Which was hard when even now the pull of that gorgeous bod in the narrow little bed was like the gravitational force of an entire planetary system.

How could it have been this good? Feel this intimate? Truth was, despite her once-love of Tinder, she'd passed on the casual sex thing recently. Which was probably why when Jake ditched her—gently, but firmly—because he'd fallen in love with Lou, it had hurt more than she'd imagined.

Not because she was in love with Jake—God no, never that—but it had been warm and safe and *nice*.

But, here, even more significant than having her mind blown by the most amazing sex, she had the sense she was in a circle of safety. With a guy she didn't even know.

Like they *fit together.*

Which, frankly, was enough to scare the crapola out of her.

It had been okay with Jake because it had started with clear rules, years ago. And despite enjoying his big-bear warmth and his ability to know which buttons to press to satisfy her, there had never been that extra zing.

But with Solo—holy cow, it was one big adrenaline rush.

And at the same time so comfortable and easy and just plain fun; he made her smile and laugh and...

Polly sank her head in her hands with a groan.

This was the problem with chemistry. You could never trust it. She'd had it big time once before, when she was sixteen. And he'd promised her the world. Shite, she'd only just been legal. When she'd followed him to Perth, she'd found out she was nothing more than a notch on his bedpost. The barely-legal virgin he'd bedded and then boasted to his mates about. What a coup. And the biggest humiliation of her life.

She rubbed her forehead as a tight band started to form over her eyes.

Oh yeah, she'd learned the lesson; from the way Dad treated Mum, from her first love: all men were bastards. She'd vowed she'd never let herself trust one again.

And she'd stuck to that rule through thick and thin.

Maybe Alice was right. Maybe it was just her ovaries, all those little eggs dancing up and down and squealing for attention as she nose-dived towards thirty.

She shook her head and refused to meet her own eyes in the mirror as she washed her hands.

As she flicked the lock and tiptoed onto the narrow landing, she heard a loud thump coming from the stairwell. Heart pounding, Polly clutched at the material of Solo's T-shirt over her chest, fearing that he might have done some weird sleep-walking thing and fallen down the stairs. She tiptoed to the banister and peered over.

A long skinny body was crumpled against the wall, halfway down the stairs. "Fuck," it muttered, followed by a weird kind of caterpillar walk up a couple of stairs. Then, as if it was all too hard, the figure slithered in a jumble of arms and legs to the bottom of the stairs.

In a heartbeat, the carer in Polly was down those stairs and leaning over him. "Carts!"

Carts lifted his head and two bleary eyes stared back at her. A hand came out and put a finger to his lips. "Shhhhhhhtttttt, you'll wake everyone up," he muttered. Then, in some deep recess of his alcohol-addled brain, something registered and his eyes focussed. "Poll, is that you?"

Oh God, here she was in nothing but Solo's T-shirt, which barely skimmed the top of her thighs. Her choices were limited: a) Leave Carts to fend for himself, possibly to incur hideous consequences from a night crumpled at the bottom of the stairs, or b) Help him to safety and risk him recalling her semi-naked presence in his house, therefore deducing the obvious.

Summoning her professional skills, Polly did a lightning-fast risk assessment and concluded that Carts, who had now buried his head in the crook of one elbow and was gently snoring, would likely not remember her presence. The most humane choice, therefore, was to get him comfortable and then brief Solo not to let on.

After which she would run.

Crouching down, careful to keep her bits out of view, she hoisted an arm under his shoulder. "Come on, sofa for you."

Somehow, she managed to drag a grumbling, partially compliant Carts into the front room, where he draped himself over the sofa like a human hammock, legs sticking out over one end, head dangling off the other. Polly shoved a couple of pillows under his neck and removed his shoes. He had his jacket on and it was a warm night, so she decided against searching for a blanket.

Carts waved a hand in her general direction. "Fanks, Poll."

She crept closer and muttered in his ear. "I'm not Polly. And you never saw me, okay?"

"Okay." And then the snoring started up again.

Polly darted out of the room and up the stairs. When she got into Solo's room he was sitting up in bed.

"What was all that noise?" he asked, rubbing at his hair, which made him look so damn cute.

She grimaced. "Carts is home, pissed as a fart."

"Oh." He grinned. "Did he see you?" He didn't look at all perturbed. But she was.

Ripping off Solo's T-shirt, she shimmied into her bra and panties.

"You're not going, are you?" The edge of disappointment in his voice was obvious.

"I had to help him onto the sofa and he recognised me—wearing nothing but your T-shirt."

"So?"

"So, I don't want him to know I was here."

"Would it matter?"

Polly looked around for her little black dress on the ground. "I don't know. Yeah, probably."

"Why?"

"I like to keep my dates right away from my life."

His eyes rested on her, luminous and steady. "Why?"

"Just because." She glanced at him as she grabbed her dress. "Avoids complications." She pulled the dress over her head and zipped it up.

He was sitting up, clasping his knees, the sheet lightly covering his groin, and she couldn't help her eyes darting to the defined six-pack, the little v of dark hair.

Polly gulped and floundered around for her shoes.

Suddenly he was up and padding towards her and the tightness in her throat nearly strangled her.

She didn't move—couldn't—her heart pounding as his animal scent and the warmth of his body enveloped her. Something about the ease he displayed in his nakedness and the fact that she was now fully dressed was screamingly erotic.

It was hard not to turn around and beg him to unzip her.

A muscle worked in Solo's jaw and when he stroked his thumb along her jawline, she heard her own breath rasping hot at the back of her throat.

"Sorry if I'm a complication in your life," he murmured, and as if there was an invisible thread between them, she raised her face to his and felt his lips brush hers. "But, for the record," he whispered against her mouth, "complicating your life was worth every amazing second."

How she longed to jump right back into that bed and forget anything else existed but her and him. Just for one night. Except in the morning, she'd still have to navigate past Carts.

She gave a tight little smirk as she pulled away. "Just remember, I was never here, okay?"

And then, grabbing her bag with her car keys and shoes, she exited the room without another glance.

CHAPTER 15

"*D*r Jakoby, would you say sertraline or fluoxetine as a starting point for Brad Jamieson?"

Solo's head jerked up from the notes he should have been writing up.

So far all he'd managed to scribble was, "major depressive episode after break-up of long-term relationship".

"Um, yes, a trial of sertraline, definitely. According to his records he didn't improve greatly on fluoxetine several years back."

"Indeed, so it would seem." Pritchard's face was grim. "His GP arranged this hospitalisation due to his previous major depressive episode."

Solo cleared his throat. "I guess the ending of an eight-year relationship would have a fair bit to do with it. There'd be a component of grieving as well."

He tapped his pen and tried to pretend he didn't feel a pair of green eyes dwelling on him for longer than was comfortable from across the table.

It was Monday morning ward meeting hell. Friday night was still very much at the forefront of his mind, where it had been lodged all weekend.

Saturday first thing he'd come downstairs to find Carts with an icepack on his head and a gigantic mug of black coffee in his grip.

"Good night?" Solo said, going to the fridge and getting out the milk. "Remember much?"

Okay, he was fishing, but Polly's concern had been a blow to his ego, not to mention leaving him alone in a bed he'd have much preferred to have been filled with a gorgeous warm woman.

"Can't remember much past when you left the Shamrock, to be honest," Carts muttered. "Except I had this weird dream."

Solo closed the fridge with his foot. "Yeah?"

"Polly Fletcher, putting me to bed on the sofa. Very scantily clad. You're the psychiatrist. Does that mean I've got some kind of subliminal hots happening for her I don't know about?"

Solo tried to prevent the smile from reaching his lips. Despite still smarting over Polly's untimely exit, Carts' complete look of terror was really quite funny.

"The idea doesn't appeal?"

He couldn't imagine many guys not finding Polly goddamn awe-inspiringly beautiful, but somehow he got the impression Carts was one of the few.

"I know guys fall over themselves for her." Carts gulped a mouthful of coffee. "But frankly, she's a bit full-on for me."

"I think you'd know if you fancied her in real life." Shit, he had, hadn't he? The moment he set eyes on her it was like every nerve in his body stood to attention. And another part of him—best not to dwell on that right now.

"Phew," said Carts. "That's a relief."

Solo wished he could wipe away all thoughts of Polly as easily as Carts could, but here he was, unable to focus, having relived their lovemaking over and over all weekend, and steeling himself not to message her.

And of course, he'd not heard a thing from her.

Disappointment had dragged his feet heavily into work this morning. He'd had to fortify his steps and lengthen his stride as he walked in behind Pritchard with the patient files in his arms.

The atmosphere in the room right now was heavy.

Judith looked pale and swollen-eyed and Polly, sitting close and clearly protective, had shot him a "don't draw attention to it" look that he'd acknowledged with a tight-lipped nod as he sat down.

Polly's energy was spiky, tense. But frankly, so was his.

Now, Pritchard looked around the room and said, little weasel eyes gleaming, "Did you all get out of bed on the wrong side this morning? Can we have a bit of enthusiasm here? Okay, Jakoby, sertraline it is. Add a bit of short-term Xanax for the anxiety. Next case."

"Bernie Bullman," Leon said with an eye-roll.

"What?" Pritchard frowned. "Didn't we discharge him on Friday?"

"Yes," Polly supplied. "Apparently he didn't turn up at the hostel I organised for him. He was found on the nineteenth floor of the Queen's building, insisting he was Spider-Man."

Pritchard sighed and ran a hand through his thinning hair. "Ah, Bernie. What on earth are we going to do with him?"

Everyone sat around, frowning and clicking their pen tops. They were definitely running out of solutions when it came to Bernie. He was outwitting all of them.

Finally, the ward round over, Solo exited the room and strode along the corridor making conversation with Leon. The more he got to know Leon, the more he liked the guy. His morose façade was just that, a façade, beneath which he was big-hearted, and infinitely kind to the patients. He was laid-back to the point of being almost horizontal, except in an emergency, when he fired on all cylinders.

"Been hearing about your knitting prowess." Leon grinned.

"Ha." Solo barked out a laugh. "News travels fast."

"Esme is calling for a Solo Jakoby knitting circle every Friday."

Solo couldn't help a smirk, especially as Polly and Judith were gaining on them. He wanted Polly to be impressed; it was stupidly childish, but there it was.

Deep in his pocket his phone rang. He stopped and drew it out.

Emma. His heart lurched in his chest.

He took it and said, louder than he needed to, "Hi, Em."

He felt Polly's attention on him as she came level; it was almost imperceptible, unless you happened to know how her ears could flap.

"Solo, I didn't really expect you'd pick up." A month or so back Emma's voice would still have caused pain, but now he was far more aware of a fleeting impression of wide green eyes as Polly shot past, followed by a toss of her head.

His stomach tightened as that curly head bobbed off into the distance. He pressed the phone to his ear. "How are you?"

"I'm good."

He forced out, "How's Drew?"

A long pause. "He's finally responding to the medication regime, they think." He could hear the tightness in Em's voice, like a stretched rubber band.

"I thought as much."

"How did you know?"

"He's stopped sending me hate messages."

"Oh no, Solo. Was he doing that? I had no idea."

No, because I chose not to worry you with it. "Private hospitals don't tend to take celebrity's phones away from them, so…"

"Were they really bad?"

No point sugar-coating the pill now. "Yep."

"I'm so sorry," Emma's voice was nearly a whisper.

"It's not your fault."

Another awkward silence

"Look, um, the reason I'm phoning is I have a modelling job in Perth in a few weeks. Could we, I mean, would you be up to meeting me?"

Solo's jaw clenched. Was he ready to see Emma again? He wasn't sure. It was like his brain had been scrambled with Polly and now nothing seemed the same anymore.

"Okay," he said, injecting warmth into his voice. "That would be good."

"Are you certain about that? I mean, if you'd rather not…"

"Em, don't worry. I'm not angry about it, okay? I'm doing fine. How are you two going…?"

He sensed her moment of hesitation. "We're... okay... good, I think, now he's more himself."

Before, those words would have hurt like hell. Now the whole sordid business felt distant, hazy. Unreal. Like it had happened to someone else.

Solo stifled a sigh. Filled his voice with smiles, so she'd hear he was fine. "That's great news."

"Are you enjoying Perth?" Emma asked.

"I am."

"The job and all? You've made some friends?"

"Yep. Job's good. And yes, I've made some friends." He'd count Carts as a friend, and Leon was someone he felt he could warm towards. And then there was Polly.

What on earth would he call her? Frenemy? Sexemy?

"Anyway, got to go, Em, I've got patients to see. Text me the date. Are you set for accommodation and everything?"

"Oh yes, I've got a hotel. The Sheridan."

"It will be good to show you around Perth."

"That would be nice. And it's good to talk to you, Solo."

"Good to talk to you, too, Em."

"Bye then."

"Bye."

When he'd pocketed his phone he glanced along the hospital corridor.

Polly was nowhere to be seen.

HI MIM,

Fingers hovering over the keyboard of her laptop, Polly chewed on the inside of her cheek. What the hell should she offer to bring to Dad's seventieth?

It was a mere two weeks away, and she hadn't even thought of a present.

A new shirt? Dad wore the same old things on the farm, his blue overalls with a white Bonds T-shirt underneath. A shaver, to get rid of his beard? Maybe a clean shave would do him good. A book from The Book Genie? Dad had started reading once and had actually gone through some classics. They'd even managed to have some good conversations, but the problem was that other than the farm—and drinking—Dad hadn't developed many hobbies. Sure, the farm took his time, but he was a man without a rudder. A man whose past would never quite set him free. He never spoke about Vietnam, but Polly knew his experiences there had broken him. Broken his relationship with Mum, which had—according to the occasional conversation she'd had with Gran on the subject—been so vibrant and romantic before he left, only to turn into a nightmare of mood swings and drinking binges when he got back.

The only thing that Polly could remember between her parents were long periods of tense silence punctuated by raised voices and smashing crockery.

She stuck her chin on her fist and sighed. She knew what he'd like her to give him, and it made her heart curl into a tight little knot. His favourite Irish whisky. But it had been years since anyone would buy Dad alcohol.

She wasn't a great cook, so baking anything was out. Then an idea struck her. The decorations. A big 70th sign. She'd make it after work in the OT department. That would do. And she'd take some snacks, nice cheeses, gourmet crackers. Hardly imaginative, but better than subjecting the guests to her cooking.

Smiling, she started to type the email again, then stopped, chewing at her lip once more. God, how these two had managed to get this far was anyone's guess. When Mum had taken off over east when Polly was fourteen, Mim had moved in barely nine months later. Polly had nothing against Mim, she was a nice, warm-hearted woman. She took Dad's flack most of the time, always came back to him after the occasional spat, and she'd been good to Gran in her final year of life. Yeah, Mim had put up with a lot.

Polly straightened. She'd never do that. Put up with shit and keep on smiling and forgiving. She'd go to her death for a friend, but not a lover.

She'd meant it when she'd told Solo friends came first. She'd learned to value friendship over any liaison, no matter how good it felt. Once burned, twice, thrice, a thousand times shy.

Sex was just that. Sex.

Except it didn't feel like *just* sex with Solo, did it?

She wriggled her butt into the seat. It had been so damned good. But there was also this really pesky emotional thing happening, wasn't there? She actually felt drawn to him as a person. And that was simply not on.

Which made everything awkward. They were in this kind of weird limbo-land of brief steamy looks and stilted conversation. And then there'd been that call in the hospital corridor yesterday that had drawn Solo to an abrupt standstill, the sudden smile as he said the word "Em". And you could bet it wasn't frigging Emanuel or Emmerson or whatever male names began with Em.

It was a woman.

So what? She wasn't interested in anything long-term, so if there was some girl lurking back in Sydney, all fine and good.

Polly flicked a defiant curl out of her eyes and typed.

Hi Mim,

I'm going to flex my creative muscles and make a big 70 glittery sign. Also, I'll bring some cheeses, dips and crackers.

Let me know how many coming. I have a disco ball somewhere. Do you want it?

Anything else you need, drop me a line.

Expect I'll get there midday on Saturday.

Polly xx

A tightness constricted her throat at the idea of going up to Wadgigaree. The sparse flat country, the parched eucalypts. The dry riverbed. In winter it was green and pretty enough, but it was the end of summer now and even the pink galahs would be straggly and irritable like a gang of delinquent teenagers, the cattle lacklustre, the colours of the bush burned out by the unrelenting sun.

And dust everywhere. So freakin' dusty.

No wonder Dad found it hard not to drink. The only fun spot was the old Wadgigaree pub with its wide verandas and the jacaranda trees providing a patch of welcome shade.

She kicked back in her chair and took a sip of her lemon water. Sunday she'd made chocolate brownies from a packet mix. Ate half the tin, hated herself. Was determined to throw the rest in the bin on Monday, but when she got home after the Solo and Em conversation, she'd shoved another two pieces in her mouth before ditching the rest.

Then she'd gone for a run, which had made her want to throw up the brownie and, by the feel of her lower legs, given her shin splints into the bargain.

So now she was hobbling, had stuffed her face with nearly a pan of brownies over two days, and her punishment was lemons forever.

Polly tapped send on her computer, and was trying to work out what she was going to cook with two lemons, half an onion and three potatoes when her phone rang. "Dr J" came up on the screen. She'd jokingly put in that title one day at work.

"Wondering if you'd like to go for a quick bite?" His voice was deeper and more gravelly than she'd noticed when his face was attached to it. "We haven't discussed how we go about the PTSD group tomorrow. I don't want to get it wrong again."

Okay, she'd concede. This was merely a professional after-work meeting so that was fine, wasn't it? And besides, what could you make with a couple of lemons, half an onion and a sprouting potato? Nada.

"Okay." She schooled her voice to neutral and ignored her pounding heart. "There's a decent Vietnamese between my place and yours."

"Great. Send me the address and I'll Google how to get there."

After Solo hung up, she'd texted the address with oddly shaky fingers. Unable to breathe at all steadily, she dashed into her room, ripped off her tracky pants and T-shirt and hopped in the shower. Because, for goodness sake, you had to be clean and perfumed and dressed in the cutest little red-and-white flowered frock for a meeting with a colleague, didn't you?

Forty-five minutes later, she walked through the door of Saigon Corner and scanned the crowd. Her stomach bottomed out when she realised there was no short, spiky hair in sight. She was a few minutes early, though. She sat herself down and gladly took the menu from the waitress.

Her mouth was watering over Cau Lau and beef pho when she sensed a presence and looked up to see Solo in a crisp white shirt and blue jeans. His hair looked newly washed, and now that his stubble was shorter she could see he had a marked dimple in his chin. It was altogether too delicious a sight as it met the strong tanned column of his neck.

Polly swallowed the saliva gathering in her mouth.

All these new little things she was noticing about him were such a turn-on. The subtle nuances that made her greedy for more. More exploration, more little treasures she'd only just begun to discover.

Enough!

If she had a wooden spoon she'd rap herself over the knuckles just like Gran used to when she tried to poke her finger into the cake mix. But despite that she longed to reach out and wheedle a finger between the buttons of his shirt to the velvety skin. Tweak one dark nipple.

She gulped.

They were here to talk work. Not to indulge her sexual fantasies.

"Hi," she said, trying to sound casual.

"Hi." His eyes lingered, as if he too wanted to stick a finger in the cake mix, so to speak.

"Glad you could make it."

"I had some stuff to sort out but decided I could spare time for a quick bite. For the sake of our co-therapy role."

His lips twitched. "Thanks."

When she smiled up at him, she realised she was blushing, which was clearly ridiculous.

"So, what were you doing?" he asked as he sat down and she hid behind the menu, too busy focusing on controlling her body's temperature gauge to answer.

Solo supplied, "You said you were sorting stuff out?"

"Oh, um—" Polly floundered, unable to think up a fib. "I was helping plan my dad's seventieth."

It would hardly count as comprehensive planning. A short, terse email to Mim. And the fact that her thoughts kept bouncing back to the guy who was now sitting in the flesh in front of her, that was neither here nor there, was it?

The urge to touch him almost overwhelmed her again as Solo tilted his head; the striated muscles in his neck fluid as he ordered their drinks. She could almost imagine the warm, sweet scent of him on her nostrils.

His gaze returned to her face and she must still have that hungry look, because his eyes narrowed and a muscle ticked in his jaw.

Polly's breath snagged in her throat. She thrust back in her chair and folded her arms. His eyes dipped to her chest. Of course they did, her breasts were her prize asset and folding her arms accentuated them. A whoosh of heat shot to her sex as he quickly averted his gaze.

She had to admit, it thrilled her, knowing she was turning him on. Even if she wasn't going to let it go any further.

"So what's happening for his birthday?" Solo asked.

"His long-term partner had the crack-brained idea we should throw him a party."

Solo frowned. "Why's that crack-brained?"

"Dad's an alcoholic. If you asked him, he'd say he's a recovered alcoholic, but frankly, they never are. He just likes to pretend falling off the wagon never happens. Denial is his default mode."

She tried to keep the bitterness at bay but it was hard, and she could feel Solo's eyes boring into her as he asked, "Is that why you used to play peacekeeper?"

She picked at the edge of the paper menu. "You remember me saying that?"

He nodded

"Yeah. I didn't do a good enough job of it, clearly."

"Maybe it wasn't your job to do."

She glanced up to see his eyes glowing soft, caressing her. Taking a breath suddenly hurt. "Maybe."

"So where's your mum now?"

"She left when I was fourteen, went off in a campervan around

Australia, met a nice guy on the way and shacked up with him in Far North Queensland."

"That must have been hard."

If Dr J was trying to give her therapy, he could forget it. She shrugged. "No, not really. Mum and I were never close. It was Gran who did the nurturing of me and Joe."

"Your brother?"

"Yeah, he's six years older than me. He helps run the farm now."

"Is your mum still in Queensland?"

"No. She and Trevor bred chihuahuas for a while, but she was a smoker, ate crap. Never looked after herself. She'd had digestive problems for years that she'd never had looked at, and by the time she did, it was too late. She died of pancreatic cancer ten years ago."

"Hence your dislike of me smoking."

"Not you especially. Just anyone." He wasn't going to get her to admit she actually cared.

"I'll remember to avoid the cancer sticks around you, then."

She narrowed her eyes at him. "Just avoid them, end of story."

"Yes, ma'am."

Polly couldn't help a grin. "That's better. I like compliance in a man."

He threw himself back in his chair. "Wait a sec, I think I have a little studded collar somewhere in my pocket, do you want me to pop it on now or later?"

Now she was laughing. Oh *fuckity fuck*, and blushing again. She fanned herself with the menu. Time to get right away from the personal stuff. "Can we talk about something else? Like, not dredge up all the personal shit?"

"Sorry." He didn't look sorry. "I guess we haven't really had much of a conversation, despite..."

He trailed off, and she wasn't going to fill in the space that was full of all the unsaid things that were clearly going on in both their heads. She forced her shoulders to relax. Come on, she asked people questions about their lives all the time, so why was she so churned up?

As the plates of aromatic food arrived, crowding out the space on the chequered tablecloth, conversation halted until the waiter left. Solo motioned for her to go first.

She took a thumbnail of rice and two tiny mouse-sized portions of gorgeous, sticky caramelised pork, hesitated, then took one spoonful of the beef pho. Her stomach grumbled desperately.

"Is that it?"

She broke apart her chopsticks. "How do you mean?"

"Is that all you're having?"

"Yep. I've over-indulged lately." Heat burned holes in her cheeks. "With food, that is."

'You've got a distorted view of your body."

"I do not!"

"Your body is beautiful." He said the words quietly, firmly. His eyes seared into her, almost angry.

They stared at one another for a long beat. A vein throbbed in her neck, until the throb extended lower, like molten liquid. It was all she could do not to say "forget dinner, let's move straight along to bed, shall we?"

But she didn't. "I beg to differ," she responded stiffly, wielding her chopsticks.

"Yeah, because maybe if that little girl had been perfect back then, she could have stopped her parents from fighting. Right?"

The comment stole the breath out of her lungs, left her hand waving the chopsticks in mid-air and her mouth half open. She'd always refused to dwell on it, her discomfort with just being her, the sense that she was never measuring up, but now it was like Solo had whacked a mallet between her eyes.

"Am I right?"

"I—oh. Jesus. Typical bloody psychiatrist," she blustered, gripping the chopsticks firmer and digging them into her plate of food. "You can't help but analyse, can you?"

"I just don't get how you can seem so confident but want to change exactly what makes you who you are."

Polly stared down at her plate; a coil of curls fell over her eye and she flipped it irritably away. He was right. She hated her damn curls too, even though most people said they were her crowning glory. Literally. "I guess, like everyone, I'm a complex mix. I mean, look at you, Dr J. Blood phobic, knitting fiend, with a past you're running away from."

"What makes you think that?"

She shrugged, not looking at him. "A hunch." How to explain? Other than tell the truth. "Carts said you'd been getting some pretty heavy phone messages."

Solo's features tightened. "How does he know?"

She pushed back her shoulders and looked him squarely in the eye. "You left your phone in the kitchen and the texts kept coming in so he read a stream. Don't blame Carts. He wasn't purposely prying, he just thought it might be urgent."

"I see."

They stayed silent for a long moment, both of them scooting food around their plates, then she couldn't help asking, "Were they from an ex?"

He barked a little laugh. "You could say that. Ex-friend."

Her mind flew to the photo in his wallet. The boy with the world-conquering smile.

"The photo in your wallet. Is that him with you and your pop?"

"So you saw it."

"I had to check inside to see whose wallet it was."

He didn't seem surprised. Or that worried. In fact, he looked almost relieved.

And then she did something she'd do if Solo were her friend, someone who she cared about, not just a guy she'd had mind-blowing sex with. She reached across the table, put her hand on his arm and asked softly, "Do you want to talk about it?"

CHAPTER 16

Solo looked down at the hand on his arm. Neatly manicured nails on slim fingers, so damn pretty, so damned good at eliciting an immediate response from his body.

And now she was asking for a completely different one.

She was offering to listen. This was the side to Polly he'd glimpsed on the ward, a woman who displayed a huge heart and the most generous listening ear.

"Yes," he said. "Actually, it would be good to talk." He glanced around the brightly lit jam-packed restaurant. "Maybe we should finish up here and go somewhere quieter for a drink."

The green eyes that met his were serious. "Okay."

"For now, let's discuss tomorrow's PTSD group."

"Sure." She dimpled. He loved that puckish little smile, so full of mischief. "Let's get one thing straight, though," she said. "It's my turn to bring the Tim Tams…"

Half an hour later, neither of them had finished their meal—maybe Polly because of her food hang-up, and him, because he'd lost his appetite with the Drew stuff hanging over him—but at least they'd sorted out the PTSD group. Polly was planning a discussion on trust, and they'd agreed that they would allow feedback on medication issues for half an hour.

As they split the bill, he realised how tight the knot had been in his stomach for months. Would talking to Polly untie it? Or would opening up to her add a whole heap more complications?

They walked onto the busy street and Polly said, "There's a really great wine bar five minutes' walk from here, it's low-key. I go there when I want a quiet chat with colleagues."

"You and quiet in the same sentence?"

She smiled. "It happens. Probably a lot more than I let on."

When they'd both got a glass of wine, they sat down at a table in a secluded corner and Solo got the sense Polly was just letting him settle.

He had the ridiculous urge to take her hand in his, thread his fingers through hers. If she was his girlfriend... *Eghhh...* just forget it...

He drew in a deep breath. "Have you heard of a guy called Drew Faulkner?"

She narrowed her eyes as if in thought, then a look of comprehension dawned. "The soldier from Afghanistan who saved that convoy from a suicide bomber?"

"Yep. The very one."

"Oh my god. He left the army after that, though, didn't he? Wasn't he on *Survivor* a couple of seasons back?"

"Yep."

"And..." She screwed up her nose as if trying to remember. "He got all that flack from the media for exploiting his fame, and then, shit, he attempted suicide not long ago, right?" Her hand flew up to her mouth. "Oh, Jesus Christ, is he the guy in the photo with you in your wallet?"

Of course she'd remember the story. Events like that stuck in mental health workers' minds. Potential suicides—those were the things that stopped you sleeping at night. Praying that you were never the one on watch when some poor soul slipped through the net.

Except, thank god, Drew's attempt hadn't succeeded.

Polly's eyes were growing wider and wider as he saw her piecing the threads together. "He tried to jump off the Gap, like, six weeks ago, didn't he?" she said. "And some guy—a doctor—stopped him... that—that was you? The doctor who stopped him?"

He nodded,

"Fuck!"

"He was very unwell," Solo explained. "And he's been hospitalised ever since."

"What happened?"

"Oh, Christ, where do I start?" Solo flexed his fingers in his lap.

"Maybe at the beginning?"

"Huh, how long have you got?"

"As long as you need." She gave a crooked smile. "No charge."

He gave a tiny push with his shoulder into hers, felt the pressure back. Somehow, that little gesture helped the words to flow.

"Drew came to live with us when I was nine and he was ten. His mum worked on and off for my nan and pop, in lambing season and helping with odd jobs. Most years she'd turn up. She was pretty itinerant, but her kid and I hit it off. Then, one year they came—they used to stay in a cottage down the end of the paddock—but after a couple of days she just disappeared, leaving Drew alone. I was too young to really understand it, but I gather she went off to be with some guy in Sydney. He was a drug dealer and she was a pretty heavy user herself."

He heard Polly inhale sharply. "After a fair bit of toing and froing with his mum and the authorities, Drew lived with us full-time. Nan and Pop became his foster parents. So then they had both of us." He smiled at her sadly. "We were close before, but after Drew's mum left, I guess we became like brothers. We did everything together. And Nan and Pop let us have pretty much free rein. We went to different schools but we'd spend our holidays together. I guess Drew brought me out of my shell, taught me to be more adventurous, daring." He laughed ruefully. "I was a bit of a boffin, into reading and science. He was the one who taught me how to ride a motorbike."

"He didn't manage to cure you of your blood phobia, though?"

"No. That had to wait for Professor Crayshaw."

"Did you teach him to knit?"

Solo grinned. "Funnily enough, knitting wasn't Drew's thing. He used to give me serious flack for that, not that it ever stopped me. I knitted him a beanie as an act of revenge before he left for Afghanistan." He paused. "So, anyway, I went to medical school. And Drew went into the army. It was all he ever wanted. His dad had been in the SAS. Killed in a routine exercise that went wrong, as I understand it. I think Drew felt he had to prove himself. For his mum."

"Is she still in his life?"

Solo shook his head. "No. She died of a drug overdose when Drew was fifteen. That hit him real hard. But anyway, he was determined and got into the SAS, saw service in Afghanistan. We stayed close during that time, got together whenever he was home." He took a sip of his wine. "Anyway, you know what happened with the convoy of trucks. How he dragged the driver and two other soldiers to safety. He came back a hero, but that just papered over the cracks that were forming. After a while I sensed he wasn't doing great. When he decided it was time to go back to being a civilian, I encouraged that. For a while, as you know, he was flying high. Everyone's darling. He was great with the media and that's when the reality TV roles started rolling in."

"Wasn't he touted to be the next *Bachelor*?"

Solo smiled grimly. He didn't need to go into what had brought that to a halt.

"Winning *Survivor* made him plenty of dough, gave him the glamour status. But he couldn't keep up the façade. Behind it, his life was turning pear-shaped. When he admitted to me he was taking a cocktail of cocaine and amphetamines, I wasn't surprised. He'd changed. His behaviour was unpredictable. I helped organise a place at a private clinic. Kept everything away from the media. He didn't take it up. Pretended he was okay, that he'd got off it all himself. I didn't believe him, but I couldn't force him into treatment either."

Polly made a noise, like she understood. Despite the fact he barely knew her, she was the only person he could imagine confiding all this in. Even so, he couldn't tell her all of it. The stuff with Emma. Some things were too hard to speak out loud.

He tightened his lips. "So he kept hiding his shit from the world, and that's when he got a contract with Channel Ten for *The Bachelor*. But by then, his drug use was seriously escalating. And then, when Pop died suddenly of a heart attack, *BAM*. I think Pop was the last thread that held Drew onto reality. He lost it completely after that. That's when the psychosis set in. After Pop's funeral he turned up at my apartment, ranting and raving, and I knew then things were really bad. I tried to stop him getting in his car, but the drugs made him potentially violent. The only thing I could do was follow him and call 000. I got to him as he reached the Gap. I had to talk him down until the police got there."

"Jesus, Solo, you put your own safety at risk."

"I wasn't thinking about my safety at that moment."

Polly shook her head. "I remember the footage, with the police cars and ambulances on standby... You were there too!"

"Yes, though I managed to keep my face out of view. I didn't need to be known as the guy who saved Drew Faulkner from killing himself."

"Oh, that's horrible. No wonder you got on your motorbike and rode off into the never-never."

"Yeah, it was a pretty good incentive to get the hell out of there. The thing is, I would probably never have left except Drew started to send all those texts. He was out of his mind, furious that I stopped him from killing himself. I didn't blame him, but I knew with Pop dying and now this, I had to let other professionals treat Drew. Disappear for a while."

"You did the right thing," Polly said. Her eyes were soft, almost mossy, and her hand came back and squeezed his arm. He liked it there, wished she'd keep it there. He touched her fingers lightly, and she intertwined hers with his.

It was so tender his heart lurched and sputtered in his chest.

"There's something else, isn't there?"

Her eyes were lasering into him, and he had to look away quickly so she wouldn't see, that yes, there was more; more hurt, more betrayal.

"No," he lied. "That's the only reason I'm here. I've heard Drew's responding to treatment. The messages have stopped. But I don't want to risk contacting him. Not yet."

"You have been the best friend he could ever wish for. Someday he'll realise that. Do you think you'll be able to mend the rift?"

Tentatively he stroked her fingers. How soft they were. "I don't know. But I hope so."

"And you'll go back to Sydney, after this locum job is over?"

Solo heard himself laugh, a hollow sound. "I don't know. Maybe. I'm not sure if I'll be ready to return to Sydney. But I have to put Nan and Pop's farm up for sale at some stage; there's a manager in there at the moment."

"You could become a rural GP."

He shook his head. "I've toyed with the idea of hiding out in the bush. But I've got ambitions. I'd like to get into neuropsychiatry and I can't imagine my options to do that would be great in a country town."

"Maybe not."

They sat, and she slowly removed her hand. He wanted to grab it back. Wanted to tell her that despite only knowing her for a ridiculously short space of time, she'd somehow buried herself in his heart.

Did she feel the same? Somehow his logical brain doubted it.

"That's some confession, Dr J," she said after a moment. "No wonder you were keen to let the PTSD group know their options."

"Yeah, I let my own stuff take over there a bit."

"I doubt if a support group would have been enough to help Drew," she replied thoughtfully. "I've been working in mental health long enough to know that sometimes a person needs hospital and meds first to relieve the worst symptoms."

"What worries me about Drew is how much early trauma there was in his life," Solo said. "You know, he was this amazing star beaming through the sky, but sooner or later, with that amount of adulation, he was always going to burn up. He had this side to him you could never touch, never reach; a side that made him take risks when he shouldn't. A darkness. It was eating away underneath that great big smile, the bravado and military swagger. I saw it. But I don't think anyone else did, not even Nan and Pops." He shook his head. "I'm so glad Pops didn't see Drew at his worst. It would have broken him."

He drained his glass. "Anyway, I've talked enough about my shit. Maybe I should let you go."

"Maybe." She smiled and glanced at her watch. For another moment neither of them moved. The air prickled.

What he would give to bury himself in her beautiful body again tonight. But then, he sensed the rules of the game would change, and he wasn't sure Polly was ready for that. Talking had been good, but it had also brought up all the rawness of the past months.

If Polly rejected him now, then where in hell's name would he go from here? A wave of loneliness engulfed him, and if he hadn't been sitting down, Solo was sure it would have knocked him right off his feet.

"I really better go," he said.

He hadn't meant it so abruptly. It was a defence mechanism. She should know all about them, she had enough of her own.

Obviously not, because he felt her stiffen next to him. Her features drew into a polite, tight mask.

"I've an early start tomorrow," he explained, feeling lame. But he had to protect himself, glue all the bits back into place that were at risk of falling apart. "Pritchard wants me to review a couple of patients with him first thing."

"Of course." She bent and picked up her bag. Their evening of intimacy almost felt like it had never happened; it had been a heavy discussion for both of them. Now maybe it was time to beat a retreat. He reminded himself that he didn't know her, not really, but he appreciated the moments of bright sunshine she'd brought into his life.

"Thanks for listening," he said. "Where's your car? I'll walk you there."

She laughed. "You sound like Carts with Judith."

It was a relief to have something else to focus on as they walked. "Does Carts know Judith's split with her man?"

"God, no, don't mention it, he'll be over with flowers and chocolates before you can blink."

"Maybe that's exactly what she needs."

"What Judith needs is a period of mourning. She was with the guy twelve years."

"That's hard."

"How about you?" Her voice was feather-light. "Did you leave someone special behind in Sydney?"

He said quickly, "Nope. No-one special."

They walked in silence for a minute. Suddenly he couldn't stop himself from asking, "And you—no-one special in the past?"

"Nope."

Subject closed.

Solo stifled a sigh. Face it. She was a firecracker in bed, a great listener, but she wasn't interested in anything more. And she wasn't going to share her reasons.

Suck it up, Solo, mate.

So when he reached her car, and she leaned her back against it and looked up at him with that glint of invitation in the depths of the green, he gritted his teeth and kissed her on the cheek. Tried to block out the seductive scent of her perfume.

"Thanks for listening," he said, barely able to take the sudden shuttering in her eyes. Knowing that if she was disappointed they hadn't ended up in bed, he was a thousand times more so.

He just couldn't face any more rejections right now. And sooner rather than later, he was sure there would be one.

"See you at work tomorrow."

"Yep," she said tightly. "See you at the salt mines."

He didn't dare look at her face again, just turned on his heels and walked away.

CHAPTER 17

*P*olly was sitting in the occupational therapy craft room slathering a large cardboard "7" with gold paint. She could easily have bought the numbers 70 at a party shop, all covered in glitter for ten dollars, but somehow it felt important to make them herself.

She hadn't gone to so much effort for Dad in years, even though he'd done his best to hand out the olive branch. Maybe it was time…

Everyone else had gone home, except Judith, who was flitting around tidying up after the art therapy session. Polly flicked her a glance. The last two days Judith had seemed a little more cheerful, her shoulders less defeated. Polly had even caught her humming to herself.

Surely Judith wasn't getting back with Mark?

It happened all the time though, didn't it? People deciding to break up, then backing away from the finality of it all and limping on for another round. Even deciding to have a baby, as if that would magically fix things. And then there it was, another innocent little life brought into the mix.

Mum had told Polly once, in her totally insensitive way, that she was the result of a make-up fuck. That if Polly hadn't come along, Mum would have left years before.

She was just one huge mistake, responsible for prolonging her parents' misery.

Polly swiped too much paint onto the brush and watched it dribble a big arc across the table.

"Tsk." Judith was by her side with a cloth. "Put some newspaper down, you mucky pup."

"What are you so chirpy about?" Polly commented darkly. And then wanted to unsay it, because it broadcast the fact that she was personally about as chirpy as a crow with a broken wing. Of course, she was happy that Judith's mood had improved, just not if it involved that douchebag Mark.

Judith gave a little giggle.

Polly put down her paintbrush with a suspicious frown. "What's going on?"

"Nothing."

"You haven't taken him back, have you?"

"Technically, he hasn't gone anywhere to take him back from. I mean, he's still living in the house, we just have separate rooms."

"Jude, I really don't like the sound of this."

"It's not what you think."

"What then?"

Judith fussed around washing paintbrushes and laying out paintings to dry.

"You haven't agreed to give it another go, have you?" Polly asked suspiciously. "Don't believe him if he says he wants to try again; it's just fear of change, not a change of heart."

"I know, I know. In fact, Carts warned me about tha—"

"*Carts!*" Polly's eyes popped wide. "When did you see Carts?"

Judith was hiding behind her hair. "I bumped into him in Woolworths. We had a discussion about whether you could make that fake mince taste as good as real mince in a spag bol. I said you could and Carts said you couldn't."

"Really." Polly couldn't help a little smirk. They would probably have both talked that through for a good ten minutes, very seriously.

"Yes. And then he asked me how I was going and I—um—burst into tears. Which was kind of embarrassing over a tray of Cumberland pork sausages."

Polly's eyebrows flew up. Judith kept hiding behind her long, blonde hair.

"I can hear what you're thinking, Polly," she said after a moment. "And of course I'm not going to do anything rash. It's just that he's nice. And kind. And he listens like he's interested in what I have to say. I'm not used to being listened to."

Polly gripped the paintbrush and zipped her lip. She'd been just about to tell Judith it was too early, and that besides, Carts was not the kind of guy to have a rebound relationship with. But seriously, as if she was in any position to pass judgement. Her head had been going round and round for the past week over Solo's revelations. The evening had started off fun and turned heavy, and she'd been so close to asking him home and humiliating herself. It had come as a shock when he'd gently but firmly turned her down, not in words, but certainly in actions. Never had a peck on the cheek felt more like a slap.

He'd been friendly but distant ever since. The vibe was nothing close to what they'd had. And the truth was, she missed it like crazy. Missed the touch of his hands, missed his lips, missed his kisses, those eyes weaving themselves into some crazy place inside her that she thought she'd managed to stamp out for good.

She'd not slept properly; she'd even lost her appetite. At least that was a small bonus. She'd got on the scales this morning and found she'd lost two kilos. In a week. *A week!*

Any other time she'd be air-punching.

As an act of defiance, she'd gone partying with some old friends from university on Friday night, a crowd who she saw less often but who were fun and frivolous. Sure, it had been a blast and she'd had a humdinger of a hangover on Saturday morning, but it hadn't filled the space inside her that had Solo written on it.

Somehow—when she'd finally dragged herself out of bed to get some shopping—she'd found herself in a craft shop, staring at knitting needles, because if you were going to be an auntie, you had to knit something for the baby, didn't you? But after the mess she'd made of a single blanket square, the poor kid would probably be a teenager before Polly got something finished. And worse, she kept seeing Solo's hands in her mind's eye, and what she had them doing didn't remotely resemble knitting.

So work had ticked by with stilted conversations over morning tea and Solo rushing off after PTSD group yesterday saying he had something urgent to do. What was urgent at 9.30 on a Wednesday night? Officially, she was losing her mind.

Sighing, Polly laid the 7 out to dry and started on the 0.

"Carts is a really nice person," she said without knowing whether she meant it as a warning or encouragement.

Clearly Judith saw it as the latter. "He said yoga might help, that it really calmed his mind after a major break-up. Do you know what happened?"

Polly made a careful stroke with her brush. "He got engaged, or rather, didn't. Anyway, he's... he's not that lucky with women."

Judith swivelled, surprise on her face. "Why ever not?"

"Way too nice."

"Oh, that's sad. He's got lovely eyes." Judith removed her art apron. "Anyway, I said I might see him there tomorrow night. The Thousand Petalled Lotus, at the surf club on the beach."

"Jude, your voice has got that sing-song note it gets when you're pretending you don't want a piece of Leon's apple strudel."

Judith skipped around with jam jars of paint water, clattering them into the sink. "Why don't you come too?"

Polly looked at her askance. "You're joking, right?"

"No, you've been really jumpy lately. I reckon some deep breathing would do you a world of good."

What she needed, Polly decided glumly, was some wild tantric sex. With somebody who seemed to have opened all her chakras, then slammed the lid shut when he got to the most important one.

But maybe Jude was right. She needed to centre herself. Regain her inner focus and re-align herself with her single status.

Which was why, Friday after work, Polly found herself lying with her back supported on a bolster, arms out to the side, palms up and her legs in a weird, froglike pose, feeling like she was at a pre-birthing class.

"Breathe deep into your belly.... feel it expand... now let the breath go in three stages... belly... ribs... shoulders. Fully empty the lungs of air... Beautiful... That's right. Imagine the air reaching your fingertips as you breathe back in."

The woman sounded like she was in some kind of mesmeric trance. Polly squeezed her eyes closed, because otherwise she'd see Judith or Carts doing the same weird froggy thing and she might get the giggles.

Like this, with her bits practically swinging in the breeze, it was hard not to think about Solo. How could he totally open up to her and then suddenly withdraw? In fact, if you wanted to really explore it, that's what they'd done since they met, hadn't they? Both of them. Night one, Solo exited the stage; night two, she'd done a runner; potential night three, there she was slathered against her car door, panting, and he'd turned and walked off.

So now she knew who the guy in the photo was. And it filled in some pieces of the puzzle. But not all of them.

Because who the bloody hell was Em?

He wasn't telling her everything.

Oh, shit, now where was she? Breathing in or out, ribs or belly?

She wriggled her back into the bolster, which started her thighs cramping. This was actually really anxiety-provoking. Not at all freakin' calming.

Focus on Miss Mesmeric.

After what felt like an hour of pan pipes, Polly was practically ready to claw her Lululemons off. She rolled off her bolster in an ungainly heap, rolled up her mat and was out of the room already waiting when Carts and Judith exited.

They were both looking remarkably floaty and enlightened. Which clearly meant the problem was with her.

"That was *divine*," Judith enthused. "All the tension has left my body. Just from doing nothing but breathe for an hour."

"Fern's an amazing teacher," Carts replied. "I come in here all wound up and leave feeling like I'm walking six inches off the ground."

It was tempting to say he'd hit the ceiling if that was the case, but Polly's nasty little demon needed to be kept in check. What the hell was wrong with her?

Whatever it was, restorative yoga wasn't the fix she needed.

Carts said, "Why don't we go for a quick drink at the pub?"

"Won't that undo all the good?" Judith frowned.

"No way," Polly said, suddenly feeling much brighter. "I think it would be the perfect end to the evening. I'm happy to OM before I take a sip of gin and tonic."

"Silly," Judith said, but she was playing with her messy up-do and glancing sideways at Carts from under her lashes.

"Would you like to?" he asked Judith shyly.

"Oh, all right then. You've twisted my arm."

If that was a twist, thought Polly, *I'm a yogi.*

Before long they were seated at a table at the Shamrock, yoga mats at their sides, a pint of lager, a glass of mimosa, a gin and tonic, and a dish of peanuts in front of them.

For the first time in a week, Polly actually felt her shoulders relaxing.

Carts settled next to Judith. "I thought we should even up the numbers," he said. "So I messaged Solo and he's coming to join us."

Polly nearly bolted out of her chair. "Oh, you didn't need to do that. I'm not staying and then there will be three of you again, so all that trouble for nothing." So awkward. And her showing off her blubber in her Lululemons, too. Though her baggy T-shirt covered the worst of her thighs.

Which was utterly crazy since she didn't seem to have a problem about her thighs when they were wrapped starkers around Solo's butt. Maybe he was right, maybe she did have a case of distorted body image.

Carts and Judith both gave her puzzled looks. "But you said you had nothing on this evening."

"Got to finish planning for Dad's birthday."

"Wow, that's sounding more and more like a military exercise," Judith said. She turned to Carts. "Polly has made a banner for her Dad's birthday party. It looks pretty but she's messier than a three-year-old when she paints."

Carts smirked indulgently at Polly then gave Judith a moony look. "I'd love to be more artistic. I'm like, colour by numbers. Could you teach me?"

"I'm not really an art teacher, I do art therapy."

"Like that ink-blot stuff?"

"Rorschach, you mean?"

He nodded and Polly felt like she was in the exclusion zone.

"Not really. That's more psychologists' realm, and it's not used much anymore. No, I use art as a means of helping people to express their emotions, you know—grief, sadness, anger. Getting the feelings out onto paper can really help."

"Wow."

"And you're an accountant, aren't you?"

Oh, here it went, the sussing out a potential partner game.

"'Fraid so, hence the lack of artistic genius."

Judith gave a cute shrug. "Doesn't follow. People don't slot so neatly into categories. Why shouldn't you be an artist and an accountant? I bet there's hidden talent in there."

Carts blushed.

Polly started to plan her escape—maybe the ladies' loo window? Either that or another drink. She should leave, before Solo got here, but... she drained her glass. "Anyone for another?"

"We're fine, thanks," Judith and Carts chimed in unison. Polly did an internal eye-roll as she sidled over to the bar. She waved a desperate hand at Paddy, who was still serving someone else and winked at her.

He was finally coming her way when his gaze shifted over her shoulder and a voice that made her toes curl said, "I'll get these. What'll it be, Polly?"

Arggghhh. She wanted to gnaw on the fist holding up her twenty-dollar note.

"Oh, hi there," she tried for casual but it came out as a squeak. "I'm fine to buy my own."

"I know you're fine to buy your own." The patience in Solo's voice would have been admirable with a toddler on the verge of a tantrum. "But I'm offering."

"Right." She felt too weak-kneed suddenly to put up a fight. "Gin and tonic then. Thanks."

Even after a yoga class, two drinks wouldn't be considered over the top, not in the circumstances.

"I've hardly seen you all week," he said, leaning on the bar next to her.

Huh, it wasn't her who'd dashed off on Wednesday night after the PTSD group, was it?

"Oh, you know how it is with a full ward, we're all running around like headless chooks."

"Yeah, you're right, it's been pretty crazy."

They took their drinks and went and sat back down.

There followed another twenty minutes of Judith and Carts hitting it off big time, and Polly and Solo sitting quietly and rather awkwardly sipping their drinks. When Judith made moves to go, Carts jumped up just as Polly did the same.

"My car's parked near yours," Polly gritted through tight lips. "I'll walk with you, Jude."

Judith didn't look enthused by the idea. "Really, Poll, I'm fine."

Carts was jangling his own car keys. "Yep, I'm actually going. I'll walk you. Bye, guys."

Judith flashed him an exclusive show of teeth, leaving Polly gaping after them as they left, both instinctively ducking at the doorway.

"Interesting body language," Solo said as she sank reluctantly back down.

She stared at the squished bit of lemon at the bottom of her glass. "I'm not sure it's a good thing."

"Why not?"

"Judith's not ready yet, and Carts is always ready."

Solo laughed in a way that made her body tingle from head to toe.

"I told him after Alice to back off women for a while and he did fine. He focused on his own wellbeing, hence the yoga. But he's smitten with Judith. And if events were different, I'd probably say they're well suited, but…"

"Quite a matchmaker for someone who doesn't believe in love."

She shrugged. "I make no secret of the fact that I enjoy it for other people. It's just, I think I happen to be—"

"What?"

"Incapable." It came out almost on a little sigh, not how she'd meant it at all.

"I don't think I buy that."

Polly tightened her lips one more notch. "Believe it or not, it's the truth."

His eyebrows lifted. "Because of your mum and dad? Our parents aren't our destiny." She flicked her eyes up and saw that delectable sideways twist to his lips. "Otherwise I don't give much for my chances."

She huffed out a laugh. *"They fuck you up, your mum and dad."*

"Ha, not only your parents. I reckon there's more to this than you're telling."

Her scalp prickled. "Like what?"

"Like something—or someone else."

Polly scoffed, way too loudly. "God, you love to dig around, Dr J." She turned to face him on the bench and hoisted a leg up, held onto her ankle. His eyes flicked to her sheeny leggings then away quickly.

Yep, he was still interested. One up to her.

"Okay, I'll make a deal," she said. "You tell me your heartbreak and I'll tell you mine."

His chin retracted and his eyes clouded for a second. "Not sure if that's fair. You've got a lot more dirt on me so far than the other way round."

"Oh, come on, I've told you all about my fucked-up childhood."

"Hardly. You're a tightly closed book masquerading as a full-page spread."

The obvious double meaning made her smirk and he grinned up from under his lashes. It was disconcerting how he seemed to get her, but it felt good somehow, like a pair of warm arms enveloping her.

She drew in a big breath. "Okay. The reason I left home at sixteen was, yeah, I couldn't stand being around Dad, and partly because of a guy."

"Knew it!"

She cast him the stink-eye. "Stop looking so smug. It's not that incredible a deduction. Teenage girl, unhappy at home, looking for an out. Go figure."

They grinned at each other.

"Okay, so I was pretty infatuated, I'll admit it. Gave the bastard my virginity. I thought I was in love. He was a musician. Danny O'Dougherty; played in a band called Streets of Dublin. Irish, of course, super-cute, and did the bastard know it. I met him when his band was on a tour of outback pubs. He'd finished his tour in our town, so he stayed on for a month or two working on Dad's farm. He basically seduced me. Told me I was his everything and, guess what? My sixteen-year-old hormonal brain believed every word. So I followed him to Perth. Only to turn up at his house to find Danny's naked butt grooving on top of some other desperate little groupie."

"Jesussss!"

She flicked him a glance, saw those silver eyes spark, and it made her heart do a hop and skip.

"What did you do?"

Polly pushed the hair away from her face with both hands. "In a very un-me-like fashion, I backed quietly out of the room and sat down in an alley and cried for three hours."

He didn't speak, but his eyes were immeasurably soft and that made a little hiccup of pain rise up in her throat. Amazing how you could plaster it all over until someone cracked you open so that all your gooey middle was ready to spill out.

"Then I went and got a tattoo."

"The, er, one, on your...?"

"Yep, my serpent. It cost me most of the money I'd brought with me, but I didn't give a rat's. And then I went looking for a job. I got turned down by about twenty places and then I walked into this weird, second-hand book shop, with this big blonde woman bustling around inside. She took one look at my face, said 'you poor little darling, in you come'... and that was it... that was my new mummy hen."

"That's whose house you live in now?"

Polly nodded, swirled the ice in her glass. "Rowena Montgomery. And Alice, her daughter, is my very best friend."

"And she's the one in England with her fiancé, who you—"

"Yes, but that's a long story."

Solo smiled. "For another day, right."

"So, now I've bared my soul, how about you? Who broke your heart, Dr J?"

He stared into his pint for long moments. "I had a long-term girl-friend since university."

She'd known as much. He was rebounding. "Did it end recently?"

"Roughly nine months ago."

"What happened?"

He shrugged. "We grew apart. I guess we were like Judith and her boyfriend. Comfortable. We'd been together a long time."

"So was it you or her? Who broke it off?"

He was stroking patterns in the condensation on his glass, his head averted. She saw a muscle tic in his jaw. *He's not over her,* she thought.

"Her. But I could see the sense of it."

"Very magnanimous of you."

He gave a downturned smile and she just couldn't leave it there. "Was there another guy involved?"

"Nope."

He was lying, you didn't need a degree in social work to tell that. Suddenly, she didn't want to play this game anymore. There were sharp little needles stabbing into her chest.

"I see," she said. "You know what, two G&Ts on top of yoga and I'm pooped. I think I should go home."

"Yes. Right. I'll walk with you."

"Nice of you to always offer, Dr J, but I'm quite capable..."

"You think I want to sit here drowning my sorrows on my own?"

She felt her shoulders sag. "I'm sorry, I didn't intend to have another heavy conversation."

"Maybe we should do something fun for a change?" he ventured.

Her heart betrayed her by bumping hard against her ribs. "What—you mean now?"

"No, not now, over the weekend, maybe? I don't know, maybe we should go somewhere, out into the bush, explore a bit."

She sighed and gathered up her belongings. She wanted to say it was too confusing, all this advancing and retreating. Like some kind of weird dance that neither of them knew the steps to.

"Oh, I don't know... you know how I don't date—"

He finished for her "—work colleagues. Yes, you told me already."

Which was a joke really, after the other night, and they both knew it.

As they made their way onto the street, Solo moved ahead, walking backwards in front of her, arms spread wide. "Come on, we enjoy each other's company, what's to lose? I'm only here for a short time, we're good together"—he waggled his eyebrows and she couldn't help laughing—"and we're both walking wounded apparently, so..."

She tilted her chin. "Speak for yourself. My wounds are long healed, thank you."

"Okay, scarred then. And both big, grown-up people; we know the score. Why not enjoy some no-strings time together?"

Why not indeed? She had no logical argument against it. At the end of his locum, Solo would go back to Sydney, and she'd... she'd go back to being a party girl. Yeah. No strings attached, a free spirit.

She tossed a raft of curls over her shoulders. "Okay, what have you got in mind?"

"How about we go for a bike ride?"

"Put me on the back of that thing? You have got to be joking!"

"Have you ridden pillion before?"

She actually hadn't. In all her adventures she'd never once been on a motorbike, not even Joe's dirt bike on the farm.

"No. Besides, how could I? You don't have another helmet do you?"

"No, but I can get you one. Just let me have your head measurements and I'll buy you one."

"For one ride?"

"Maybe it'll be more. Who knows?"

Her spirits lifted. Yes, it would be fun. And lovely to get out of Perth, go up the coast to the pristine northern beaches. The weekend after this was Dad's party and that wouldn't be fun at all, so spending time with Solo, maybe even in bed afterwards... Her body buzzed suddenly like a kid who'd just been promised a ride on the big dipper.

She beamed up at him. "Okay, then you've got a deal."

CHAPTER 18

Solo killed the engine

Pulling off his helmet, he planted his feet either side of the bike and let his gaze take in the neat weatherboard house with its rim of rosebushes. It provided another piece to the jigsaw he'd been putting together of Polly. Homely and quaint, it made him think of scones and jam and cream. Somehow he'd imagined she'd live in some trendy art deco apartment, all boho chic and crammed full of quirky ornaments, but this was more homespun charm.

So this was where she now lived with her "adopted" family. And yeah, now it made sense, her need for somewhere safe. He'd seen the chinks of vulnerability peep out from the depths of those green eyes. Then down would slam the shutters to keep him out.

He'd worked out the game he had to play.

Casual. Cool. The problem was that nothing in his body, or his brain, seemed to want to play by the rules. As he walked up the path, excitement revved, a steady hum low in his belly. He'd even bought a pack of condoms. Just in case. And when he knocked on the door, his heartbeat sounded as loud as his fist on the wooden surface as the pad of feet on the other side got closer.

Like always, whenever Polly was near, his breath got knotted in his throat.

The door flung open.

Her hair was tied up, but softly, in a casual up-do that encouraged little ebony curls to tumble around her face. In a checked cotton shirt, she looked like a fresh-faced jillaroo and suddenly he could picture her on the farm. It did nothing to calm his libido.

He lifted an eyebrow, trying for cool. "Ready?" He handed her the helmet.

Polly took it and frowned. "It's heavy."

"It needs to be, to protect your assets."

She held it against her chest with a suggestive raise of an eyebrow and he burst out laughing. "Not those assets." He grinned, feeling his face flush.

And, boy, did he want to take her into his arms and crush those gorgeous assets against his chest.

"Come in then." She cast him a smug little smile.

They went into the kitchen and Solo took in the room. It was cosy and inviting, a big wooden table in the centre, cluttered shelves and photos haphazardly stuck on the fridge. A coffee machine and an array of teapots all different sizes and shapes sat on a shelf above the stove.

"Someone likes tea."

"Rowena and Alice are tea addicts. Me, I'm a coffee girl. I need a proper caffeine hit."

"Never anything by halves, right?"

"You know me." She bit her lower lip, a mottled flush appearing on her cheeks. Quickly she changed tack. "So, now, how do I put this thing on?"

She was fiddling with the straps, scowling at it like it was some kind of slain animal that Solo had brought to her as an offering. Grinning, he took it from her and their fingers brushed. A zing of lust hit his groin, and the room suddenly felt thick with expectation.

"Like this." He untangled the straps, slipping it onto her head, avoiding inhaling too deeply of her perfume and that sweet, musky something that lurked just below it. He forced himself to focus on the straps and not the nearness of her breasts almost brushing his chest.

Their combined breathing seemed to fill the space. His hands felt too large, clumsy as he pulled the strap around her chin. "You need to not have hair around your face."

"That's impossible with my hair," she grumbled.

He grunted, focused. God it *was* nearly impossible, getting those curls to behave. Like their owner.

Gently he tucked the tendrils in.

"Feels weird," she mumbled. Her cheeks were bunched by the helmet and it gave her a cute chipmunk look.

"All done," he said gruffly as their lower bodies bumped.

Before he could stop himself he did something totally unexpected, even to him, and dropped a feather-light kiss on the tip of her nose.

Polly sprang backwards, one hand rubbing fiercely at her nose like he'd decked her.

"I warned you not to do that!" But she was grinning, pink in the face as she swiped his arm. And suddenly the energy was light and playful, like they'd finally negotiated a space that was okay to enjoy each other in.

"So where are we going?" she asked.

"I've been looking at maps and I reckon we should go north."

"Good idea. The beaches up there are beautiful."

"Crowded?"

"No way." She laughed. "Most people still call Perth a big country town, sandwiched between the desert and the ocean. I reckon it won't be too crowded."

"Granted," he said. "Sometimes it's hard to get my head around how isolated it is here."

"I love it. So much space," Polly said. "Shall we go? I don't think I can cope inside here much longer without the wind on my face, I'm getting claustrophobic already."

She grabbed her denim jacket, a little backpack, and they exited the house. When they reached his bike he said, "I have snacks, and water."

She nodded, eyes big in her face. Solo climbed on the bike and then instructed her how to get on behind him. "You can either hold the panniers or hold on to me. I'll go slow, but the rule is to move with my body. If I sway to the left, so do you."

"Okay, Capitan," came her muffled voice in his ear. A pair of arms snuck around his waist and he tried to ignore the corresponding thrill that snaked its way down his spine.

"Hold on tight." He started the engine, took it slowly, moving off with the easy grace of someone used to living in the saddle, and soon he felt her relaxing into him. Her thighs braced his hips as they made their way through the city streets and along West Coast Highway.

The heaviness of her body, the feel of her arms around him, the sway of her thighs, was a lovely backdrop to the great swathe of turquoise sea and low bush as the city fell away. After half an hour he stopped, they took off their helmets and he broke a muesli bar in half and handed a piece to her. "How are you feeling?"

"I love it." Her eyes sparkled; big bright emeralds in her flushed face. "I could keep going forever."

It suddenly struck him that riding off into the sunset with Polly pillion was an idea he could get used to.

"I'm going to show you to a special, secluded beach," she said to him, dusting crumbs of muesli bar off her chest in a way that had him telling himself to keep his eyes firmly on her face.

"Yeah. How far away?"

"Another twenty minutes ride, I guess." They got out their phones and she showed him on Google maps. "It's not that hard; take the turning to Yanchep, and then follow your nose. You can't miss it, there's really only one road."

"Okay."

He tried not to let excitement take hold at the thought of pristine secluded white beaches, but his body pulsed out an unmistakable beat. And then, with a shared smile, they were slamming down their visors, and Polly climbed on behind him like she'd been doing this her whole life, and they were off, with the wind in their faces, until they reached the sign for Yanchep.

When he caught sight of the ocean, Solo's breath hitched. Sure, the beaches over east were beautiful, some of the best in the world, in fact, but it was the absolute wildness, the white sand and turquoise sea and dune grasses sweeping off as far as the eye could see, that made his soul sing.

And now, with the most beautiful woman riding behind him, Jesus, what more could a guy want?

His heart felt like it might just explode right through his leather jacket as he got off the bike and unzipped it.

"Okay," said Polly, ripping off her helmet and jacket. "It's swim time."

He looked at her, aghast. "Hell, I didn't even think about bringing bathers."

She grinned, and the dimples danced in her cheeks. "Ah, Dr J, looks like you just might have to skinny dip then."

POLLY HADN'T EXACTLY STARED but she hadn't averted her eyes either as Solo stripped. She rifled through her backpack and brought out her teeny-weeny red bikini and a towel. She knew she was one of those women whose curves always looked better the less she wore, and as she tugged off her jeans and T-shirt and shimmied into them, Solo, in full sunshine, looked pretty damn good too as he got naked.

He'd turned slightly away from her and his lean, tight butt and long muscled thighs dusted with dark hair made her mouth water. His back was beautiful, all the muscles perfectly defined like some classical Greek statue, and she remembered how he'd felt under her fingers, strong and hard, his skin velvet-smooth.

Firecrackers of longing crackled between her thighs. Maybe they could forget the swim?

When he turned around holding his bunched-up jeans in front of his crown jewels, she burst out laughing.

"What if someone sees me like this?"

She swept an arm out towards the empty beach. "Take a look, Dr J. The crowds are overwhelming."

Solo's gaze skittered up and down the beach, followed by a relieved smirk. "Okay, guess I'll take your word for it."

With a giggle, she yanked at the hand holding his jeans. Obligingly he dropped them. Polly's eyes skimmed over his assets. God, no wonder he'd felt so magical inside her, in broad daylight it was obvious how seriously built *down there* he was.

Their eyes met, his molten with something that made her breath hitch and her inner muscles clench hard. But no, she'd dared him to a swim, so swim they would. She wasn't going to behave like she was desperate for a shag or anything.

His fingers were warm in hers as she grabbed his hand and pulled him across the soft sand, her toes squeaking in the fine icing sugar powderiness of it. And then they were tumbling into the waves, laughing, splashing one another, fooling around like two kids.

Solo dived with the ease and grace of a dolphin; she caught the flash of his buttocks, then he was up, several feet away, throwing back his head so droplets glistened in the sunlight, and calling, "Ha, ha, can't catch me." And she was diving after him, giggling, spotting him under the water and grabbing his ankle. A wave tumbled them, and they landed in the white water, a heap of arms and legs and laughter.

And then Solo took her in his arms and kissed her.

Salt and water and strong biceps bound her to him, the salty taste of his mouth, the coolness of his lips a mind-blowing contrast to the heat of his tongue as it explored hers. When she wrapped her legs around his waist, his cock butted hard against her skin and, as another wave hit, somehow they kept kissing, deep, hungry kisses that made her body thrum with want.

Another wave, bigger this time and Solo pulled back, then smoothed the wet hair out of her eyes.

"You look like a drowned puppy." He grinned.

"At least you didn't say seal."

"Why a seal?'

"All my blubber."

"Oh, for Christ's sake, woman!" She felt his hand smoothing around her buttocks. "This is the most beautiful butt in the world, you know that?" The eyes in his wet face were bright silver with lust, his black lashes clogged with water. His hand cupped the gusset of her bathers, and her clit obligingly throbbed out a response.

She gasped as he palmed her, soft yet firm, right here in the shallows, until she was desperate and pushing against the heel of his palm for release.

"I brought a condom," he muttered thickly in her ear. "In my jeans pocket."

"Oh, you did?" she managed against the wet skin of his neck, and loved how rich and ripe the sound of her own laugh was. "You wicked, wicked man."

"Should we find some little secluded nook over in the sand dunes?" he said.

Couldn't he tell she was going to explode if they didn't? "Uh-huh."

He removed his hand, and if she hadn't known more treats were in store, Polly thought she'd probably cry from teetering so close to the edge. Anticipation pulsed inside her as they ran up the beach. Solo grabbed their shared towel and dried her, paying particular attention to her breasts and thighs, and she replied with little mewls of frustration and need.

But despite that, she returned the favour, taking the towel from him, biting at her lower lip as her ministrations caught on the very jutting evidence of his desire for her. She let her hand play up and down him under the towel; Solo let out a groan and his head kicked back.

He gritted out finally, "Lay the towel down."

For once she was overjoyed to do as she was told, and soon they were tumbling around on the ground, kissing.

And, oh, God, how the guy could kiss. These were A-grade kisses, the kind that would make a woman come if they kept going long enough. And when his hand joined the party, fondling her breasts, tweaking her nipples into tight peaks, trailing across her still-damp belly and finding the sweet spot between her thighs, all she could do was arch her back and open her legs wider and let him stroke her towards heaven. Effortlessly, his touch pushed her higher, pulled her tighter, spun her around and around, until finally she came so hard all she could do was scream as her thighs scissored around his hand.

"Oh, sweet Jesus," she whimpered as she floated slowly back to earth. She could feel sand in her hair from where her head had thrashed off the towel. She'd have to spend hours washing it out and she didn't give a flying fuck-a-doodle; she just wanted—needed—him to fill her right up with his glorious cock.

"Condom now," she gasped out.

Solo reached for his jeans and in moments was prepared. He tore the foil pack between his teeth, eyes shining as he muttered, "God, you drive me wild when you come." Then he shifted his weight over her and Polly opened to him, the last waves of her orgasm pulling him towards his own peak so fast that it was barely any time before Solo was shouting his release.

"You're going to give me premature ejaculation problems," he gasped on a laugh. "Being inside you feels so damned good."

"I don't think a guy who gives his woman a humungous orgasm first can be accused of that."

Fuck! Had she just said *'his* woman'? Like… like she belonged to him, or something? Had her orgasm-numbed brain just made that connection?

Solo had slumped heavy on top of her, but clearly he felt her tense up because he lifted his head. "What's wrong? Am I hurting you?"

Was he? *Could he?*

That was the problem, wasn't it? That's why she'd frozen. Because Solo was getting right into places he had no right to be, places she never gave a guy permission to go.

Polly shifted, pushed against his chest. "Maybe you should move, you're getting a bit heavy."

It was a lie. Of course it was, but a naked girl in the sand dunes who'd just had her brains blown needed to protect her anatomy.

Not her vagina. Not her clit. They were all fine and dandy.

No, it was her heart that she was shit-scared about.

∾

168

SOME WHILE LATER AS THEY sat side by side, now partially dressed, and finished the last muesli bar together, a strange little melancholy descended between them.

It felt as if clouds were forming out to sea and rolling in like sea mist.

Except the day was still perfect as the sun dipped lower towards the horizon and the blue of the sky intensified to a deep violet streaked with pink. A lone seabird dived repeatedly into the water, looking for its supper. Somewhere in the distance its mate called for it.

Solo leaned over his knees, jeans loose around his hips, no T-shirt, his freakin' gorgeous pecs and the perfection of his biceps and forearms still taunting her. He was so artistically put together it made her throat constrict with something almost painful.

"Where's your dad's party being held?" he said suddenly.

She turned her head to look at him. "Up in the wheat belt. About two hours inland from here. Why do you ask?"

"Oh, nothing, just realised you won't be around next weekend, that's all."

Her heart leaped but she reined it in sharply. "Why's that a problem?" Okay, she was fishing. Fishing like that seabird right out in the waves. What did she want him to say? That he'd miss her? And then what?

He'd picked up a smooth piece of driftwood and was passing it around in his fingers. Beautiful, long, sensitive fingers, with slightly bony knuckles. Just how very sensitive, she knew.

As if on cue, her clit spasmed, damn the evil little thing.

She sensed he was smiling. "Despite you looking like a blubbery seal, I find I'm wanting to spend more time with you."

She whacked him teasingly.

"Ow!" He rubbed his arm. "Watch out, I have a weapon here." She went to swipe the piece of driftwood from him and they landed back down in the sand. Sensing his plan, Polly clapped her hand over her face.

As he tried to prise her fingers away, they rolled around, giggling. He managed to squeeze his lips through her finger and thumb and, when Polly felt the soft pull of his mouth on hers, she gave in, let her hand skim round the back of his head and dove into the sweetness of his kiss.

When they finally surfaced again, she found she was looking into his eyes and he was staring unblinking back, and something way too deep passed between them.

And, as though she had absolutely no say over her brain-to-mouth connection, no censorship left at all, out popped, "Would you like to come to my dad's seventieth?"

CHAPTER 19

here was something calming about a pair of adoring brown eyes staring up at you. It beat a cigarette, Solo decided, chuffing the border collie under the chin yet again. If his hand stopped for more than a second a nudge accompanied by a soft snort seemed to say, "Come on, mate."

"You'll be doing that all day if Charlie has his way," Mim commented, as she bustled around the kitchen grabbing cups and filling the teapot.

Solo grinned. "It's okay, I'm used to dogs. I grew up on a farm."

"Yeah, Charlie probably senses that. We reckon he's psychic. He always knows where I hide the treats, no matter how cunning I am. Here you are." Mim plonked a big mug of steaming tea on the table. "Polly's just taking a shower, she'll be here any sec. Sugar? Milk?"

Solo tried to block the thought of Polly showering. "Just milk, thanks."

The outer screen door of the kitchen banged and another woman appeared, a lot younger than Mim, with thick auburn hair piled onto her head. She was carrying a couple of bags full of shopping, and as she placed them on the table he noticed her belly was rounded with early pregnancy.

"Oh, hullo, you must be Solo." She smiled. "I'm Kate, Polly's sister-in-law."

Solo tried to stand but Charlie's chin stayed firmly glued to his leg, pinning him to the chair.

"Ha, I see you've been Charlied." Kate laughed.

Solo grinned ruefully. "And I thought I was special."

"Everyone's special to Charlie."

Already Solo liked these two women; they were no-nonsense, straight to the point. Mim, with her big smile and salt-and-pepper hair, was your earth mother type. Kate was clearly practical and calm, he decided, as he watched her methodically unpacking the bags, putting things in the cupboard, and leaving out others with a quick word to Mim. "This is for the cake icing. I bought double the eggs for the frittata."

The smell of cooking already pervaded every corner of the kitchen.

Solo's nostrils quivered and he laughed, glancing down at Charlie. He wasn't much better than the dog, totally led by his stomach. It was his nan's fault for being such a good cook. His chest contracted as the memories flooded in. Nan's kitchen was not unlike this one. Solo guessed farm kitchens were often pretty similar. A large jarrah wood table in the centre, mismatched chairs, a pile of Blundstone boots near the door next to hooks loaded with coats. A jam-jar of wildflowers in the centre of the table with a dog lead and a pad of paper covered in notes. A cosy mish-mash of what made a place home.

He sighed. That was all gone now. Pop's and Nan's farmhouse in the hands of a stranger. How quickly life could change.

And then it changed again as Polly flew through the door in a very short, red, kimono-style dressing gown with Betty Boop emblazoned over one breast.

She stopped abruptly when she saw him and pushed the curls off her face.

"Oh, you're here already. I didn't expect you until much later."

Not exactly the welcome he'd been hoping for. He kept his eyes carefully averted from those beautiful white thighs, barely covered by the silky number that was totally incongruous with the friendly farmhouse vibe.

"You've met Mim and Kate already then." Her cheeks were pink, maybe from the shower but he thought not. When her lips suddenly tilted and that lovely dimple grooved her cheek, tingles sped right down his spine.

"Dad around?" she asked of Mim.

She came over and leaned on the back of a chair, pushing it down with her palms and rocking it onto two legs. And he realised suddenly she was feeling uncomfortable. Sure, she was hiding it, but he was getting used to catching glimpses of this other less confident Polly.

"He's probably gone to ground," Mim said in a resigned tone. "Worried about controlling the—" She bent her arm in a gesture of putting a glass to her lips. Polly's features tightened and she tugged at the hem of the kimono thing.

"Is that what you're wearing to the party?" Kate grinned.

Polly cast Solo a glance and he quickly flicked his gaze from her mesmerising legs to Charlie. Did the freakin' hound just wink at him?

"It was all I could find in the cupboard. I think I last wore it when I was sixteen. And no, don't be silly. I just didn't know we had company."

Company? That was weirdly formal after the wildly intimate things they'd gotten up to these past couple of weeks.

"Solo's been well looked after," Mim said. "We've had a nice chat about Sydney and his work. Though why you made the poor guy drive up on his motorbike when he could have come with you…"

"I had things on this morning," Solo said quickly. The reality was that driving up first thing this morning in a confined space with Polly's legs in his peripheral vision for two and a half hours was not something he needed to subject himself to.

So when Polly had said she would be leaving at the crack of dawn and maybe he should come up on his bike, he'd gladly agreed. The ride would blow away the tension he was feeling. They hadn't touched since Saturday at the beach. During the week professional Polly, all brisk and businesslike, was back. It was like playing the dating equivalent of Dr Jekyll and Mr Hyde.

"I'll show you to your room, if you like," Polly addressed him.

Solo slurped an obligatory mouthful or two of strong tea and got up. Charlie let out a whine of protest and backed away, then started to wag his tail in anticipation of what might come next.

Polly bent down and chucked him under the chin, pulled his ears. Solo averted his eyes from the way her hemline nearly rode up to expose... no way could he trust his body to behave if he got a glimpse of what lay underneath.

"You bad, bad boy..." she crooned. Solo nearly groaned at the husky tone of her voice. "You leave Solo alone now."

"See you later, Mim, Kate, thanks for the cuppa," he said. The two women were already making plans for the food and gave him a cheery wave. "Anything else I can do to help?"

"Joe will probably need a hand in the barn with arranging the tables and chairs," Kate said. "I'll let Polly show you where to go."

Dutifully he grabbed his overnight bag off the floor and followed Polly. The farmhouse, with its rabbit warren of rooms and bits built on different levels, reminded Solo so much of Pop's and Nan's that a shot of nostalgia hit yet again. And then a wave of sadness. He suddenly remembered how much Drew had loved the farm; it was always where he'd seemed at peace, and now it looked like it was going to be Solo's burden to sell.

Another wedge that would be driven between them.

He pushed aside the thoughts as Polly threw open a door. "This is where you're staying. It used to be my gran's room."

Solo moved past her; taking care not to swing his bag into her meant their bodies bumped instead. It was like they were both holding their breath.

He couldn't help smiling as he took in the interior.

By now Polly had walked around to the other side of the bed and was watching him, arms crossed against her chest.

"What's funny?" she asked.

"Not funny. It's just—" He put his bag down on the floor next to the bed and swept his arm in an expansive gesture. "It's exactly like my nan's bedroom. Same candlewick bedspread, only hers was white, not pink;

the dressing table with the three-way mirror. Even..." He moved over and touched the little white vase with the spray of delicately moulded porcelain flowers on the side. "Even this... Nan always had wild roses in hers."

In the mirror, Polly's image reflected back at him. She was clasping her elbows, rubbing her arms with tight fingers. Her face looked so young and vulnerable.

"It's kind of reassuring," he said quickly to cover his desire to circumnavigate the bed and pull her into his arms.

"In what way?"

"Our grandparents' worlds. When I was a kid, those things kept me safe, like after Mum and Dad died and I'd come into Nan's bed for my morning cup of tea and there would be her stuff, her ornaments, and, you know, every time I smell lavender, even now it makes me feel good."

Polly gave a little laugh. "Gran's clothes always smelled like lavender. She had those things, what d'you call them, pomanders or something. Made of gauze and full of dried lavender flowers."

He nodded. He remembered.

She sat down on the bed. "See here."

He went over and sat next to her, watching her hand smoothing over the coverlet.

"This is where I picked out bits of yarn. And here." She bent down and pulled up a corner of the bedspread and showed him where it was threadbare two rows from the bottom. "When Gran told me off for picking at it, I secretly picked at the hem. It was really, really addictive."

Solo laughed, he loved these little morsels Polly kept throwing him. He was no better than Charlie, really, was he? Living in hope of the small crumbs. She moved her leg a little closer and his breath scrambled, a pulse beat hard in his temples. He was contemplating taking her hand in his when there was a commotion, Charlie barking and a loud yelping.

Polly jumped up.

"That'll be Dad home for lunch, I'll introduce you. I'll just go put some clothes on first." She pulled at the tie of her dressing gown and he stood too, so they were facing each other. She bit on her lower lip and the little pillow it made under her teeth made him want to throw her on that bed, Gran's room or not, and make wild passionate love to her.

"Must you?"

Now she licked her lower lip and it glistened. "Ahhhh—that would feel kind of weird, like, in here."

"Yeah, of course. I didn't actually mean..."

She raised a hand and stroked a finger around the opening of his shirt, along the line of his neck. He stifled a shiver, barely able to stop himself pulling her close.

"I really appreciate you coming," she said quietly. "I'm just pretty wired about tonight."

Now her fingers were at his collar, neatening it. He gulped hard. "What are you worried about?"

"That Dad's drinking will get out of control. That he'll make a complete idiot of himself. That he'll ruin it for everyone. He's always been good at destroying things and really bad at putting them back together again."

"Surely Mim, and your brother and Kate wouldn't have planned this if they didn't think he'd cope?"

"Mim lives in hope. But, yeah." She patted down his collar. "I guess it's been a couple of years since his last big blowout. He's been trying. He's even been to see me in Perth a couple of times. It's always felt kind of awkward."

He gave in to the longing and covered her hand with his. Her fingers fluttered before she slipped her hand out and backed away. He stifled a wave of disappointment. At the door, the old coquettish Polly was back, head on one side, dimple pinned to her cheek. Safe, now she'd got away from him.

But he was far from safe.

"Guess I'm not going to behave the same here as back in Perth," she said. "So don't expect, you know..."

"Is that why you've given me your gran's room?"

"To keep temptation at bay. Absolutely. I'll meet you back in the kitchen." And then she vanished.

Solo hoisted his bag onto the bed. Took out his toiletries bag. He knew what was in here with his toothbrush and hair gel—those little foil packets clearly weren't going to get a look-in this weekend. He smiled at the way his balls kept leading his brain astray. What had he been thinking? That they'd actually be rolling around in the hay together all weekend?

Shaking his head, he hung up his gear. He could do with a shower after his ride. They'd left him a towel and a guest bar of soap but it could wait. It was more important to meet Polly's dad.

And, okay, if he'd been effectively tossed into the friend basket for the weekend, he was liking getting to know these other facets of Polly Fletcher's life. Perhaps a little too much.

WHEN POLLY ARRIVED in the kitchen, Dad was sitting at the table eating a doorstop-sized cheese and pickle sandwich and reading the paper.

He looked up and his face took on that mix of overly cheerful and apologetic. Like he was always trying to repair the rips he'd torn in the fabric of their relationship but hadn't got a clue how to sew.

She hauled in a breath and gave him a hug. His arms came around her, he smelled of axle grease and grass, and she wished she could feel something more. But there was just that familiar knot in the pit of her stomach. She tried to return the hug but her arms felt like they were being operated by remote control.

She made an effort and squeezed.

"Hi sweetheart," her dad's deep voice rumbled in her ear before she pulled back. "Looking good." His eyes skimmed over her, that same embarrassment, almost like he'd never got used to the idea that he was her father.

"You too, Dad."

"Yeah, Mim's been keeping me busy. Never lets up, that one."

"Gah, get away with your grumbling," Mim growled.

Ted's eyes, the same deep shade of green as her own, skimmed past Polly and she swung around to see Solo standing in the doorway.

Her dad's head jerked. "Is this your lad?"

"No, Dad, just a friend." Had she imagined it or did Solo stiffen? "This is Solo Jakoby. We work together—he's a doctor on the ward."

The dogs were up and both sniffing around Solo again. They'd been in their baskets, knowing they might as well not waste their time with the family.

"A shrink?" Ted grinned—he'd fixed up his front tooth, thank Jesus. He'd left it missing for years, never owned up to how he lost it, but Joe had told her it was in a drunken brawl at some pub in another town.

"Afraid so, but a relatively normal one."

"No such thing as a normal shrink," Ted said.

"Dad!"

"Only joking. Nice to meet you, son." He got up and winced. His knee was obviously giving him gyp. He shook Solo's hand heartily. "Nice you could join me to celebrate the big one. Never thought I'd see it, to be honest."

Polly internally groaned; when Dad was nervous he tended to say too much about the past. Luckily he thumped his chest. "A few ticker problems, but sorted for now with a few drugs."

"Ah-ha. Good to meet you, Ted." Solo's smile was so warm, so embracing, her own heart fluttered weirdly behind her ribs.

Then the back door banged and in breezed her big brother. Joe was big in every sense of the word. Broad-chested and over six-foot-three, he filled up the space. "Hullo, Poll." He strode over and enveloped her in a bear hug. "Good to see you, sis."

"Hi, Joe boy."

Joe held her back from him with two beefy hands on her arms and surveyed her face with bright blue eyes that were just like their mum's, but without the constant resentment that had always seemed to shadow hers.

Now it was Polly's turn to introduce Joe to Solo. She saw Joe and Kate's eyes appraising him, weighing up whether he was someone to get their hopes up over. Honestly, you could almost hear the cogs in their brains whirring.

Wish on, guys.

Introductions over, another wave of sandwich-making from Mim, and they all sat down for a late lunch. It was hard to swallow, hard to think. Already Polly was wishing she hadn't invited Solo. The expectations were weighing on her, not just about whether he was her boyfriend, but whether she'd have to jump in later—appease a guest Dad had said the wrong thing to, calm Mim's feathers. God, why did Mim keep trying to get Dad to jump through these hoops?

And now, if it all turned pear-shaped, Solo would be here to watch another Fletcher bun-fight.

And yet... oh, fuck-a-doodle, it felt good to have him here. She glanced over and a little hip-hop dance played out behind her ribs as she saw him laughing and talking tractors with Dad and Joe.

Shit, what couldn't this guy do? Knit, command a group, kiss like a sinner, make a girl scream the house down with her orgasms.

Bake a cake. He couldn't bake a cake. A spluttered giggle escaped her and suddenly those silver eyes were on her; he cocked an eyebrow and warmth spilled through her body.

Polly jumped up. "We had better start getting ready," she said, knowing she was a tad wild-eyed.

"I could do with some help arranging the hay bales in the barn and getting the dance floor in place," Joe said.

Dad got up with a grumble and both dogs lifted their heads from their baskets, ears pricked, ready for the afternoon's work. "I've got to go and check some fences," he said.

"Don't you disappear anywhere. You've got to be back here in good time to spruce up," Mim warned, turning from where she was preparing a bowl of icing for the cake.

"What for?" When Dad popped his eyes with that mock innocent look, Polly knew they resembled one another. A little knife twisted in her gut. She really wished she'd seen more of that humour when she was a kid. But those moments had been few and far between; the hurts far more frequent.

And in the end, it was the hurts that you remembered.

Solo got up on cue, piling up plates and taking them over to the sink. "Do you want a hand washing these up, Mim?"

The guy sure knew how to suck up.

"No, Solo, luv." Mim patted his arm. "You'd be more help in the barn with Joe."

"All this bloody fuss," Dad muttered and ambled out, whistling to the dogs.

"Be back by five," Mim called after him.

"Yeah, yeah," he called back.

Joe stood up too, kissed Kate and laid a hand on her belly. His face lit up. "I just felt a kick. Here, Poll, come and have a feel."

Solo's eyes were burning holes in her. She felt her cheeks firing up. What the hell was wrong with her? Her lips seemed to be shaping into a silly grin, the kind of smile women got when the broody hormones kicked in. And then her hand was reaching out like it was magnetised towards the lovely round mound of Kate's belly.

"Here," Joe said. "A bit lower." He took hold of Polly's hand and gently re-arranged it. Sure enough, a little *thump thump* pushed back against her palm through the cotton of Kate's T-shirt. Polly jumped and giggled. Kate's eyes were shining.

Polly's throat constricted. "Aww, that is so cute. Is it happening much?"

"All the time," Kate said proudly.

"Blimp is on the move," Joe said.

Kate thumped Joe on the arm. "Not Blimp. Our Little Miracle."

Polly made the mistake of looking over at Solo and their eyes locked. And suddenly there was a painful thump going on inside her own belly.

It wasn't a phantom baby.

It was a huge great stab of envy...

CHAPTER 20

Stripping off, Solo stepped into the shower cubicle and grinned as he pulled at the rope that promptly dumped a bucket of warm water on his head. Heck, he'd forgotten how much he loved bush showers. Makeshift wrought-iron shelters, the water heated by what got to be called a donkey by bush folk, but was actually a wood-fired burner, and then hoisting the water up in a metal bucket and *whoooshhhh*.

He wiped rivulets of water off his face and, grabbing the bar of soap, lathered away the sweat and dust from a solid afternoon's labour.

Working side-by-side with Joe and Polly had felt good, reminded him of those days when Drew and he used to help Pop on the farm, rounding up the sheep for the shearers. He'd kept watching Polly out of the corner of his eye, the play of her strong, shapely arms, the curve of her beautiful butt cheeks in her jeans, the little display of belly when her T-shirt rose and the glint of her belly button ring. And somehow he'd kept the yearning and the throb of desire in the background.

He blinked water—and the images of Polly—out of his eyes and soaped over his abdomen and there it was again, a frigging half mongrel between his legs. He did his level best to ignore it but it clearly had a mind of its own as it bobbed into a salute. Once a week wasn't keeping his libido in check, not with the fresh air and exercise and constant nearness of her. She must feel it too, surely?

He yanked the towel off its hook, stepped out... and *oomph*, a body bowled straight into him. Curls tangled in his mouth and stuck to his damp skin, arms flailed wildly. Both of them reeled backwards.

Polly's eyes flew straight to his groin. Oh shit, he still had an erection. It was true, when you blushed naked, it didn't just stop at your face.

"Jesus, Polly!" It came out gruff, because his dick was now tenting the towel he'd slung round his midriff.

"I—oh?" she panted. Her eyes rounded and then shot to his face and that's when he realised something was wrong.

Not turned on. Or even amused. Scared.

Twisting the towel into a tight knot round his waist, he asked sharply, "What's wrong?"

"It's Dad. No-one can find him and he's not answering his mobile. I was wondering—would you—could you help look for him?"

Solo sprang into professional mode. "Sure. I'll just throw on some clothes."

The tension was ebbing out of her, flowing into him, stoking his body with adrenaline.

She said, frowning, "I'll um, just wait outside."

When he got out she was standing with her arms bunched over her chest.

"What's going on?"

"No-one can get him on his mobile. Which is Dad all over, of course, but he promised Mim today he'd keep it on. And he was supposed to be back well over an hour ago. The guests are due to arrive soon. Mim's out of her mind with worry."

"Okay. Where was he working?"

"Joe's gone to check the far paddocks. Though, to be honest, the most likely place he'll be now is his den. I said I'd check, but I— I don't want to find him..."

He looked at her, alarmed. "You don't think he'd harm himself?"

She shook her head. "No—I don't think so. Not nowadays. Ask me fifteen years ago, I'd say something different, but, eshhh." Her shoulders hunched nearly up to her ears, her hand came up and she chewed on the cuticle of her thumb. "Drinking, I bet." The eyes that met his were dulled by dread. "But the thing is, when Dad starts... he doesn't stop..."

"Fuck!"

"Yeah." Her laugh was mirthless. "Not a good look, punching your guests' lights out."

"Would he?"

"He used to get aggressive. Mostly, as he's got older, he just gets maudlin and loud and embarrasses his family."

Solo braced. "Okay, tell me how to get to his den."

"It will take three minutes on your bike. It's the building you can see on the road in, just before you get to the farm gate, with the eucalypts around it."

He remembered seeing it.

She grimaced. "I know this sounds pathetic but can you check it out first? I'll follow in my car and you can phone me and let me know if..." Her voice trailed off and he saw fear pinching her features.

"It's, um, just—" Her lower lip quivered. "I can't face him like this without a warning first... too many memories..."

He moved closer. "I get it. Hey, I get it, okay?"

Her face turned up to his and his heart slammed against his ribs. Tears swam in her eyes. Something inside him cracked open with tenderness. He bent his head, kissed her just beside her ear and whispered, "It'll be okay," before striding towards the house and his bike.

Did he know that? Of course he didn't. He just couldn't bear to see her fall apart.

No more than seven minutes later, Solo drew up outside Ted's shed. It was grey jarrah, worn and beaten by the weather, with bits of farm paraphernalia—old wheels and twisted tractor axles—hammered onto the outside. The large doors were shut. It looked deserted, then Solo saw Ted's old ute tucked around the back.

A gunshot rang out.

Shit!

He was off the bike in seconds and sprinting, no thoughts, just pure adrenaline.

Another shot.

"Christ." Solo got to the doors and his fingers, suddenly shaking, dragged a couple of times on the metal handle, before he pushed it roughly open, blinking to adjust to the dimness inside.

There was an eerie stillness. Eyes wide and scanning, Solo advanced slowly. If Ted had shot himself... Christ... the implications were too much to take in, the present moment and the rasp of his amplified breath filling his ears.

Then there was a rustle as a figure moved somewhere in the shadows.

"Ted!" Solo called.

A grunt. Was he injured?

"Ted!" Louder this time.

"What is it, lad?" Solo's highly tuned ears registered that the voice didn't sound injured or in pain. Just slightly irritated.

"Ted, are you okay?"

"Yeah, yeah. Just needed some quiet time."

Solo didn't point out that firing guns was hardly freakin' quiet time.

His legs almost gave way with the surge of relief, and then, as his eyes took in more, his stomach dropped. His nostrils registered the pungent scent of what—whisky? Mixed with something else, sweeter. Rum?

Anger surged in Solo's belly. How dare he do that, the selfish old bastard? After all the trouble his family had been to...

He knew to hold himself in check. Advanced slowly, cautiously.

Ted's bulky frame was slumped in a chair on the far wall. Lined up on the bench in front of him were bottles of alcohol. At least half a dozen.

Solo's foot squelched into wet straw, then scrunched on broken glass.

He looked at Ted and realised the guy had a gun; *he was still holding the fucking gun.*

His body brittle, his mind switched into icy professional psychiatrist mode. Smoothly, he said, "Perhaps you could put the gun down, Ted."

Ted stood up, his big body looming.

Solo swallowed, his throat dry as dust. "Put the gun down, Ted."

"Shit, boy, you don't think I'd shoot you, do you?"

Solo watched, all senses on high alert as Ted brandished the gun.

"Put—the— gun— down, Ted," he repeated.

"What, you thought I'd shoot meself?" Ted sounded incredulous.

"I don't know, Ted. Were you planning to?"

The older man let out a harsh laugh. "Smell that?" He pointed the gun barrel at the bottles. "I used to think that was nectar of the gods. Now it's the devil's brew, son. That's the enemy. I've been shooting the fucking bottles."

Solo nodded. "Okay."

"It was that or drink the bastards. And where would that have bloody got me?"

Solo nodded again. "So now you've done it, you can put the gun down."

Ted sighed. "Guess I'll have to clear all this bloody mess up now, won't I. Still..." He barked out another laugh and relief flooded Solo as, finally, Ted placed the gun against the wall. "Better than clearing up the mess I'd make of myself, Mim and the kids if I drank the stuff."

Ted slumped back in his seat with a big sigh. "I'm just trying to put off going to that bloody shindig, to be honest. When I came up here it was 50/50 I would drink myself blind, or get rid of it all."

Solo advanced slowly, eyes scanning between the gun against the wall and Ted's hands, now in his lap. "You decided to do the latter."

"Yeah."

Solo registered the thud of his heart slowing as the adrenaline ran its course. He was close to Ted now, but not too close, not threateningly close.

Ted looked up and a sad smile twisted his mouth. "You want to sit for a bit, lad?"

Solo hesitated, feeling for his phone in his jeans pocket. "Sure. But can I just let your family know you're okay first?"

Ted's face in the shadows looked surprised. "Were they worried?"

"It's nearly time for the party to start, Ted."

"Oh, bugger." The older man hung his head, stared at his clasped hands. "Time loses its meaning sometimes, when… Yeah, call Poll. Let her know. She'll smooth it over with the others."

Yes, thought Solo. Polly the peacekeeper. He moved away and dialled her number. She picked up straight away.

"Have you found him?"

"Yes, he's safe."

"He hasn't been…?"

"No. No, sober as a judge, aren't you, Ted?" Solo made his voice jovial. "I'm just going to stay here with him for a while, but tell everyone he's fine."

"Is he coming to the party?"

"Soon."

"Okay." She clearly got the message.

"I'll text you if we're going to be longer than half an hour."

"Right. Thanks so much for doing this." Her voice sounded small, exhausted. So unlike the usual ebullient Polly that his heart almost broke as he put his phone away.

"They're not upset?" Ted asked.

"No, they're cool." It was a lie, but clearly it wasn't going to make Ted feel better hearing they'd been worried sick.

"I'd offer you a drink, but…" Ted said.

They both laughed, a flimsy token but a start. Ted motioned to the chair next to him. "This one at least has a seat."

Solo parked his butt on the old busted chair, felt the ping of a spring up his arse and chuckled. "Not much of one."

"I only get the things that are thrown out. Bit like me, on the scrapheap."

"Don't say that. Your family love you."

Ted sighed. They sat in silence for long moments. "You know what the irony is? The thing that makes me want to drink the most is knowing how much I've let them all down. The shame. That's what I try to drown out. That, and the memories."

"Pretty bad, huh?"

"Vietnam. Did Poll tell you? You being a shrink and all, she's probably told you everything about my fucked-up life." Ted's voice had an edge that Solo sensed would need careful handling.

"Yes, she mentioned you were in Vietnam. My best friend served in Afghanistan. It roughed him up a lot."

Ted turned his head and looked at Solo, his eyes glinting in the dim light. "So, you've seen what it does to someone first-hand?"

"I have. It's not pretty."

"Telling me." Ted leaned back. "I get them less now, you know, the flashbacks. That sound, though, *phtpht phphhht, pphhhttt*. Helicopters. Even now, if I hear one I want to flatten to the fucking ground. I keep away from the bastard things. And that stuff, the magic elixir"—he waved his hand at the lined-up bottles—"helps you forget. All you want, all you need, is to forget. It's a battlefield... only up here." He tapped his head.

"That's pretty much how my best mate described it."

"Shit, is the poor bugger okay?"

Solo paused. Was Drew okay? He couldn't know for sure. "He's getting treatment." That much was true, at least.

Ted sighed. "Did Polly say I drove her mum away, too? With my drinking, my verbals. I hit her, once, twice at most. Lowest points of my life. It was mostly words, but I guess words can be just as bad. Poll, she was a good girl, always smiling, always forgiving, hugged me as she cleaned up the freakin' mess afterwards. Told me 'you'll be okay, Daddy'. Then her mum left. And her gran died. She adored her gran, our Polly did. That's when it changed. She stopped talking to me. Scarpered. Can't blame her." Suddenly his shoulders shook. "I want to tell her..."

"Tell her what?" Solo asked softly.

"That I'm sorry... For what I did." Ted's voice choked up. "For what I didn't do... how I, you know, wasn't a real dad to her all those years."

Solo turned towards Ted, his body language open and accepting. "You were unwell, Ted. It's hard to treat people decently when you're suffering. And no-one can see psychological wounds."

"Dead right. would have been better if my bloody legs had been blown off. Then they'd have seen it."

"PTSD is as bad as losing limbs," Solo pointed out. "Maybe worse, because nobody can see when we lose part of our mind. They just feel the effects."

"Yeah, like a fucking great mine blowing up in their faces. I tried to get help, several times, and then, you know, you feel better, you think, 'Christ, stop being a sook, you don't need these bloody pills. Man up. Just get on with it'. And I'd ditch them down the loo. A week later be back on that stuff." He waved a hand at the bottles again. "Just got to shoot the rest and I'm done."

"Maybe not, Ted."

Ted hung his head. "Ah, it felt good smashing the buggers."

"Empty them out instead."

"Gah, you young 'uns. No sense of adventure."

"Not around guns, no." Solo dared to grin now the mood was lightening. "Now, motorbikes, that's a different thing altogether."

"Thought I heard an engine coming up the hill. What is it, a Honda?"

"No, Ducati Monster."

"Used to have a Bonneville."

"Really? You lucky man."

"A real beaut, that one. Rode it pissed as a fart one day and that was it, written off and one broken collarbone."

"You were lucky."

"Maybe. Maybe the world would be better off without me."

"No, Ted, never."

Ted heaved another heavy sigh then landed his big hands on his thighs and stood up. He cocked his head as he looked down at Solo.

"You going to let me ride on the back of the Monster? Reckon it's the only way you'll get me back to that gig."

Solo laughed and stood up. The danger had passed. "If I agree to it, we'll be going at a snail's pace."

"What, because I'm a fat bastard?"

"No, because you won't have a helmet on."

"Okay, I'll accept that. And, lad, thanks for the chat. It's eased my mind."

"It's not too late to get some help for this, Ted," Solo said as they walked out into the evening air. The horizon still glowed red from the setting sun. Ted's features softened as he looked at Solo in the deepening light. Solo pressed on gently. "Especially now with your first grandkid on the way."

Ted scratched his head. "You mean the touchy-feely talk-talk stuff? The stuff our Poll does?"

"Well, obviously not with Polly. But there's good people out there."

Ted looked at him hard. His eyes were so like Polly's, suddenly soft and clear. "If I give you my number, could you ask around for me? Get a name? Not going to ask Polly, not appropriate. But it would be good, maybe, if Mim and I could see someone together and sort a few issues out." Ted hesitated, his eyes almost pleading. "Would you mind?"

"Of course not," Solo said. "I'd be happy to help."

He swung a leg over the bike. "Hop on, but I'm warning you, this isn't going to be the Grand Prix."

"Jesus Christ, spoil an old man's fun on his birthday, would you?" Ted huffed. "All right, lad, all right."

"AND I WANT to thank my long-suffering partner, Mim; my big ugly son, who's worked his arse off for this place; and his lovely wife, who's going to make me a very proud granddad shortly..."

Polly held her breath as Ted's eyes sought hers across the crowd, "And my beautiful daughter, Polly."

Dad's big hand trembled on the microphone. He looked down at the floor. What was he going to say next? Please god, don't let it be embarrassing.

Ted gave a wavery laugh. "She's an amazing girl. You know, as a kid, she always used to know the right thing to say. Knew how to make a bad situation better. And, er, I'm not proud to say, but at my age I can admit it, there were a few of those. Guess that's what makes her amazing at her job... she's a... she's a social worker, most of you know... and ah, a great artist." A thick thumb jerked up to the swinging wonky 70 sign she'd made... Another embarrassed laugh then, gruff as old boots grinding on pebbles, Ted said, "I've never told you, Poll, but I love you, girl."

Polly's lower lip wobbled dangerously as a round of applause and whooping filled the air.

"Come up here, my four favourite people, and give a gnarly old seventy-year-old a hug."

Polly's legs felt like someone had removed the bones from them, but she got up there somehow and found herself in a group hug with Joe and Mim and Kate and... Dad.

And her heart felt like it might just jump right out of her chest. More cheering and laughter and someone—Dad's old friend Bill, who'd stood by him all these years—hollered from the back of the crowd: "A toast to Ted Fletcher, the old bastard. May he live forever." And suddenly it struck her—they all loved him. This community of Wadgigaree who had dragged him out of the gutter countless times and driven him home and got him out of the lock-up a couple of times, they all loved her dad.

Her head kicked back and she heard herself laughing and cheering, and then her gaze snagged on Solo standing quietly, one hand in his pocket, the other holding his beer and a look... a look so warm and soft and *loving* on his face that suddenly she couldn't breathe.

The laughter got caught in a strange little hiccup in her throat and in that moment, she knew, she *fucking knew*, she was at risk of falling for Solo Jakoby.

Sometime later he found her by the drinks table.

"Your dad's done amazingly."

"Yep. He's stuck to no-alcohol beer all night."

"And that speech. Straight from the heart."

"Did you hypnotise him—cast some weird Dr J spell on him?" she managed lightly, adding chunks of ice to her glass and pouring in non-alcoholic punch. They'd kept a table full of non-alcoholic drinks to help Dad along and she'd kept him company. It was the least she could do in the circumstances.

She turned to Solo, sucking on her straw, feeling weird and kind of coy—the same feeling she'd got just after she'd met him, like she'd dance in a field of corn with her hair in bunches, all dressed in gingham if he asked her.

He smiled down at her, shook his head and an arrow stabbed repeatedly into her heart.

A muscle at the corner of his jaw tightened. Just one side. Oh, the blissful asymmetry of his face. She'd never get bored looking at it. Her fingers itched to reach up and trace around his jaw, feel that muscle tighten and twitch, lose herself in the way his mouth softened, his eyes darkened, just before he kissed her.

"I haven't, um, had a chance to properly thank you," she managed to croak, breaking the spell because it hurt, really *hurt* to want to kiss someone this badly.

"You don't need to thank me. I would have done it a thousand times over if you'd asked me."

"Shit!"

"What?"

"Why do you have to say something like that?"

He looked momentarily bewildered. "Sorry, I—"

She laughed shakily. "I mean, why do you have to be so... so fucking nice to me?"

Relief flooded his face, his jaw relaxed. "What would you prefer—I put you over my knee and spanked you?"

Now this was the language she understood. It chased away the stupidity that had sent her brain soft there for a moment. They were good together in bed. Short term. Forget all the soppy shit.

Brain funk sorted.

She chinked her glass against his and let the familiar energy zap down her spine and run sweet between her legs.

"That's more what I'm used to."

He bent his head close and murmured, "Okay, give me a time and a place and I'll be there."

His mouth nuzzled against her ear and she let herself sway into him. Then he whispered, "Want to dance?"

Chris Isaac's "Wicked Game" had just started up. Like, seriously, what was she supposed to do?

Polly gulped hard. "Sure."

He took her hand in his, and when his thumb-pad stroked her wrist as he pulled her close, she suddenly had an image of herself as one of those self-saucing puddings. Like Solo had just plunged a dessert spoon straight into her middle.

She sank against him as his arms bound her close. And God, why did he have to hold her in that old-fashioned way? Her arm sandwiched against his chest, fingers intertwined, his chin resting on her curls. She could feel the beating of his heart against her breasts, and her nipples jumped to attention.

She didn't dare look up. She'd disintegrate.

The words crooned across the dance floor.

How did Chris Isaac know that she, Polly Fletcher, would be right here trying to resist that very thing? Clearly the universe and all that crap about a butterfly's wings starting an earthquake in Tokyo was absolutely, one hundred per cent true. Because right now, it felt like that earthquake was right here, that her world was going to collapse into Solo's arms and never find its way back to normal.

And then his lips moved softly down her neck, and the swell of her belly registered the hard ridge of his desire. And it was all. Just. Too. Much.

Polly pulled back. Gasped out, "Sorry, I've got to go—um—yeah, I forgot—I'm in charge of the cake."

Black lashes blinked over luminous silver, then the light extinguished and her sinking heart knew she'd blown something truly magical.

Blindly, she dashed through the crowded dance floor. Someone said, "You all right Poll?" and she realised it was Joe, dancing with Kate.

"Fine. Just forgot, I have to get the cake," she said and fled towards the house.

In the kitchen, Mim and her friend Mira were putting the finishing touches on the cake: a tractor and seven large candles—one for each decade—plus a big 70 sign and a little plastic farmer.

Smoothing down her dress with palms that trembled, she asked, "Need some help?"

"I think we've got it pretty much under control." Mim looked so happy. She'd finally been rewarded with the man she'd always hoped for after all these years. Wasn't that what love was about? Sticking in there, warts and all, good times and bad times, ups and downs.

Polly had no faith she could do that. No trust that she had it in her.

And then it hit like a lightning bolt, nearly blowing her back out the door she'd just entered.

It wasn't that she didn't trust herself. She just didn't believe anyone could love her the way Mim loved Dad. That anyone would ever stick around that long.

WHAT THE HELL JUST HAPPENED?

One minute they were wrapped around each other and everything was perfect, and then she'd ducked and run with some lame excuse.

Solo stood at the side of the dance floor, squeezing his beer glass until it threatened to smash. What had he done? Just nuzzled her neck, held her close… nothing compared to their other wild pursuits. Was it that they were in view of her family? That she didn't want them to think—

Jesus. He ruffled a hand through the short spikes of his hair and let out an exasperated breath.

Bloody Polly Fletcher, constant mixed messages like a bag of mixed lollies. It made him remember a story Pop had told him when he was a kid. Pop and his friends had been nicking lollies, so one day the old guy at the corner shop had emptied out the fondant centres and filled them up with hot English mustard.

That was exactly how it felt with Polly—just as he thought it was safe to sink his teeth into that wonderful softness, she turned it all into something that left a horrible taste in his mouth.

Fuck, she annoyed the hell out of him.

And then he saw her marching out with the cake held up in those luscious arms, a big smile on her bright red lips, and he couldn't be angry with her. She was beautiful and complex and totally confusing. Could he put up with the mustard centres for a bit longer, in the hope that eventually he'd hit something sweet and wonderful and long-lasting?

The pull of her was so strong, Solo realised he didn't have a choice.

"Where are you, birthday boy?" Mim's strident voice bellowed over the microphone. "Come and blow out these candles, you bloody slacker."

More laughter and Ted was pushed forward. Hands clapped his back as he made his way to the front.

Solo watched Polly, a hundred and one emotions playing out behind that smile. He raised his glass in a salute and realised that finally, he was getting better at reading her.

And then another thought struck—she knew that, didn't she? Knew he could see behind the games she played to the real Polly. And that, he realised, scared the bejesus out of her.

Later, much later, when the guests had gone and the party had been dissected over cups of tea at the kitchen table and Ted had gone to bed, Solo and Polly were skirting around each other, playing at helping, when finally Mim said, "Off with you both, you're as useless as tits on a bull. Besides, I like clearing the kitchen on my own. It's my little pre-bed routine."

Polly's gaze met his and then slid away, which was what had been happening since the dance-floor incident. He'd catch her watching him, then when he returned her gaze she'd look away, like a hummingbird flitting from flower to flower, refusing to settle even though the nectar was sweet.

Sure, he was pretty damn sweet. On her. He was sure she knew that. His sense it was reciprocated was getting stronger, but hell, this had been an emotional day all round and it wasn't the right time to pursue it. Plus, he was dead beat. The incident with Ted earlier had taken him right back to Drew's suicide attempt. Made him jagged and raw inside.

Which was why he carefully kept his distance as they walked down the corridor to their rooms. Not that it did much to stop the pulse in his temples and an answering one in his groin as they faced each other at his bedroom door. He leaned on the doorframe, let his fingers reach for the door handle to show he was ready to turn in.

"Good night, Dr J."

"Good night." They both looked at their feet, then up simultaneously and laughed in unison.

Polly the seductress was nowhere in sight. Instead, fatigue smudged shadows under her eyes. With her lipstick all eaten off and the dusting of freckles on her nose, she looked like a teenager returning from her first party.

"I owe you," she said, and he noticed the way her fingers twisted together in front of her in a gesture he'd never seen her do before. Was this some little throwback from childhood? "You handled Dad amazingly."

"He's a great guy. I was happy to help."

"Yeah, like you go in and wrestle a weapon from someone every week." She stopped, bit her lip, and said, "Sorry, I didn't mean to remind you of..."

"I'll admit I had a bit of a trip wire happening, when I walked into the barn."

She nodded. "I'm sorry, I just sensed you'd know what to do—and—" She hesitated and he longed to fold her hands in his, stop her torturing those fingers. "I—I just met a brick wall inside myself. I couldn't go look for him."

He caved and covered both her hands with his. The finger twisting stopped. Her head was bent but he could tell she was biting her lower lip.

"Hey, it's okay to not know what to do. To be—" Would she bristle if he said scared? He chose "vulnerable" instead.

Didn't she know that her vulnerability was leaking out of every one of her pores right now? The desire to put his arms around her became a physical ache. To hold her close and comfort her.

Her head shot up; her smile radiant, incongruent. "Vulnerable. That's a novel one for me, isn't it?" And then, gently but firmly, she tugged her hands from his grasp.

He smiled back as his heart plummeted and he said, "Guess I'll turn in, as my nan used to say."

'Sure, me too," she murmured, then reached up and kissed him lightly on the mouth.

He returned it, felt her lips respond for a split second. Then she stepped back. "Better not."

"No. You're right. Gran might be watching from above."

"She would definitely not approve of shenanigans in her bed. Good-night then, Solo-man."

He cocked an eyebrow. "Where's Dr J gone? I was getting to enjoy that title."

"Doesn't do to be predictable." And then she swivelled on her heels and, with a toss of those dark curls and the words "sweet dreams", she was gone.

He watched her shimmy off down the dimly lit passage; a part of him, the part that would never get enough of her, almost crying with frustration at the gorgeous tilt of those hips in the silky green dress, moving out of reach.

"Goodnight, Miss Unpredictable," he called. She held up her hand and wiggled her middle finger, which he guessed was the bird, Polly-style.

Yeah, Miss Unpredictable—the name sure suited her.

CHAPTER 21

"It's my birthday in two weeks," Carts said as he bounded into the kitchen, pulling off his tie and throwing it on the bench top. Solo was cooking himself a quick omelette before heading off for the last of the Wednesday night PTSD groups.

"I've decided to have a party, on the Saturday night." Carts' grin was that of a man who had experienced a Eureka moment on the way home from work.

"Is that a warning to make myself scarce?" Solo asked, tipping the omelette onto a plate. Carts' face took on an expression of hurt. "No, mate, it's an invite."

Solo smothered a smile. "Dinner party?"

"Nah, cooking's not my thing. Drinks, nibbles." Carts' features took on a slight flush. "Just, um, thought it's time to give my social life a bit of a kick-start."

He put his case down by the door and shucked his long arms out of his jacket. "You're seeing Polly tonight, aren't you, at that group thing you run?"

"Yeah, why?"

"Can you ask her?"

Solo stiffened. They'd been back in odd work mode since the weekend. Frankly, it was getting to him. "We're not dating, you know." Then he kicked himself for even saying it.

Carts' brown eyes widened in surprise. "Never said you were."

Solo sat down and shovelled omelette into his mouth. "Sure, I'll tell her," he said, and quickly changed the subject.

As he left the kitchen a short while later, Carts said airily, "Back to the party issue. It's just I've asked Judith and er, you know, don't want to look too keen, so if you and Poll are there too, as my friends, no wires crossed, get my meaning."

"Right, got it," Solo said, and zoomed out the door like all the bats of hell were in hot pursuit.

When he arrived at the community centre half an hour later, most of the participants were there and Polly was arranging Tim Tams on a plate in the kitchen. She gave him her "we are only professionals working together do not forget that" smile.

He flashed his teeth back at her. This was their last group together. Ben would be back next week, and since they'd called a truce, it was like they both had to work extra-hard at being colleagues to be sure that nobody would guess they were anything but. The result was this awkward spiky energy between them.

He sighed.

"Tim Tams again?"

She shrugged. "You can't go wrong with Tim Tams, can you?"

"Any no-shows?"

"No, I think since you came on the scene full attendance has been pretty much a given. You're popular, Dr J."

"Thanks. By the way, before I forget"—he cast a furtive glance into the room but the participants were laughing and talking among themselves—"Carts is planning a party Saturday week. For his birthday. He's invited you, and me. Not as a couple or anything. And Judith, of course. Guest of honour, I think."

Polly rolled her eyes. "God, he does not let up, that guy."

"Are you playing romance police?" It was hard to keep his irritation from surfacing.

Polly crushed the Tim Tam wrapper, opened the pedal bin with her foot and shoved it in. "It's just that I'll have to pick up the pieces when it goes pear-shaped."

He swallowed the irritation bubble. "They're grown-ups, I'm sure they'll work it out. Here, do you want me to take some cups out?"

"Sure."

He put the cups and teabags on the tray and took the plate from her, carefully avoiding their fingers touching. They hadn't touched since Sunday morning when she'd tapped his arm before he rode off on his motorbike.

He ached for her.

With a sudden surge of courage, he moved along the bench until their bodies nearly touched and she seemed to move into him a little. Their elbows nudged, and a little bit of electric magic travelled up his arm, into his scalp. Her perfume made his head spin, like a man deprived of oxygen.

"So, will you come?"

"Mmmm?"

"To Carts' party?"

"I guess to keep Jude from being gobbled up alive—" He sensed her smiling next to him.

"I'd like it if you did."

"Does Carts suspect anything? You know, after I rescued him from the stair incident?"

It stung that she still seemed worried. "Nope. He still thinks he dreamed you."

Now she gave a low, soft laugh. "Okay then, I'll come."

Suddenly he was ridiculously chuffed, like he'd achieved something way more than a party invite acceptance. As they exited the kitchen a few heads turned and, as if she remembered she wasn't supposed to be walking quite so close, Polly veered towards the table at the front of the room with her usually chirpy, "How's everyone's week been?", leaving Solo to arrange the tea stuff on the trestle table.

He sensed a figure sidle up next to him. "Put the Tim Tams away, doc."

Solo laughed. "Sounds like an order."

He looked around to see Grant holding a cake box.

"Got something much better here," Grant said with a grin.

Solo realised the other participants were crowding around. "Open it, doc." Grant motioned with his head.

Feeling self-conscious, Solo took the box and flicked up the lid.

Chocolate cake met his gaze, covered in thick buttercream icing and the words "Solo, you rock doc" scrawled in confectioners' icing.

A lump formed at the back of Solo's throat and his eyes smarted. A grin threatened to hijack his face. He gazed around the assembled group of ten. Everyone was here tonight and that made his heart swell.

"Aww, thanks, guys," he said, blushing. "I'm really touched."

"We don't want you to go, doc."

"I don't want to either, but endings, like beginning, are just part of life. You've been a great bunch; thanks for opening up and sharing your triumphs and struggles so honestly. I've felt honoured to share a little part of the journey to recovery with all of you these past four weeks. Keep up the great work and thanks, I'm—I'm – er—gobsmacked, to be honest."

As his gaze swept the smiling faces, he caught Polly's eyes glowing emerald, a smile curving her lips that spoke more than words, and he inhaled sharply. That look wasn't indifference, it was warm and intense. Like being immersed in a bath full of rose petals.

Crazy.

He composed himself in case the whole PTSD group saw him shooting Polly the look of love in return and said, "The sooner we get started, the sooner we get to have a slice of this amazing cake. Guess it makes up for torturing your tastebuds with my cake that first night. And thanks again, you guys. If I may say so, I think you all rock."

At the end of the group, as Grant came and shook hands with him, Solo looked into his eyes and saw how the haunted look had eased. There was a new vitality in the gaze that returned his.

"I want to thank you personally, doc. I got in to see my psychiatrist last week and he's changed my meds. Already I reckon there's not so many flashbacks."

"That's good to hear, Grant."

"I reckon I can speak for all of us when I say we'll miss you, Doc Solo."

Something twanged inside Solo's chest like someone had snapped a glow stick next to his heart. He put a hand up and pinched the bridge of his nose, shook his head to hide just how touched he was, just how much this meant. That in some small way it made up for the fuck-up with Drew. Even though he knew he'd done everything right by saving his friend's life that day, part of him couldn't let go of wondering if he could have done it better, saved Drew the humiliation of being carted off in an ambulance with flashing cameras in his face.

But these past four weeks, with this bunch of brave people, he felt like he might just have put some of that to rights.

After everyone had left, Polly and Solo stacked the chairs and cleaned up the tiny kitchenette. They locked up the centre and strolled towards their respective vehicles.

Arriving at Polly's car first, they stopped and faced each other. Polly slung her bag on the bonnet and Solo leaned a lazy elbow on the side of her car, which kind of stopped her from opening it. A ploy, admittedly, but he didn't want her to go home and he sensed she didn't either.

"Fancy a drink and a de-brief?" He hitched an eyebrow, and she laughed.

"That is exactly the eyebrow waggle you gave me the first time we met."

"Not surprising, you were muttering to yourself like a crazy old woman."

"I'd just monumentally humiliated myself."

"I never did find out why you called yourself an idiot. What had you done, thrown your drink over someone? Hurled insults at the bride?"

She grinned sheepishly. "No, just said something embarrassing out loud without realising it."

"Fancy telling me what?"

"No."

Now it was his turn to grin. "So, then you went on to insult a poor defenceless guy who'd just arrived from over east."

"Defenceless my butt, you were fully in control of the situation and you knew it."

He liked that she was complimenting him in this way. In his head he rarely felt like that super-cool biker guy she'd taken him for. He cared too much about people to ever be Mr Macho. And he was okay with that—except when he seriously had to impress a beautiful woman.

"Seems like it worked," he said.

She shook her head, still smirking, and he watched the light of the streetlamp on her hair almost turning it into baby serpents. It made him think of the one on her thigh. Medusa. "Could it work again tonight, maybe?" He resisted the urge to touch a curl, wind it round his finger.

Her eyes met his, dark as a forest and sultry, and he wondered where they were in the game—was it her turn to back off next? Make him advance? Playing emotional chess.

She looked down at her feet and he realised her toe in her pretty pumps had advanced and was touching his foot. He'd never realised before what a turn-on a foot nudge could be. Heat rushed up his leg, swirled into his groin.

God, he wanted to fuck Polly tonight. Go deep inside her, lose himself, forget there was a world outside of him and her, wrap her up in his arms afterwards and hold her close until morning.

"Why don't we go back to my place?" she said. "I've got lemons and gin and probably a bottle of tonic. Unless you need to eat first?"

"I've eaten enough chocolate cake to sink a ship and I made myself an omelette earlier."

She laughed.

"What's so funny?"

"I don't know—it's kind of cute, or a bit sad—you in Carts' kitchen making an itsy-bitsy omelette for one."

"I'll have you know I make very good omelettes. And if you're worried I need company, I could always make a two-person omelette for breakfast."

"Now that's a thought..." Her lips parted to show a tantalising glimpse of tongue. He wanted to kiss her. Take her against the car bonnet. Do all manner of things that were illegal in public. Libido brain bypassing all those logical synapses, knocking them out like skittles in a bowling alley.

"You know how to get to my place from here, don't you?" she asked.

He gulped hard, because his throat was dry as sandpaper, nodded, touched her fingers lightly and felt hers coil around his for the briefest second. If she'd wrapped her hand around his cock it couldn't have made every cell in his body jump higher. Pure elation hit like a drug.

"Sure do. See you in ten." And with that, Solo turned and strode off towards his bike, his groin pummelling his brain into a delightful hot mess of anticipation.

WHEN POLLY GOT HOME she whizzed into her bedroom, threw the pile of clothes on the bed into a cupboard and slammed the door. Turned on the bedside lamps. Smoothed the bed covers—though why, when they were about to ruck them all up again, was anybody's guess.

Her body was a thrumming, throbbing, delightful group of cells all bumping against each other with excitement.

In all honesty, since the weekend, she'd been kicking herself for not sneaking into Gran's bed and wrapping her arms and legs around Solo like a sex octopus. On Sunday she had stayed all day with Dad and Mim after Solo had left early. She'd let Dad show her round the farm, made lunch with Mim, and when she'd got home it was late. Solo had left her a text asking how it went and saying he'd enjoyed it, and she'd messaged back saying all fine. Frankly, her feelings were confusing the hell out of her. The lust she could handle, but not the *like* that was threatening to tip way too far into something else. Something more intimate and too beautiful.

She ran into the bathroom, rubbed toothpaste round her teeth, fluffed out her curls and bit her lips to bring colour to them, and when she heard the familiar deep roar of his motorbike, her heart rapped against her ribs.

She undid two buttons of her blouse. It would make access just that bit easier.

Then he was at the door and she gave him the kind of awkward polite welcome she'd give a vacuum cleaner salesman. She'd never felt so coy around a guy.

"So, about that drink." She obviously wasn't going to drag him straight into the bedroom. That would be kind of crass, even for her.

He strode into the kitchen and laid his helmet down on the table. "Yeah, about that drink."

She grabbed ice out of the freezer, trying not to notice just how nice his crotch looked in his tight jeans, and the way his thighs ran into his calves and into his bike boots. He took off his jacket and his biceps flexed invitingly. She turned to the glasses with an internal whimper, and threw together ice, gin and mixer haphazardly.

"Cheers." She tried to look nonchalant, hips against the kitchen bench, and they both took a few sips. Lowering the glass, her eyes locked with his as he stood by the table. His Adam's apple bobbed as if swallowing was an effort, the silver of his eyes deepening to storm-grey.

In two strides he was at her side. Gently he prised the glass from her fingers and put it on the bench. Next, he took her hands and slowly, deliberately, tucked them one at a time around his waist. As if hypnotised, she moved into his embrace.

The hard pouch in his jeans pressed into her belly. The fact that he was already so turned on by her made her suddenly wild.

With a moan Polly climbed his body like a kitten scaling a tree.

Solo grabbed her butt, anchoring her close as they kissed like crazy things. And, ah, how she'd forgotten in a week how badly she needed his kisses. They were like the elixir of life itself, she decided, as his tongue forged into her mouth.

Teasing him a little, she ran her tongue along the seam of his lips until he growled and bit then licked her lower lip.

"Bedroom?" she finally husked against his mouth.

"Or we could do it right here." He'd turned so macho, and it was such a turn-on.

She rifled her hands through his hair, slithered down his body. "Why not."

He gave a lascivious grin and, as if to torture her, slowed the pace, undoing the buttons of her shirt one at a time. They both gazed down at the creamy flesh begging to escape the confines of her bra. He pushed down the cups and she sighed as his fingers grazed over her nipples, before dark spiky hair was all she could see and all she could feel was his lips teasing her nipple into a hard little nub of delight. He gave the other the same lavish attention. Her back arched as he sucked, then, unable to bear it any longer, she pushed him off, ripped off her neat little work shirt, and then made light work of his.

Running her hands along the ridges and planes of his chest, she gasped, "I just want you inside me. Now."

"What happened to foreplay?" he murmured, tiptoeing his lips down her neck, hungry fingers ruching up her skirt until she shoved a thigh between his and rode him like a rodeo queen. That worked. He groaned, his erection grinding into her belly.

"Like this—" She turned around, not caring that her skirt was still bunched around her waist, and wriggled her butt cheeks up at him as she splayed her hands on the benchtop. "I want you like this—"

"Oh fuck, you are magnificent." Behind her she could hear the awe in his voice and she heard the zipper of his pants before he was back, pushing down her panties, his fingers stroking between her wet folds. She gasped as he found her clit.

"Oh yes... more..." Tight knuckles clasped the edge of the bench as he stroked her with expert precision.

Then two fingers dipped inside her and she bucked, heat building at her core, while his other hand anchored her hips.

"Oh, god—I—like, now!" She groped for her bag—luckily she'd thrown it on the benchtop nearby—and pulled out the condom pack. Twisting her head, she glanced up at him.

Desire filled out his lips, his nostrils flared, his eyes almost other-worldly. Her internal muscles clenched, knowing he was the most beautiful man to ever take her like this, rough and wild and untamed. Her hips spread wider and his strokes grew faster. It was almost unbearable, as the heat swirled and gained momentum, she was teetering so close to the edge.

She needed him inside her. "Stop torturing me."

"I won't be able to hold out for long."

"You won't have to."

His hand moved away to grab the condoms on the bench and the loss of his touch made her bite her lip in frustration. She heard the rip of foil. The wait was unbearable. She angled her hips higher. When the head of his cock nudged her entrance, she let out a low moan.

Anchoring her hips with his hands, slowly at first, he thrust. With a happy groan she felt his hand resume its task, the pressure of his fingers just right, like somehow he just knew what she needed without words. Was this what being perfectly in tune with someone was all about? It had taken months to train Jake to get it right, but Solo took her to the edge so fast; a few magic strokes and it was like a tornado had taken over her body.

Polly's knuckles tightened on the bench, his body following where her rhythm led. Everything dipped and dived and her vision behind her closed eyes went red, then purple. They were fucking like wild animals next to the kitchen sink and it was the most amazing thing in the world. There was no-one to see or hear them, and *ooooohh fuck, yessss, just there* —that last perfect thrust and she was flying, right up there in the stratosphere of super orgasms. The kind that blew your head right off your body and sent your pussy into a dance of cosmic joy.

With her internal muscles bunching around him, sucking him deep, that did it.

"You're going to make me come so hard." His gritty, harsh words set her on fire, made her wring every last drop of pleasure out of him, until finally Solo's sweat-sheened body collapsed onto her.

Polly couldn't move, limp as a rag, Solo's belly against her butt cheeks, his chest heavy on her back, his lips feathering kisses on the back of her neck.

"Mmm, you smell delicious," he murmured in her ear before he pulled out reluctantly and disposed of the condom.

Some time later, now fully undressed, they'd managed to make it to her bed and lay facing each other, their joined hands sandwiched between them just like they'd been on the dance floor swaying to Chris Isaac; only now, of course, they were horizontal, not vertical.

It was all she could do to not let stupid, crazy, dumb words spill out of her mouth.

Words that had one wicked four-letter word squeezed in the middle. A word that hadn't been in her vocabulary since she was sixteen and naïve enough to believe it actually meant something

She bit down on it like a shark swallowing a school of unruly little fish.

And then he kissed her nose.

CHAPTER 22

*S*olo lay back and grinned at the ceiling.

She hadn't tried to fend him off. Instead, she giggled and snuggled into him, her curls squashed under his chin and her cheek nestled on his chest.

Her toes curled against his calves, like a kitten making pillows with its claws.

"My toes are tingling," she said.

"Is that good?"

"I guess it shows there's been a fair bit of blood circulating." A glance up, a peek of green before long lashes swooped down.

He shifted onto his back and brought her with him. Now her head rested against his shoulder, her fingers stroking circles between his pecs.

Solo opened his mouth to speak, shut it, opened it again; damn it, she might as well know.

"I'm finding this, whole thing—you know, us—pretty toe-tingling all round, to be honest."

"Which means?"

"Which means I like you. A lot."

"Oh."

Long silence. Solo racked his brain. Then he realised she was feathering kisses down his neck. "I quite like you too." Barely audible.

He guessed he shouldn't push his luck, but he did anyway. "Meaning?"

"Meaning, I like you. I think you're hot."

"That makes me feel objectified."

"And you're a really nice, kind person."

"Which sounds like any moment I'm going to be friend-zoned."

"Jeesh, there's no pleasing you." She giggled and slapped his chest. "Okay, for the record I'm enjoying this; really enjoying it. And I guess, yeah, I could keep it going for a while longer."

"What's a while longer in Polly Fletcher terms?"

"Until you head back to Sydney."

"Wow, thanks! Another couple of months."

"That's long-term in my books."

His chest tightened. He tried to keep his tone light. "So, you don't see any further than that. For us?"

He felt her shoulder against him bunch in a shrug. "I don't know. I try not to think too far ahead."

"Why?"

"What's the point? It never turns out like you imagine anyway."

"So after Danny there was no-one who floated your boat?"

"Not really. How about after Emma?"

"That didn't end so very long ago, there's only been you since."

He sensed her grimace. "Urgh, I'm getting rebound vibes here. You said it was mutual, but in my experience it's never mutual. How did it really end?"

He stiffened. And she felt it. She glanced up. "You don't actually have to answer that. I just can't help being a nosy cow."

"No, it's fine. She met someone else. But I guess we were already growing apart, so…"

It was true, they'd drifted into habit. A nice, warm habit, but after these few weeks with Polly, he realised he and Emma had lost that special something, long before Drew. He was the devoted type; the kind of guy who would have stuck by Emma without questioning it. So why couldn't he tell Polly the truth?

She said, "But you wouldn't have left first, right?"

Holy cow, her intuition was unnerving. He wasn't going to tell her about Emma and Drew. Sure, it was pathetic ego stuff; not wanting to be seen as the loser who'd lost his girl to his best mate. Wanting to maintain his stud-muffin status in her eyes. And why the hell not? It was, as Polly had pointed out, only going to last for a month or two.

"No, I probably wouldn't have left first." He kissed her forehead. "But then I would never have met you."

She didn't answer, then changed the subject. "Tell me your career plans. You mentioned neuropsychiatry the other day. That sounds exciting."

She was playing him, typical social worker, getting him to talk about himself.

"I can specialise in neuropsychiatry in Sydney. I'd like to get more involved in research. There is a position I've applied for. I'm waiting to hear whether I've got an interview."

"Great!" She said it like it was the best news she'd heard all day.

Solo's heart did another dive. This was crazy. They weren't even an item. Christ, how were you supposed to do this? After ten years with Emma, he'd lost his knack of navigating new relationships. And was that what this even was?

Not according to Polly.

He tried to sound casual when he asked, "How about you? Where do you want your career to head next?"

"Oh, I don't know. I've been asked to apply for management, but that means less clinical work and I love seeing clients. I guess I might go travelling... who knows... I could go rural, but... Oh, this is boring..."

"No, it's not. I'm interested."

She pulled away, lay on her back. "I'm not used to talking about myself."

He kept his arm around her shoulder. She wasn't escaping that easily. "I've noticed your tendency to focus on other people's happiness before your own."

"Bullshit. I am totally hedonistic and utterly self-obsessed."

"I don't mean the superficial stuff. Like losing a centimetre or two off your thighs."

"Try ten."

"Jesus, see what I mean? I mean the stuff inside. The stuff of dreams."

"Wow! Dr J, the romantic. You should have been a poet."

He laughed, some little seed of masochism pushing for more. "Go on, tell me a couple of your dreams."

"Oh god. All right. Travel the world, marry off my friends—it makes them happy, and I'm kind of good at it."

"Marry off your friends!" He scoffed. The question on his lips felt like walking into a field of unexploded mines. "Don't you want to get married eventually?"

"Marriage ruins your sex life. Why would I want that? Especially after the orgasm you just delivered, Dr J." She curled into him again, put a hand up to his cheek and brushed her lips to his. "Let's stop talking, shall we..."

Her tongue circled his lips and his body shuddered an immediate response. He hustled his disappointment into some dark recess of his brain, smoothed a hand over her hips, between her thighs and heard her little gasp.

"Let's just forget the deep and meaningfuls." She jumped on top of him, grinning broadly and scissored his hips with her thighs. Solo's brain turned to mush as her hands pinned him down and her head moved lower. "Right now, I've got a very different kind of deep in mind." Polly giggled.

Solo groaned. Words got them into trouble.

But this... ah, this... Oh, *fuck,*

His eyes rolled back in his head.

With sex they were on the same page.

Every. Single. Time.

"APPLE STRUDEL." Judith poked her head round the door of Polly's office.

"The one and only?" Polly looked up from the computer screen.

"Nothing less than the gold-medal winner."

It was true, Leon's wife had taken the gold medal in a dessert competition for her apple strudel. It was something to do with the puff pastry offset against plump apples and raisins probably soaked in something very alcoholic, and then that thick crust of lemon zing icing on top.

It came onto Echidna Ward less often now that Maria had had a baby, but when it did, everyone congregated.

Polly felt a little zip of pleasure knowing she'd see Solo at morning tea. It wasn't like they weren't spending time together—every other night since last Wednesday, to be precise. (They'd both agreed they needed a night off in between to catch up on sleep). She felt juicy and, what had Judith once called her? Oh yes, fecund, which made her think of babies, and thinking of babies other than the one in Kate's beautifully expanding belly was alarming.

And yet... and yet, being with Solo was making her feel broody as all hell. Which made her think of a mother hen. Admittedly a very sexy mother hen, but that old nesting thing really did seem to have a biological pull.

Of course, she was resisting it.

But she couldn't resist strudel.

Sure enough, Solo was sitting in the staff room talking to Ben, both of them cramming strudel into their mouths. Solo had this way of sprawling when he wasn't in meetings that drew her attention to those long, lean legs in his suit pants, the secret knowledge of what he kept tucked in there especially for her making her feel even more fecund.

Oh, dear. This wasn't getting any easier, but she wasn't going to think further than the weekend. Talking of which... she cast a glance at Judith, who was looking pretty and relaxed and chatting to another nurse. There was going to be some action between Jude and Carts, mark her words.

Judith had sidled up to her the other day after Dr Death's ward round. "Can I ask you something, Poll? Seeing you're an expert on this stuff."

"What stuff?"

"You know, the dating stuff."

Polly had gathered up her files and watched Solo's broad shoulders in his suit jacket (god, he was just as gorgeous in a suit as a bike jacket, wasn't he?) disappear with Dr Death on patient rounds.

"I guess I'm good at the early stages."

Judith's blue eyes lit up. "That's exactly what I need right now."

"Okay, fire away."

"Sooo, if you've kind of been seeing someone at, like, yoga, and having a drink after, and the vibe is good and then they invite you to something—"

Polly raised an eyebrow. "Wouldn't be a birthday party, would it?"

"Yeah, obviously, durhhh, I'm not trying to hide who it is. You *are* going, aren't you?"

"I have been invited, so yes, probably." Like with bells and whistles on, though how she'd keep her and Solo quiet after this, god only knew.

"So help me here, how do you take it to the next level? Like, imply you're interested?"

"Don't you think he knows?"

"We're both so shy. I think he's interested in me, but he's so polite and gentlemanly. But oh, Polly, he has the nicest eyes and"—Judith rolled her own now—"his smile. That little snaggly tooth of his, it actually adds to his attractiveness."

Polly smiled to herself. Wasn't love the sweetest thing? Carts wasn't exactly male model material but he had a lovely smile, that was true. How superficial of her to think that way. "Maybe you just need to ask him to dance."

"Me ask him!"

"Jude, don't go all 1950s on me. For god's sake, woman, yeah. It's always been up to the woman, she's the decider, but nowadays there's no need for the silly games to bolster the guy's ego and pretend he's the one making the decision."

"Really, *we* decide?" Judith straightened her shoulders and almost preened. "Never thought of it like that." Her face fell. "Made a bum decision with Mark then, didn't I?"

"Maybe it was the right decision for back then."

Judith's mouth twisted into a wry smile. "Maybe. We were seventeen, he helped me with maths and I wrote his English essays for him."

"Mutually beneficial, then."

"Just shouldn't have stayed twelve years."

"How are things going between you guys now he's moved out?"

"We're talking. He's happy as a pig in poo in his new apartment; all his computer screens set up for gaming for hours on end. And honestly, Poll, I don't know why I hung around all those years, when the intimacy left and the sex fizzled, cooking and cleaning and being there for him."

"Hmmm," said Polly. She reminded herself that after twelve years, she and Solo would quite probably add up to something similar. Both slouched on the sofa after a long day at work with a TV meal and not much to say to each other. And a bed that didn't get to see tangled sheets and waking each other up in the night multiple times because they simply couldn't get enough of each other.

And then Solo glanced up with a piece of strudel halfway to his lips and that wicked gleam in his eyes, and her resolve immediately went AWOL. He winked at her and she felt heat creeping up her neck.

She flicked her gaze away and dived on the strudel.

As she cleaned up her plate not long after and went to leave for ward meetings, Solo was behind her. He held the door so she could pass through, his body brushing against her, and the scent of him, the warmth of his body, was electric.

She couldn't help smiling up at him as they walked. Being around him made her happy, it was that simple. And that complicated.

"God, that strudel's good!" he said, smacking his lips.

"I know, divine." She rolled her eyes. They ground to a halt outside the doctor's office.

Solo grimaced. "I've got to go and write three discharge summaries. Are you around later?"

"For a professional chat?" She glanced up at him flirtatiously.

"Exactly." He was standing too close as Judith and Leon walked past and Polly stepped back, feeling them both casting meaningful glances at them. Were they being that obvious?

Solo didn't seem to notice. Or care. "Want to join me for omelette?"

She hid her delighted smirk. Omelette was now code for staying over. Last night her bed had felt big and empty and she'd woken up practically humping her pillow, which was kind of teenage crass.

She gave a little nod. "I could do."

"Great." He grinned, that flash of white teeth against his dark stubble so enticing, the way his eyes crinkled at the corners, those brackets in his cheek. It took so much effort to resist. It occurred to her that it would be so much nicer not to have to try.

Then his phone trilled. He dragged it out of his pocket, glanced at it, then flicked it off and pocketed it, but something about the tightening of his lips made her ask, "Was that Drew?"

He shook his head. "No, no-one important."

But when he looked at her she knew he was hiding something. A knot tightened in her stomach.

She shrugged it off. What did it matter if there was another woman out there somewhere? So what? He'd be going back to Sydney soon.

Bye bye, Solo.

She ground back on her heels and slung her bag over her shoulder, tossed her head. Was tempted to say she was staying in to wash her hair tonight. But she couldn't—just couldn't.

She managed to keep her smile casual. "Text me later, and I'll decide if I'm free."

He looked at her, as if suddenly perplexed by the cool change, then he shook his head and grinned. "You sure like to keep a guy guessing."

She winked, gave his arm a playful punch. "How it should be." Then she sashayed off, loving the fact he was watching her arse for sure.

ONCE HE'D CLOSED the door of the doctor's office, Solo drew out his phone and looked at Emma's message.

I'll be arriving Saturday evening. Can we catch up Sunday? Drew is keen to FaceTime when we're together. He really wants to talk to you.

He frowned. Saturday was Carts' party, so he was glad she hadn't suggested that, but if Polly and he spent the night together, what then?

Why couldn't he just come clean about Emma? Because he knew it would be an awkward conversation. Any wrong move and Polly might back off. And now, to make life more complicated, it seemed Drew wanted to communicate with him via Emma. Was that Drew's way of holding out an olive branch? There had been no abusive messages for two weeks now. Maybe that was a sign that Drew's mental health was improving?

Gah, he needed to tell Polly and be done with it. What was he worried about?

It wasn't anything to do with his feelings for Emma. He knew he was over her. But the precariousness of the whole thing with Polly felt like a pack of cards. Add one more complication and the whole thing might collapse.

Besides, he reasoned, Emma being a reed-thin model wouldn't be something Polly would exactly be cool with. Behind that façade Polly was deeply insecure. He loved that about her, the complete contradictions of her personality. But the last thing he needed was her retreating because of some great big hang-up about Emma's completely different brand of beauty. The fact that you could count Emma's vertebrae even through her clothes wasn't something any woman needed to envy in his book. And quite frankly, now he'd experienced Polly's delicious curves, there was no going back.

Sometimes with Polly it was like dealing with a wild animal; as though he'd got her almost trusting him, and then, *poof*, one wrong move, and all the ground he'd gained was at risk of being lost.

He rubbed his forehead. He'd tell Polly Saturday after the party that he was catching up with Emma. He needed the next few days to build on their growing intimacy. To coax that shy, wild creature out into the light. To let her feel what it was like when a guy really fell in love with her.

He stared at the pile of papers on his desk. Yep, he was in deep. He'd fallen in love with Polly Fletcher. Every damn glorious, infuriating inch of her.

Quickly he texted Emma back.

Cool.

I'll pick you up at your hotel.
Send me the address.
Any time after 10 a.m. is fine.

He startled as Pritchard put his head round the door. "I need you to go to ED, Jakoby. There's a new admission, a young man with psychosis; they're treating it like it's drug-induced, but it sounds more complex to me. They need some psychiatry input."

Solo sighed. Discharge summaries would have to wait again. But he'd bloody well work through his lunch break, because nothing was going to ruin his evening with Polly.

CHAPTER 23

*C*arts was frothing.

That was really the only word to describe his behaviour. He'd been bounding around with the vacuum cleaner all morning, and now he was running in and out with boxes of food and drink. Solo went out to the car to help him.

"How many did you say you were inviting?"

"About thirty. Mostly work colleagues, a few from university, Dan, Poll... my best mate Aaron's still in the UK, which is a pity, cos you'd get on... And um, a few women and of course, urmmm—Judith."

Solo's lips twitched and he hefted out a carton of beer. "Good move."

Carts gave him a furtive glance. "I'm going to ask her out tonight. I reckon I stand a better chance on my birthday."

"Why?"

"Pity date. Turning thirty and all, she might feel sorry for me..."

"Oh, Christ, mate, that means I'm a lost cause at thirty-two."

Solo plonked the beers down on the island bench next to boxes of dips and cheeses and crackers.

Carts frowned at the food on the benchtop. "Do you think this'll be enough?"

"More than enough.""

"Great. Can I run my outfit past you?"

"Sure, mate, of course." Solo grinned at Carts' eager face. Every day he was getting fonder of Carts. The guy was six-foot-six of kindness, rather awkwardly put together. And according to Polly, he had the worst luck in love. Solo hoped he wouldn't be rebuffed on his birthday. But then, the way Judith acted around Carts, like she'd been lit up from the inside, Solo reckoned the odds were in Carts' favour.

"I've got two different shirts and I don't know which one." Carts' eyes were awash with excitement. He looked like a kid trying to decide which treat in the toyshop he should buy. Somehow Solo guessed it would have to be one of those science kits that grew crystals, not the Action Man with a machine gun.

Why couldn't more women see the merit in that?

He nodded. "Sure, I'll just put the beer away. Call me when you're ready."

After Carts disappeared, Solo squeezed beer and wine bottles into the already tightly packed fridge. Carefully stacked the dips and put the cheese and meats in the cold drawer.

"Duh-duh, what d'you think?"

Solo straightened and turned to see Carts doing a catwalk slink around the kitchen table, one hand slung casually onto his hip, his long chin coyly dropped to his chest, eyelashes batting.

Solo burst out laughing.

Carts followed suit. "You mean you don't like my seductive look?"

"Maybe tone it down slightly. The shirt's great, though."

It was a really nice shirt, Solo thought with admiration. Subtle white and grey shapes that resembled feathers on a black background, and a slim fit that was in at the moment. With his pencil-thin jeans and shiny black shoes he did actually look pretty sharp. Tall, but sharp.

"Okay, that's close to a ten in my books. Show me the other one."

Carts scooted out the door and Solo laid copious bags of chips and snacks out in a neat line on the bench. He hoped Carts had thought about buying some bowls to put them in.

Carts' second number was also pretty snazzy. A bit on the wild side for Carts, which made Solo mildly suspicious. "Did someone help you choose?"

Carts blushed. "Polly. I texted her some shots."

Solo turned away quickly. Something like envy stabbed his gut.

Be realistic, mate, these guys go back to uni. But it still needled him.

"Poll's got great taste," Carts said.

Solo focused on the psychedelic purple and pink patterns in the shirt. "This one's a bit busy. I'd go for the first one. More sophisticated."

"But which would impress you more? You know, if you were a woman?"

Solo felt his lips hitch. "I don't know, mate. Women are a complete mystery to me."

Carts sighed. "Okay I'll go for the first one. Or maybe I'll text Polly and ask her. What do you reckon?"

"Yeah," said Solo, slamming the last packet of chips onto the bench. "Don't trust my opinion. Ask Polly."

POLLY MET Judith at the end of Carts' street at 8.30 p.m. sharp.

Judith was wearing a flowing cornflower-blue dress dotted with little yellow flowers. She'd clearly been to the hairdresser. Her long hair hung in perfectly styled waves, bronzer highlighted her cheekbones and her lips were a perky candy pink.

"Wow, you look a million dollars," Polly enthused.

"Thanks." Judith gave her a quick hug. "I am soooo nervous."

Polly stepped back. "You're crushing badly, aren't you?"

Judith bit her lip and gave a little nod. "Is it that obvious?"

"Only to me. You know my antennae for these things."

They started walking.

"Talking of antennae, my underdeveloped one has been sensing something," Judith said. "Are you and Solo dating?"

Polly laughed too loudly. "God no."

Judith glanced at her sideways and shifted a wave of blonde away from her face.

The blotchiness marched its way up from her cleavage. "We're just having a bit of fun, that's all."

Judith gave a little nudge with her elbow. "Are you sure it's only fun?"

"Why would it be anything else?"

"I've seen the way he looks at you." Polly said nothing, the heat intensifying into her neck, sneaking over her chin. "And the way you look back," Judith finished.

Polly let out a snort.

"No, I have, Poll, you go all misty eyed. I've seen it across ward round, in the tearoom, when you're—"

Her cheeks must now resemble a Californian sunset. "Okay, okay. Enough, I don't do serious, you know that."

"Oh, shame," Jude sighed. "Maybe one day you'll realise falling in love is worth it."

Polly chuckled. "I can't believe you, of all people, are saying that right now."

"I'm not a cynic like you."

Polly blinked. "I'm not a cynic." Doubt lodged in the back of her throat. "Am I?"

"Not for other people. Only for yourself," Judith said, then added with a quick glance, "You do deserve love you know, Poll."

Polly stared at her sparkly toes in her Louboutin look-alikes. And how come her Gigi Young dress suddenly felt too tight around her ribs? (Too many omelettes for breakfast and too much strudel, clearly.) She'd let herself relax into her curves since Solo seemed to worship them so thoroughly.

Worship? Seriously, she didn't use words like that in relation to men. And why the sudden warm glow spreading out from her middle? Grrrr!

As they walked up the steps to Carts' door they could hear the music blaring. The party was already in full swing. A thousand tiny bubbles were ready to explode in Polly's stomach at the thought of seeing Solo, which was dumb because she'd seen him at work today, slept spooned against him just two nights ago.

She was at risk of losing her sanity.

She tucked her arm tightly in Judith's and squeezed. "Don't worry about me, I was born without the love chromosome. But here's to your dreams coming true, eh?"

Jude squeezed back and then Carts threw open the door and there was no room left in Judith's world for anything but the man standing in front of her.

Cute. *Not.*

In the kitchen, Polly's gaze found Solo like a homing pigeon. He was pouring drinks for Dan and another guy she recognised from the odd pub session, and as if he'd sensed her presence, his head came up and he shot her a dazzling smile.

Her vagina did a happy dance. Only it wasn't just her vagina, was it? It was all of her.

She wended her way over as casually as she could. "Hi Dan. Hi—um." She racked her brains.

"Chris," the guy said with a smile.

"Sure, Chris." She pressed her hand to her cheek. "Remind me, you work with Carts, don't you?"

"Yeah, in revenue management. We've met a few times at the pub." His eyes behind his glasses shot to her cleavage and then back, and the poor guy looked like he'd just stepped on a wasp's nest.

Polly felt sorry for him. It was so hard for guys these days, you couldn't be seen to be ogling. She gave him a flirtatious smile and he looked relieved, then flattered, but really, truthfully, she was just trying to make Solo a little bit envious.

And she didn't even know why. Because Solo had been behaving impeccably, made all the right moves in and out of bed, whispered things in her ear that would make any normal woman melt like hot caramel. She cast a glance to see him watching her intently, a tiny frown pleating his brow, and her heart sped up.

Another moment and Polly excused herself and strolled over.

She picked up an empty champagne glass and held it out to him. "Are you the waiter tonight, Dr J?"

He grinned, and she sensed him relax. Had her little flirtation worried him? The idea made her tummy do the bubble bath number again.

"Seems I have been given that role, yes," Solo agreed.

"Then I'll have a champers, thanks."

He inclined his head, a salacious little smile playing around his lips as he murmured, "Madam's wish is my command."

As he handed her glass to her, she moved closer and whispered, "I'm not wearing any panties."

She loved his sudden intake of breath. "I might have to punish you for that later."

"Bring it on, Daddy."

They both laughed, and she brushed against him and he pulled her close for the briefest second. The hard planes of his body, the strength of his arms made her feel—what? Kind of cherished. Special. She forced herself to focus on the pulse between her legs. This sexual thing between them was insane. And totally within her comfort zone.

Love? Okay, so her mind had toyed with the idea at Dad's party. But a cat could toy with a mouse. Didn't mean it loved it.

Phhtt. Honestly, Judith should keep her opinions to herself.

As she shimmied out of Solo's embrace with a quick, "There's a line waiting to be served," Polly saw Carts talking earnestly to Judith in a corner of the room, so engrossed he wasn't even greeting his other guests. Now, that was just plain rude.

Polly sighed, spotted another friend she hadn't been in contact with for a few months, and went over to say hi. She needed to ration herself where Solo was concerned. Otherwise it would all burn out before he even returned to Sydney.

But it was only ten minutes before he joined her. Someone had turned the music up.

"Will you dance with me?" His head bumped close to hers.

"Okay."

It was a boppy number and they skirted around each other. Polly was good at dancing, clubs had been her happy hunting ground for years. Solo, she noticed, had the same fluid athletic moves when he danced as he did when he walked or rode his bike, or made love...

Polly shimmied harder to push away that four-letter word.

At least there wasn't any Chris Isaac playing. It was all nineties bop, but then Angus and Julia Stone's "Big Jet Plane" came on and Solo moved in and put his arms around her. His forehead touched hers. The silver of his eyes, those dark lashes, seemed to cast a spell on her. Losing all capacity for self-control, her hands slid around his waist. She almost swooned with the deliciousness of their bodies swaying together. Like this was where she belonged.

In her periphery she caught sight of Judith and Carts linked together.

"Don't stare, but I think those two are getting it on," she whispered.

Solo laughed low in her ear. "Didn't see that one coming." His voice was laden with sarcasm.

"I guess the energy's been pretty intense."

"A bit like you and me."

Polly stiffened. "No, we're different."

"In what way?"

"We're—" She hesitated, what were they? They weren't exactly a fling, there was too much emotion for that... friends? Fuck buddies? It felt like someone had glued the words to the back of her tongue.

"We're—"

For some stupid reason she lifted her head off his shoulder and looked at him. One eyebrow shot up, in synch with the deep groove in his cheek. They stayed like that, Polly mesmerised, lost in the softness of that silver gaze. He was going to kiss her and she wanted him to; so, so much. The words she'd been trying to say disintegrated. Her eyes watered as other words she couldn't possibly say kept flashing in front of her eyes like Broadway lights.

Just then something caught Solo's attention, his eyes shifting past her. She felt his whole body stiffen. Polly's head swivelled to follow his gaze.

The most beautiful woman she had ever seen was hovering in the doorway, her eyes scanning the room.

Her dark hair hung straight and heavy to her waist; she was tall, but perfectly proportioned, almost waif-like; two huge blue eyes peered out of the perfect structure of her face. A silky chiffon dress hung beautifully on her bone-china frame. Everything about her was exquisite.

What wasn't exquisite was the way Solo was frozen like an ice statue, eyes wide and unblinking.

By now Carts had dashed over to the woman and was pointing towards them. Polly stumbled back as the girl's eyes skimmed past her and landed on Solo, sudden relief spreading across her face.

Polly stared at Solo. He'd gone ashen.

It felt like a car smash was happening behind her ribs.

"You know her?" The words punctured out of her mouth.

He gave her a fleeting look, cloudy, indecipherable, but somewhere in there she was sure she saw regret. And shame.

And now she knew what the car smash was all about. He'd taken her for a ride. Just like fucking Danny O'Dougherty.

Solo nodded. "Yes," he said, and she saw how he swallowed as if his mouth was dry; cheeks that a moment ago were white flushed a deep, dull red. "It's Emma."

And then he strode across the room towards the vision of loveliness.

CHAPTER 24

*S*hit, shit, shit.

What the hell was he supposed to do now? Solo pitched towards Emma like someone trying to avert a tsunami with a bucket and spade.

From across the room, Polly's eyes lasered into his spine as he managed, "Em, hi, this is a surprise!"

Next to Emma, Carts bounced on his heels, looking apologetic. "Sorry, mate, I completely forgot to tell you, with all the party excitement."

Solo could only stare at him, perplexed.

"I rang," Emma explained, placing a hand on Solo's arm. It was all he could do not to jerk away from her touch. "Carts picked up and said you were in the shower, and"—she gave a nervous laugh—"invited me to come to his party tonight. He said he'd tell you. I didn't do the wrong thing, did I?"

He smiled and shook his head, though his features felt like they'd crumple right off his face. Emma's eyes travelled past him and somehow — Christ, the thought made him want to punch himself repeatedly in the jaw—he needed to introduce Emma to Polly, explain this debacle to Polly. And still retain his balls.

"No, no, look, I'll introduce you to some people. Drink?"

"That would be nice," Emma said, following him.

In the kitchen, Polly was leaning against the sink with her champagne glass hovering around her nose. He went over and muttered, "I'm sorry, I didn't know she was coming."

"Of course you didn't." Her eyes were like iceberg chips over the rim of her glass. When she looked past him, her smile took on angelic proportions. "Hi, you must be Emma. I'm Polly, I work with Solo at the hospital. So lovely to meet you; Solo's told me such wonderful things about you."

"He has?" Emma's brows rose as she cast a quick glance at Solo.

Polly shrugged a shoulder. "Just in chatting, you know how it is. Anyway, I'll let you two catch up, sooo lovely to meet you, Emma."

Solo tried to will Polly to look at him. His telepathy attempts bombed. She sashayed past, her movements fluid, shoulders pinned back, but he wasn't fooled for a second. There were poison arrows darting at him from every cell of her body.

Fuck! This was the price you paid for hiding the truth.

He stifled a groan as he handed Emma her drink and glanced quickly past her to see Polly deep in conversation with the Chris guy, whose face looked strained just from the effort not to gawk at her breasts.

A spasm of violent rage tore into his gut. He'd happily take the guy by the scruff of his shirt collar and throw him out, but he'd asked for everything he got. And if Polly chose to leave with this guy, it would serve him right.

The rage was directed at himself, not the poor man who was being razzle-dazzled by Polly's charm. Heart in his stomach, Solo turned back to Emma and forced a grin. "It's great to see you, Em," he lied.

SHE DIDN'T MEAN to be rude to the Uber driver, but thirty minutes after her major humiliation Polly couldn't help snapping out her address to the poor guy like a volley of ammunition.

She threw her bag on the seat and ripped off her stupid fake designer shoes because her toes had gone completely numb. That's what you got for investing in fakes.

And hate it though she did, yeah, absolutely hated it, she was having to face the fact that she was hurt.

No. Scrub that. Fucking devastated.

All the memories of being sixteen and staring at Danny's naked arse as it gyrated on top of some faceless girl came flooding back, but the one thing she remembered with clarity was how long and slim the legs were that were wrapped around his butt.

And so, okay, Solo hadn't got that far—yet —but you bet later tonight he would be shagging that stunning twig.

She ground her back teeth together until she was sure they'd turned to powder and tried to stop the violent stabbing at the back of her eyes; the huge lump that was strangling her ability to take in oxygen.

She gulped hard, fixed her gaze on the passing scenery.

The buildings blurred into a moving haze.

Oh, Christ, she'd promised, *promised* herself she would never, ever cry over a guy again.

She stared down the big blob of a tear that was threatening to dangle off her eyelash. If she let this one out there would be a flood and the poor Uber guy would be sloshing water out of the back of his car for hours.

Polly blinked hard. Squeezed the monster tear back into her eye somehow and forced air into her lungs.

After flirting madly with Chris until he was almost panting, she'd not been able to stick around any longer. Solo had been trying to catch her eye, which she avoided, but after holing herself up in the toilet for ten minutes, he was waiting for her when she exited. She'd tried to push past him but he followed her, his face taut.

"Polly, can we talk about this?"

"Nope."

"I was going to tell you. Emma wasn't due to arrive until tomorrow."

"Oh, fantastic, kiss me goodbye in the morning, shove me out the door and offer Emma the next spot."

"Christ." Solo was tunnelling into his hair with agitated fingers. A girl squeezed past with a loud, "Excuse me, but I'm busting." They shifted.

Polly searched for her jacket on the rack.

"You're going?" he asked.

"Yes."

"Please stay."

"Give me one good reason."

"Because I want you to."

She grabbed her jacket and spat out, "No, what you want is a cat-fight in the middle of Carts' party. Typical fucking man. I must say, you had me sucked in that you were over her." She swung the jacket around her shoulders, dug her fingers in her bag and felt like belting him with it. "How could you be? She's just about the most stunning woman I've ever seen."

"Looks aren't everything."

"What that meant to mean? That I'm uglier than a witch, but good in the sack?"

"No!"

"No, Fuck *you*, Solo." She couldn't help it; she gave him a push in the centre of his chest with her handbag.

Solo's jaw set and his eyes sparked. He stood his ground. "You know your problem?"

She tossed her head. "I'm sure you're planning on enlightening me, so go right ahead."

"You always think you're right. The world according to Polly Fletcher. Black and white. No room for grey."

She gritted her teeth and hissed, "I've got eyes. Funny thing, but I've learned to trust them. What's more, they see in glorious technicolour."

Solo dared to smirk. "Eyewitness accounts are notoriously unreliable."

"Fuck off." Her fingers itched to shove that bag into his chest again and back him down the whole length of the hallway.

He braced his chest, as if expecting as much. "You don't know the full story."

"I think I do. It's called a truckload of bullshit"

"So you won't stick around to find out if you're wrong."

"Cor-rect."

His jaw ticked, his eyes silver slits. "Coward."

Something ripped in her chest. No-one called her a coward. "No, I'm a fucking survivor. Have a nice night with your *girlfriend*." She turned as she yanked at the door and glared at him. "On second thoughts, have a nice life together."

With that she was out the door and down the path, the sound of the Backstreet Boys ringing in her ears, wishing he'd follow her just so she could give him another very satisfying earful. But when she'd walked as fast as she could to the end of the road and taken out her phone to call an Uber and he hadn't followed her, she'd deflated like a pricked balloon.

And now here she was, dying inside at the memory.

And she couldn't breathe because there was a big metal band around her chest.

And that stupid tear was back, teetering like a trapeze artist on the end of her eyelashes.

When she got home she dropped her gear on the bench and headed for the kitchen. She grabbed a bottle of wine out of the fridge and rummaged around for the corkscrew. She was digging it relentlessly into the cork when she stopped. Froze, more like. The bottle sandwiched between her thighs and this desperate feeling rising up her throat.

The word *coward* banged around her skull like a deranged monkey.

Fuck, no!

She was behaving just like Dad. Emotional pain, running to the bottle, drowning out her feelings with alcohol. Sure, she loved a drink, maybe a bit too much sometimes, but she was a social drinker, she knew the dangers of drinking alone. But this, this was different. She wanted to obliterate the slimy black monster in her chest. The one with hideous green eyes.

Fingers shaking, she placed the bottle on the table. The opener back in the drawer.

Then she marched into her room and searched in the bottom of the wardrobe until she found it. Her purple journal, "Polly Fletcher's Journal STRICTLY PRIVATE" written on it in childish rounded hand-writing, flowers and glitter and sticky things all over the front cover.

She plonked down on the bed, pushed her curls behind both ears, and opened it.

Flicking through to the most-thumbed pages, her heart pounded as she read the entries about Danny. The outpourings of love and yearning and hopes of a sixteen-year-old. Her dreams of being with Danny, marrying Danny, riding off into a hazy sunset with Danny. The night she'd given him her virginity. *"It was beautiful, though it hurt a bit and it was over real quick, but Danny held me close and told me he loved me after."* Hearts with arrows through them, three of them, coloured in pink. She flicked through to a page four weeks later, *"I HATE HIM, I HATE HIM"* scribbled so hard in red ink the pen had punctured the page...

"I am now the proud owner of a serpent on my inner thigh. I am woman HEAR ME ROAR."

So young, so passionate, so sure she would survive.

She shut her journal, smoothed her fingertips over the glitter and transfers. Stood up. Peeled off her dress and let it fall to the ground and looked at her body in the mirror without blinking. Her inner left thigh where the serpent's tongue curled towards the little patch of dark hair, her small waist, the full mounds of her breasts and large nipples. The way her hips spread into rounded buttocks. Yeah, they were bigger than she wanted them to be, but... She turned sideways and stared at her butt cheeks over her shoulders. She had cellulite; those ripples had been there since her late teens, no matter what diet she tried, no matter how many lemons she sucked. So what. It was always going to be this way. And yes, her legs were too short for ideal beauty, her boobs way too big.

But she was *her.*

Polly.

And she didn't need anyone to make her feel beautiful. She didn't need to compare herself to anyone, however tall, and stick-thin friggin' beautiful they were. Even if she'd clearly just been a rebound fling for someone who she'd made the mistake of letting wangle his way under her skin and into her bed, and make her omelettes like a happy married couple...

Fuckity fuck.

Just as she was beginning to feel better, here came the memories of every glorious second with Solo, like a thousand needles in her brain, digging away at all that soft stuff that she'd thought she'd surgically removed years ago.

She caught her expression in the mirror, the pit of sorrow in the depths of her eyes, the sense of bewilderment and hurt.

Nope. Not happening. She'd have to bring in the big guns.

She looked around but her phone must still be in the kitchen. Barefoot and naked, she nipped down the corridor and found her phone on the kitchen table.

No messages. Really, what was she thinking? Solo would be happily entwined with the supermodel by now. His lovely, strong, muscled, lean legs would be perfect with... NO!

Her lips tightened into a hard line as she brought up the number on automatic dial and put the phone to her ear.

"Munchkin," she said, trying to control the crack in her voice when Alice answered.

"Hey, Poll, lovely to—Oh—what's wrong?"

Polly's shoulders slumped. The stuffing had been ripped out of her and she so needed someone to help her put it back, then sew her carefully back together again. And the only person who could do that right now was Alice.

"Munchkin," her voice wavered, almost cracked, but she firmed it up. "I need you to tell me I'm wonderful."

As the sun winked between the rooftops of two houses, Solo leaned on his bike handlebars and lit a cigarette. It was 6 a.m., he hadn't slept all night. And he was smoking. On a Sunday morning. As the sun rose.

Fantastic. His temples throbbed as he dragged in a slow inhalation and stared down the deserted street of neat little houses. Number 26. He could see the rose bushes poking out over the top of the picket fence from here. And any minute now he was going to walk into what looked like a sweet little English country cottage and probably have his balls broken.

But he had to talk to her. Had to have this out with her. At ten o'clock he was meeting Emma and he had to come clean about all of it with Polly before then.

Sighing, he ground his cigarette but out on the tarmac and took out his mints. Shoved a couple in his mouth and ground them down quickly under his teeth.

He couldn't add smoker's breath into the equation, he needed every one of his powers to persuade Polly that he... he...

That he loved her?

Would he, could he, go that far? He ached for her, longed for her when she wasn't with him, felt better, brighter, more alive, laughed more than he'd ever laughed before.

It was nothing like he'd once felt for Emma. The kind of reverent worship you had for a beautiful work of art you had no idea how you'd come by.

No, his feelings for Polly tore him apart, shredded him. And had the potential to make him whole.

He pushed off from his bike and sauntered slowly down the street, pretending that he felt cool, calm and collected while his hands sweated in tight fists in his pocket and his heart pounded.

Finally reaching the fence, he made his way up the path, the steps to the veranda and knocked on the door.

No answer. The blood thundered in his ears.

He skirted round the house. Polly's window was at the side, the curtains still pulled, so he went round the back, tripped over a watering can with a loud clatter-clunk, and arrived at the back door as Polly's head thrust out.

She was a mess, he could see that. She still had the remains of last night's make-up round her eyes, so panda-like, in fact, he had to ask himself if she'd been crying. Her hair looked like a thousand birds had taken up residence. His heart lurched.

Was he responsible for her looking so… so damn miserable?

When she saw him, her brows pleated and her mouth turned down. "What the fuck?"

She pulled her dressing gown round herself and made to slam the door but he vaulted over the felled watering can and got his foot in the door before she could shut it.

"This is breaking and entering," she squealed and tried to slam it again. A little tussle ensued but Solo realised he wasn't having to use any strength whatsoever before she gave in, tossed her head, crossed her arms and stomped inside.

He followed.

She turned fiercely at the kitchen bench. "I'm warning you, I have a full set of sharp knives here." She scowled.

He shut the door gently and leaned on it. They faced each other, and he suddenly sensed the weariness flowing between them; she hadn't slept either, it was obvious.

"I've come to explain."

"I don't want an explanation." But her green eyes held a different message. They were plaintive, raw, and it hurt like hell to see, but it also gave him courage.

"Well, you're getting one."

She slumped down at the kitchen table, elbows on the surface and her hand fisted close to her mouth. She wouldn't meet his gaze.

"I should have told you Emma was coming over. She told me a while back she had a modelling assignment here."

She let out a derisive snort. "She's a model. I should have guessed

Urggh. Why hadn't he just said she was here for work? Her eyes were walls. Ice-covered walls. Her face was snowed in.

He cleared his throat. "That's not relevant to us," he said and she snorted again but didn't speak. "I was going to meet with her today, she, um—she and I are going to FaceTime Drew, for the first time since he's been hospitalised."

"Does she have to hold your hand while you do it?" Her tone was cold, jeering. He didn't blame her, he'd behaved appallingly.

He took a deep breath, preparing to open himself up to further humiliation. There was nowhere else to go. Not if he had any chance to make amends.

"Emma left me for Drew. They'd been having an affair behind my back for months before I found them pretty much in bed together."

This time her eyes flew to his. Round, horrified. He braced for the caustic, "you deserved it" response.

Her mouth fell open. "You're kidding."

He shook his head.

"And you had no idea?"

"I always knew Drew had a crush on her. I didn't know she recipro-cated. It came to a head when Drew was touted to be the next Bachelor. Emma became so moody and dark. Quite unlike her—she's a level-headed kind of girl, mostly."

He felt a spike coming from Polly, could sense her comparing her volatile nature to Miss Perfection, and wanted to say how dull it was now he'd found Polly. But it would look crass, try-hard, so he kept quiet.

"We weren't seeing much of each other. She was busy with work, so was I, and then one night I went round to Drew's and he wouldn't let me in. Emma was in there with him. It all fell into place after that."

"Why would your best friend do that to you? I would never—how could she—?" Her eyes were sparking with anger and he realised she wasn't ridiculing him, she *cared* that he'd been hurt. Hope flew around his chest like some manic little bird.

Until she said, dully, "So no wonder you're not over her."

Fuck. This was not the direction he'd planned. He moved into the room. She wound her arms tightly around her waist.

"You've got this all wrong. I'm over her," he said.

"Yeah, like hell. You couldn't even mention your ex was coming to the woman you're..." She stopped and he felt his brows lift as their eyes met.

"What are we, Polly?"

She looked at him helplessly, then her eyes skittered away. She wasn't going to get out of it that easily. Not this time.

"Exactly what are we to one another?"

She shrugged, stared at the collar of his shirt.

He gave a bark of a laugh. "There we have it. That's the crux of the problem, isn't it? I don't know where I stand with you."

It was her turn to shoot out a harsh laugh. "So you just hedged your bets by having Emma waiting in the wings."

"No! Jesus Christ. No." He rafted both hands through his hair in sheer frustration. "God, are you being this difficult on purpose?" She didn't answer. "Okay." His palms came down on the table and she jumped. "Sorry," he said. "I just don't know where to go next. You block every attempt I make to talk to you about us. Every time I try and say what I feel, you just laugh it off... push me away."

"I do not."

"You do."

She glared at him now. "Okay, I'll tell you what we *were*. We *were* friends. And fuck buddies, if you want to add another minor detail. But that doesn't give you the right to hide things—"

"From where I stand, it does," he almost snarled back. "If you think your *fuck buddy* won't think of you as this cool guy anymore, that they will view you as a loser who couldn't hold on to his girlfriend, who didn't even see it coming... if you are worried about all that while trying so hard to impress the woman you're crazy about..."

He had the grim satisfaction of seeing her jaw go slack.

She wrapped her dressing gown tighter around herself. "W-what?"

"You heard me."

"You don't mean that."

He stood and walked deliberately towards her. "You better believe it. Now I've shown you mine, perhaps you could show me yours? Tell me where I stand with you, Polly?"

She stared down at her feet. The silence stretched on for what seemed like forever. Then she said, "Last night I realised you'd got to me." She spread her hands wide in a helpless gesture. "Okay. I'll admit it. I let myself feel too much for you."

"How can you feel *too much?*"

"*I* can." Her arms swung back and hugged around her waist again. He had to work hard not to reach for her. She looked so lost, bleak. "And you know what I finally worked out? The only way I can be happy is to be on my own. The only way I can control this is to not let my emotions get involved. Just. Not. Feel that stuff for someone."

"*Seriously?* You counsel people for a living—you work with feelings every day. How can you believe you can just *not* feel?"

Her smile was brittle. "I've done it brilliantly for years. I live off everyone else's feels vicariously. I—I can't take what it does to me. Inside. Feeling like my happiness depends on someone else. It messes me up big-time."

"So, what you're really saying is you're not prepared to risk it. To make yourself vulnerable enough to care about someone."

He eyeballed her, but all he got was the top of her head.

Finally she said in a small voice, "What we had was fun, Solo, okay? End of story."

"Was?" His voice was hoarse. "Past tense."

"Yeah, past tense. Seeing you with Emma, realising you had such a long-term relationship with her, I—I realised, I'm just not capable of that, you know, and even if I was, I can't cope with the fact it will turn to shit. Which it inevitably will. For me, caring for someone always turns to shit."

"Blocking off your feelings won't work," he hurled at her. "It won't protect you from getting hurt."

"Just watch me."

"It doesn't work."

"I told you, it works for me."

Rage was gnawing at his chest now, biting chunks out of his heart. He was bleeding out from gaping invisible wounds. She was willing to just discard them like some useless, soiled rag.

He hardened his bones. Braced his ribs as if fending off blows. "Seems like you and I are not on the same page then. Because despite losing my girlfriend to my best mate, despite losing my parents and my nan and pop, you know what? I'm willing to keep *feeling*. I'm willing to keep believing there is someone special out there who I can spend my life with, who I can love and who will love me back." He laughed, a harsh, bitter sound. "For a brief moment in time there, I thought it might be you."

She smiled, but it didn't touch her eyes. "Well, I'm sorry to disappoint you," she said, "but it's not."

CHAPTER 25

"*D*id I spoil something?"

Emma was surveying him over her coffee cup, her gaze solicitous.

Solo frowned. "Spoil something?" His brain was still numb from this morning's interchange with Polly.

"Last night, when I turned up. You and that girl. You kind of looked pretty close. And then I got the dagger eyes from her."

Solo shook his head, then shrugged, his fingers working round the rim of his mug of black coffee. "No." He felt Em's blue eyes on him; she knew him too well. "Okay, I guess we had a bit of a thing for a few weeks, but it's over now."

"Oh." They both sat in heavy silence. "Nothing to do with me turning up, then."

He gave her a lopsided smile. It felt like it was cracking a faceful of concrete. "Don't give up easily, do you, Em?"

She placed her hand on his wrist, tentatively. "I want you to be happy, that's all."

He put his hand over hers and took comfort from the warmth, but there was no zing. He felt like he was talking to an old, old friend. A sister, even.

"You need to stop doing this guilt trip on yourself. Maybe you turning up was a catalyst for…" He gulped. "Me and her realising we're not suited. So perhaps you did me a favour."

He wanted to howl at the moon, except outside the sun was shining and it was a beautiful day with families sipping takeaway coffees while their kids ran around the playground across the street. Beyond the little strip of park, the Indian Ocean sparkled; people were *happy.*

"That's hardly doing you a favour." Her voice was sad.

Solo suppressed a heavy sigh, added a sugar to his coffee. Unlike smoking, he'd given up sugar years ago, but something had to take away the bitter taste in his mouth.

"I'm so sorry, Solo."

"Don't be. I'll be fine. I'm moving on from here in a month."

"Are you coming back to Sydney?"

He shrugged again. "I've got a phone interview next week with The Mayfield Hospital."

"The one that specialises in neuropsychiatry? The one you've had your mind set on for years?"

"The very one." He tried to feel positive. And for a moment a little prism of something like relief gave him a tiny burst of energy. He would dive into his career, forget about those green eyes and that tumble of dark curls and the way her lips reminded him of ripe peaches, her kisses… the way she made him laugh…

Heat burned into him.

Oh *shit.* He'd just spilled coffee all the way down his white T-shirt.

Emma tutted and handed him a napkin. "If you want to talk…"

He gave a tight smile, rubbed at his chest. "I'd rather not. What time is Drew expecting us to call?"

Emma tossed back a thick strand of glossy hair and looked at her watch. "In ten minutes."

"Cool. So, fill me in, how's he going?"

Her face lit up. Why hadn't he realised years ago what a perfect couple they were? Or maybe he had and had just chosen not to acknowledge it. In fact, why hadn't he realised that he and Emma were not the perfect couple? She'd looked up to him at university. After that she'd liked the fact she was dating a doctor. And him? He'd liked the fact he was dating the most beautiful girl from their cohort. The growing apart had been gradual, insidious.

"He doesn't remember much, you know." She pulled a face, her tone suddenly awkward. "About, you know, all the abusive calls he made. He was so out of it. A complete mess."

"I know."

"After you told me he was doing that I got him to give me his phone. And I probably shouldn't have, but I erased all the messages before I gave it back. I don't want him to remember how badly he treated you when you... after you... saved him, that night."

"It's okay, I get it."

"I think it was guilt, you know, he couldn't live with himself. About what he, *what we* both did to you. And then with your pop dying so suddenly, it just sent him over the edge." She paused and Solo sensed her steeling herself. "We're both so sorry for—you know, and he's well enough to apologise. It's been eating him up."

Their eyes met and he saw the abject pain in hers. "Please stop doing this to yourself, Em," he said gently. Reaching over the table he took both of her hands in his and held her gaze. "This stops now. Here. Do you hear me? No more guilt. I've thought about it a lot and I realise now we were both ready for it to end. It's just that I was never going to face that fact. You did. You made the right choice and I don't blame you. You love him."

She didn't answer.

"You and Drew. You're okay?" He felt her hands flutter in his. Solo pressed on firmly, forcing her to meet his gaze. "I want you both to be happy. With each other. There's no ill will, Em, that's long gone."

She gave a shallow laugh. "You barely showed ill will in the first place. It would have been easier if you'd shouted at me. Said horrible things. I deserved it."

"That's not how I operate, you of all people should know that."

Except with Polly, a voice muttered inside of him. Polly could make him mad, make him hurl barbs of anger and rage. He had this morning. In fact, he had sworn before he stormed off, a blind, frustrated string of words. Not at her, not directly, he would never do that, but at the fucking hopeless situation. He hadn't looked back, just taken off on his bike, fighting the urge to weep like a kid.

Because deep down, intuition told him she was lying through her pretty white teeth.

But that didn't make the pain of rejection any easier.

He brought himself back to the present with a jolt. Heard Emma's phone ding with a message. "Drew's ready," she said.

Solo stood up. Crumpled his coffee-stained napkin. "Okay, let's go."

A few minutes later, standing on the sand, the phone rang. Emma answered.

She looked at him over the top of her sunglasses, her eyes huge. "Here he is," and she handed Solo the phone.

And then there was Drew on the screen.

The Drew he remembered. That big grin slicing his handsome features. His deep resonant voice full of warmth. "Solo, mate. How've you been?"

And it was like nothing had ever come between them. They were ten years old again, in the back paddock, down by the dam, playing with the old rowing boat. Taking two days' supply of food and their swags and sailing it down the river. Tinkering in Pop's shed, rounding up the sheep in the back of the ute. So many great memories flooded back.

Solo grinned. "Good to see you looking better, mate."

How long they talked, he wasn't sure afterwards. They discussed Drew's new health regime; exercise and therapy and healthy eating and avoiding the media. And Solo's life in Perth. Solo couldn't bring himself to mention Polly.

Finally, Drew said, "I want to go back to the farm. Pop's farm."

"Really?"

"Yeah. For a while. If you agree. Maybe six months. I need to be in nature, away from the limelight."

"I see." It made sense for Drew to go back to the place he was happiest to recuperate. And the farm was surviving under management; there wouldn't be major maintenance to do. It would put off the awful decision to sell.

Drew's face on the screen was hopeful. "So, what d'you say? You have to agree, it's half yours."

Solo frowned. "You won't feel too isolated?"

"Em will be there, between jobs, and I guess I was thinking we'd keep the manager on for another six months, and I can lend a hand. Then decide, you know, if we keep or sell. The physical work will do me good."

"That makes sense." Solo nodded. "I'm in no hurry to sell."

Drew grinned, his face relieved. "Maybe you'll make a farmer of me yet, eh?"

"I can think of worse things."

"Me too." A moment's silence, then Drew said, "I want to thank you for saving me. That night. I don't remember much, I was out of my head, you know, with the psychosis, but you always believed in me when I didn't. That there was someone good inside the fucking hellhole I was drowning in."

Solo controlled his features; inside he felt like a dam was about to burst.

But it was Drew's voice that broke. "I'm so sorry mate, for what I put you through. I don't know how you even want to talk to me."

Somehow Solo got the words out, though his voice shook. "Because you're my brother. As near as it fucking gets. And I love you, mate. Simple as that."

On the small screen he could see Drew swipe at his eyes with the back of his hand. "Love you too, mate. See you when I get out of this place, right?"

"Yeah, see you very soon."

When the phone went to screensaver, Solo gave it back to Emma.

She pocketed it. "All good," she said lightly, but he saw her lower lip tremble.

"All good," he replied. He went over to the wall and leaned over it, looking out to the blue of the horizon. "Em," he said as she joined him, "I think I would like to talk about that girl. I don't want solutions, or advice. I just want to get it off my chest."

"Tell me about her," she said softly.

Solo hauled in a breath. "Her name's Polly and she's driving me completely fucking crazy..."

~

IT WAS THE WEDNESDAY AFTER CARTS' party and Solo had been avoiding her. And no surprise, really.

She'd like to pretend she was avoiding him, but the truth was, Polly only had to walk into the room and he'd get up and leave. He studiously avoided her gaze in meetings. When she sidled up to him at the vending machine and said hi, he said a stony "hi" and sauntered off.

Yes, *sauntered.*

She wouldn't have minded if he'd stormed off all huffy. But this casual indifference was like a paper cut; it hurt so much more than it should.

And then Judith had come up behind her and bought a bar of Toblerone and said, "It's no good, I have to tell you or I'm going to burst," and her eyes were so shiny bright and happy it made Polly's gut jack-knife.

She knew what Judith was going to say but she asked anyway, "What? Tell me?" in her brightest, best, interested voice.

Judith leaned in and whispered close to her ear, "Carts kissed me. At the end of the party."

Polly had the uncharitable urge to say in a St Trinian's-style voice, "Bully for you," with a jolly air punch for extra emphasis. She didn't, of course. She smiled and made sure her eyes crinkled up and her cheeks bunched and said, "That's wonderful. If it's what you wanted, which it looks like it was."

"Oh yes." Judith was blushing. "He's got a lovely kiss. And he said he really likes me and did I want to go out for dinner."

"And you're going to accept?"

"Should I?"

Polly popped her eyes. "Whyever not?"

"It's so soon after—you know—only a few weeks, really."

"But you're keen on him, right?"

"Oh yes, he's dreamy."

"Dreamy" and "Carts" hadn't ever occupied the same thought bubble in Polly's mind. Instead, her gaze snagged on Solo's broad shoulders disappearing into the doctor's office and her heart twanged violently like a breaking violin string.

She'd blown it. She'd thought on Saturday she'd triumphed, but now her little kingdom of self-righteous victory was crumbling. More accurately, it had gone completely bankrupt.

"Look, Jude," she said with sudden feeling. "If you feel good about this, grab it with both hands, enjoy it, be open to where it will take you." *Lousy hypocrite.*

Jude beamed. "You're right, Poll. You are so wise when it comes to relationships."

Polly nearly choked. She looked at the bar of Cadbury's Fruit and Nut in her hand; she'd only bought it so she'd be able to go up to Solo, and that had backfired. What had she expected, that he'd drop his packet of salt and vinegar chips and fall at her feet, beg her to reconsider?

Judith patted Polly's arm and skipped off.

Polly stared morosely after her and threw the chocolate bar in the bin.

The rest of the week passed in a haze of misery. She spent the weekend eating cookie-dough ice-cream out of the tub and watching re-runs of *Sex and the City*. By the middle of the next week she felt like someone had gutted her with a fishing knife.

In bed at night she played over what she'd said. She kept her old journal on the bedside table, and every night re-read her entries about Danny, and Dad, and all that past stuff to stiffen her resolve.

And then on Tuesday she slammed into a brick wall.

Okay, metaphorically speaking. She'd walked into the tea room and Ben was talking to Solo. Her ears pricked up when she heard the word *"interview"*. Busying herself making a coffee, she hummed to pretend she wasn't interested, then realised she couldn't eavesdrop with her own inane, off-key version of "Baby, You're Dead To Me" in her ears, so she stopped and listened, stirring her cup.

"So, what time is the interview?" This from Ben.

"Three pm," Solo replied, "via Skype."

"Does Pritchard know to leave you alone?"

"Yes. I've told him I won't be available on the ward for an hour."

"I'm sure he understands you've got to look after your career."

"Yeah." A pause, Polly's ears pricked. "Though he's had a talk with me about something that's coming up here at the hospital. Part of a psychiatry first-response team in ED."

By now Polly was sure she resembled Dumbo. Gigantic ears flapping in the breeze. She went and got milk out of the fridge. Very, very slowly.

Ben said, "God, it'd be great if you stayed, the patients love you. Would you consider it?"

There was a long loud silence, the air buzzing with electric current. Polly plonked the carton on the bench and milk slopped everywhere.

"I don't think so." Solo's voice was clipped and hard. "Nothing for me here in Perth."

She couldn't help herself, she turned around. Two silver lasers bore into her. All she could do was stare at him helplessly.

Solo flicked his gaze away. Face blotching madly, Polly turned and focused on scrubbing at the milk on the bench.

"Hey there, Poll, come and sit with us," said Ben cheerfully.

Solo got up, washed his mug and walked out without another word.

Ben's features creased into a perplexed frown. "What's bitten him?"

Polly shrugged. "Interview nerves, maybe." Utter misery coiled into her stomach. "What's the job?" she forced out.

"The Mayfield neuropsych hospital in Sydney. A senior registrar position."

"Oh, nice," said Polly, and tried to pretend her heart hadn't just made a really loud cracking noise.

Things didn't improve over the rest of the day.

By the end of it, she'd decided she had two choices. 1) Grovel and tell Solo she missed him like fucking crazy and would he please come back into her bed. (Further than that, she refused to let her thoughts go.)

2) Forget him and go and party. Hard.

She sat in her office and let the choices percolate while she should have been writing up a family therapy session. The first option made a ball of terror barrel up her throat; the second made her feel numb and flat. She'd just decided numb and flat was preferable to death by fear when her phone trilled.

It was Dad.

"Polly, love." His voice was chirpy on the other end. "Me and Mim are up in town, we wondered if we could catch up for a bite?"

"Oh, yes." Party hard was clearly out. And strangely, she felt relieved. "Sure."

Later that evening, Polly sat with Mim and Ted in a small Italian restaurant she frequented when Dad came to the city. Ted was a man of habit: home-cooked or his one favourite Italian restaurant. That was it.

They'd just finished their first course and Ted had filled their water glasses and paused.

Why did she think there was an agenda here?

Ted plonked the water jug down and rubbed his hands together. "Mim and I are in town to see someone. We've finally decided to get some counselling. Put things properly right between us."

Polly hid her look of surprise. "Oh, that's great, Dad. How come now?"

Mim fidgeted, took hold of Ted's hand. "After the party, your dad decided he wanted to bring more intimacy, more closeness into our relationship. I'd stopped nagging a while back, sometimes you need to let people come to it in their own time. Seems like it worked." She smiled lovingly at Ted and a pang of envy hit Polly. How wonderful it would be to find this level of closeness after so many years. To keep on trying to make things better.

Ted looked a bit coy. "Yeah, I asked Solo if he could find me some names—"

Polly's eyes widened. "Solo!"

"Yeah, when we had that talk in the barn. Man to man. He said he'd ask around."

The unfairness stabbed her in the chest. All her years of trying, and in one meeting, Dad had confided in and opened up to Solo. Just like the PTSD group. How come everyone trusted Solo? He wasn't trustworthy, he was a heart-thief, or at least would be, if she'd let him.

"You could have asked me, Dad. For some names, I mean." Damn it, she sounded huffy.

Dad shrugged. "Thing is, me and Solo—I guess we hit it off. He got it, the PTSD stuff, the problems"—he snapped his finger—"just like that, he really got it. Besides, love, you're too close to all this stuff."

Polly sipped some water. "Sure."

Dad's face took on an eager look. "So, anyway, what's going on with you two?"

Her glass clunked hard onto the table. "Nothing. Why?"

"Aren't you a couple yet?"

"No, Dad, no. We most definitely are not."

"Oh." Dad sounded crestfallen

Mim gave a little tut. "Well, you should be. We noticed the vibes between you both. Everyone reckons he adores you." Polly glanced over. Mim had her smug, Mim-knows-best look on her face. "He's a keeper, that one."

"He's not a keeper." Under the table she dug her nails into her thighs. "He's heading back to Sydney."

"That's a real shame," Mim said, and made another clucking sound with her tongue. "Honey, you'll miss the boat if you go on like this."

Polly's eyes smarted. She muttered, "Thanks, Mim, but I'm not interested in getting on that particular boat."

Really, this whole conversation was pointless. because the boat had sunk. And if she had to choose a name for it, it would be the *Titanic*.

Polly gulped in great mouthfuls of air. "I think I'll skip the next course. I'm not very hungry for some reason."

Dad and Mim gave each other a knowing look. A look that said, what a shame.

Shame on them, Polly thought. Shame on them for bringing it up.

THAT NIGHT WAS EVEN WORSE than the previous ones as she tossed and turned and played through Dad and Mim's pitying looks. Sleep evaded her. She wound herself into knots in the sheets, and when she did finally fall into a doze, she dreamed of nose kisses and dynamic hot sex and silver eyes bathing her in love.

So when a message alert beeped at 6 a.m. on Thursday morning, Polly dived for her phone like one possessed.

Her heart dropped when she saw it wasn't him.

Alice: Are you awake?

Polly: Yes

The phone rang immediately. Alice's voice was breathless. "You're in love with him."

"What the fuck?" Polly sat bolt upright, all her bones aching from lack of sleep, rubbing at her sore eyes.

"This doctor guy. Solo. You're in love. I know it. From everything you've said. The fact you've called me every day for the past week and a half, making up all this nonsense about independence so you can tell me how much you're not interested in him."

"That's ridiculous," Polly huffed, kicking off the knotted sheet. "I told you, it's just sex."

"That is a fiendish lie and you know it."

Polly pushed back her mess of curls and couldn't help a tiny smile. God, she missed Alice's turn of phrase.

"I thought it from the moment you mentioned him. Your voice was different."

"Different what way?"

"Like you had suddenly been struck by awe. And delight. And fairy dust. And merman sperm!"

"Merman sperm!"

"Only joking."

Despite herself, Polly laughed and groped for her dressing gown. "You are so ridiculous."

"I am not ridiculous. You are. Stubborn as a mule, blind as a bat, and any other animal analogies you choose. You need to tell him. Before it's too late and he takes that job in Sydney."

"It's already too late. He's leaving."

"Oh no." Alice sounded horrified, which made the knife in Polly's heart dig in harder. "No, you have to go and tell him now!"

"Are you crazy? You know what time it is here, right? It's 6 a.m.!"

"I don't care. You love him. He loves you. I know it. Don't miss out, Polly. You deserve to be happy more than anyone I know."

"I—I—" But her voice trailed off and her fingers curled tight around the phone. Could Alice, her beloved friend, her soul sister, be right?

And suddenly something, some great big dam inside Polly burst, and all the feelings came tumbling out. She couldn't seem to speak, a strange little mewl came out of her mouth.

"Did you say something?" Alice's voice queried down the line.

Polly opened her mouth. Still no words. She thought about Solo leaving, flying off on that plane in less than four weeks, back to Sydney without her; she remembered their sizzling chemistry, their talks, their shared laughter. The way he held her, the way he made such a beautiful symphony of love to her.

The way he kissed the tip of her nose.

And she knew she'd never felt this way before. Would never feel it again. For anyone.

"Oh god." It burst out of her lips. "Shit. Oh, Munchkin. You're right. You're so right. I do. I love the stupid, horrible, beautiful guy."

"I knew it!" Alice's voice held a note of triumph. "Even Aaron worked it out."

Polly batted away the tear that had squeezed out of her eye. "Jesus, if Aaron spotted it, I must be running around with a love banner on my forehead."

"Yep," said Alice. "The message gamma-rayed its way from the other side of the world. Now go, you silly sausage, and claim your man."

Polly jumped up, phone still jammed to her ear as she flew to her wardrobe. "How can I ever repay you, Munchkin?"

"You have, a thousand times already, for getting me and Aaron together, you dope. Go." And Alice hung up.

Exactly twenty-two minutes later, Polly stood outside Carts' house, shivering. It was going to be warm later, the sun winking a hello over the rooftops, but it wasn't now and the first thing she had found in her cupboard was a lightweight yellow cotton dress with large red poppies splashed all over it. She'd struggled with the zipper and now, in the crisp morning air, had a sense it was stuck halfway down her back. Her hair was springing in all directions and she hadn't even bothered with a slick of lip gloss.

But it was too late to turn back now. She couldn't hide her feelings anymore, from herself, from Solo. She had to take the risk or she knew she'd regret this for the rest of her days.

She tiptoed through the gate. The curtains were still closed across Solo's bedroom window.

She picked up a handful of gravel from the succulent bed in the small patch of garden. Hurled it up at the window. A spray fell on her head. Damn, now she'd have gravel in her hair and that would be a bitch to get out.

But the tinkle on the glass told her some had hit the mark. She picked up another handful and lobbed it as the window flung wide.

Fuck, she'd just hit Solo in the face. His hand shot up as he exclaimed, "What the hell!"

"It's me, Polly," she hissed loudly.

Now Solo was leaning out the window. And oh, God, he was wearing nothing on top. The sight of his muscled torso made her mouth dry up.

"I need to talk to you," she got out.

For a moment his face remained hard, his features bunched, she could see it even in the dim early morning light and her heart stalled.

Then suddenly he ducked inside.

God, what if she'd got this all wrong? It wasn't like he'd given her a single crumb these past two weeks. Her teeth were chattering more from fear than anything as she stood waiting for him, hoping he would answer the door. Then she heard the latch draw back.

He stood on the doorstep and, sod the guy, he'd purposely left his chest bare, she knew he had. Her eyes drank in his pecs, the tiny dusting of hair on his chest, sank to the v of dark hair that descended into his pyjama pants.

She swallowed hard.

He stood back against the open door, but not before she'd caught the twitch at the corner of his beautiful mouth.

"Are you going to do more than hurl missiles at me?"

"They were meant for the window."

He stared at her, another lip twitch, but said nothing.

"I had to do something to stop you ignoring me."

"An early morning raid seems a bit dramatic."

"It's… um— because I need to… we need to… talk."

He motioned his head for her to enter. "Come inside."

"No, thanks."

She had to say it now, on the doorstep, because with him half-naked like that, if she went inside, she might just pounce and then… NO, sex was not the answer. Talking was.

She had to spill it. Open up. Communicate.

She glanced up to see a small frown furrowing Solo's brows. Hell, it made him look so sexy. Too tempting to plaster her hands all over that chest. She bit her lip, dragged in a mouthful of air.

"When you're ready," he said.

"Give me a moment," she gulped out.

He stood facing her on the porch, arms crossed. The silence yawned between them. "What do you want to say, Polly?"

She didn't dare look at him, didn't know where to start. Her hand came up and tugged at the wonky neckline of her dress. "Could you make this a little easier for me?"

He uncrossed his arms. "Is that better?"

"That's your idea of making it easier?"

"Open body language shows I'm listening. You should know that."

She glanced at his face and though his expression was deadpan, she thought she saw a softening in those silver eyes, and it made a little butterfly of hope beat its wings behind her ribs. Surely he could see that her coming here at first light must mean something really, really important?

Because it did. It meant she loved this guy with all her sad, mussed-up heart.

Get it out, woman.

"I, um, the other day, when you came around and you told me… about you and that, er, Emma." Her thumb and forefinger fiddled at the neck of her dress. She dropped her hand, tried again. "Was that the truth?"

"The truth about what?"

"The bit about you and me..."

"Which, of the many bits?"

He was going to make her grovel. Rub her nose right in the pile of poop of her own making. "The bit, um—the bit where you said..." She gulped, another collar yank. This time she realised she'd exposed a great swathe of breast. She saw his eyes drop, his jaw tighten, and the butterflies flurried into her throat. "That you were crazy about me."

"Oh, yeah, that bit."

His arms folded once more over his chest, bunching his pecs. Polly winced. "No, don't, don't cross your arms again, please. This is hard enough..."

Solo uncrossed his arms and put them behind his back, which thrust his crotch forward. Polly nearly whimpered.

God damn him.

She blurted, "So, was it true?"

The silence stretched like electric wire between them.

Finally, "Yes. Unfortunately."

"Oh." Her mouth snapped shut. Opened again and kind of hovered that way, speechless.

He squinted at her through narrowed eyes. "Is that why you're here? To humiliate me again about confessing how I feel about you..." He paused, then added softly, "Or is there another reason?"

Polly gulped in more cool morning air. She was seriously at risk of fucking this up. She shuffled on the step, nearly lost her footing and a hand flailed. "I lied. I didn't mean any of that stuff, about not wanting to feel anything, or be with anyone. I was... I was hurt and I was—am— shit scared... and..."

A hand appeared from behind his back, reached out and closed gently around the fingers that were still flapping around in mid-air. He stepped closer. His bare toes nudged her shoe. "I'm still listening."

His touch was scrambling her brain. She couldn't speak. Could barely even stand.

"Go on," Solo said, weaving his fingers through hers.

"Okay so— the trouble is, I'm in deeper than I realised. Like seriously deep. With you, I mean. And—I—I don't actually know what do about that, so—" She laughed and the sound jangled through the still morning air. Somewhere, a kookaburra laughed. "I did what I always do, I hit out first."

"You sure did." It seemed he was hitting the mark now too, his thumb-pad gently circling the soft skin of her wrist. Spasms of delight shot through her. "So, I guess I'm here to say, to ask whether... whether... you would be prepared for us to try again."

"Ahhhhaa." He was so close now his breath was stirring the curls at her ear and her mind was going to sink into her vagina and be subsumed. She'd better talk fast.

"I'm no good at this love business," she blurted.

"Don't spoil it. You were doing so well."

"I guess, I mean, I'm willing to try, if..."

With his other hand he tilted her chin. Looked deep into her eyes. "Okay, I'm going to tell you how it is, since you're clearly struggling here. I've fallen in love with you, Polly Fletcher. Which means you're going to want to run and hide. And do everything to push me away. And you know what? I'm not going to let you. So now you're here, pretty shoddily put together, if you don't mind me saying, and looking like you've barely slept because you're so fucking miserable without me. Just like I am without you—"

She almost wilted but his silver gaze wouldn't let her go.

"I need you to agree that you won't run, or hide. Not anymore."

She breathed out on a beg. "Please don't let me ruin this, just because I'm terrified."

He rested his forehead against hers, whispered, "I will never let that happen."

And then his arms came around her waist and hers snuck around his neck. For a second their noses nudged and suddenly they were kissing like they might both die if they didn't.

When they finally came up for air, Solo growled, "I'm going to carry you up those stairs and make wild, passionate love to you."

Polly peered over his shoulder into the house. "What about Carts?"

Solo's beautiful eyes crinkled. "He's not here. I think he stayed over at Judith's."

"Oh, the wicked girl, she said she was taking it slow."

"Yeah, and you told me you never dated men you work with..."

With that, he picked her up, seemingly effortlessly, and carried her up the stairs.

In the bedroom, they kissed until they fell on the bed, his body hard and hungry and urgent. They needed to get naked, now. Obviously their hands agreed, as they both started a frenzied ripping at garments.

"Jeesh, what did you do to this zipper? You've completely mangled it," Solo spluttered after a moment's tugging at her dress.

Polly giggled. "I was in a hurry. I had to tell this random guy that I love him."

Solo pulled back, eyes narrowed. "Come again."

She bit her lip, swallowed hard and tried again. "I love him" came out on a weird, husky squeak. She gazed into those quicksilver eyes, placed her hand on his cheek, felt the muscle twitch. "I love *you*."

"Oh, god, I love you too, you crazy, stubborn woman." With a triumphant laugh, Solo tugged harder at the zipper. There was a loud ripping sound. In revenge she tugged down his pyjama pants. Soon there was nothing but the beauty of skin on skin.

"We're going to be late for Dr Death's Friday ward meeting," Polly murmured, biting his neck as his body slid over hers.

"Mmm, it could look suspicious us walking in together with your dress cobbled together with safety pins."

As she pulled him closer and planted a kiss right on the tip of his nose, Polly managed her last coherent words. "You know what, Dr J? I couldn't give a flying fuck."

EPILOGUE

One Year Later...

"Can you please just pick up this dropped stitch, hon, please?"

Polly had that cute helpless look in her eyes that got him every time.

In the midst of doing up his tie, he shook his head in mock-exasperation and then couldn't help grinning at the picture of Polly, curls akimbo, a frown puckering her brow as she tried to finish a square for the baby blanket she was knitting for the Blimp, AKA Thomas.

It had been a labour of love. And *he* loved *her* for doing it.

He dropped a kiss on her hair, drank in the jasmine scent of her latest favourite shampoo (the one that now sat next to his in the shower cubicle of the apartment they'd just rented together) and took the knitting from her. A few quick and nimble moves and it was sorted.

"Now put the end of your needles in the ball of wool so it doesn't unravel and get your shoes on. We're going to be late at this rate."

Polly shoved her hair out of her eyes and pushed her lip out. They were both still flushed from a particularly frantic love-making session, the reason, far more than the knitting, why they were risking being late.

Finally they were in the Uber and heading for Kings Park.

"Feeling good about this?" Solo asked, winding his fingers through hers.

She nodded. "Absolutely. They should have done it years ago."

Solo squeezed her hand and she squeezed back. It wasn't quite time for him and Polly, though they'd had the tentative conversation about serious stuff like whether the wedding cake should be chocolate or fruit cake. Whether she'd wear a white dress.

No, Polly had pouted. Red. And lacey.

He'd laughed. She could turn up in a corset and suspenders, for all he cared, as long as she promised to stay with him forever. And every day, it was feeling more likely. They'd even discussed baby names. Once.

He was a patient man.

Finally the car stopped at the top of the hill, the grassy slopes edging down to a panorama of the city skyline. Glass and metal buildings stole the foreground, beyond which the Swan River sparkled, a great expanse of blue, dotted with sailing boats. Solo was growing to love this city with its big spaces and even bigger skies. Taking on the new role as psychiatrist to the Emergency Response Team at the hospital had also proven wonderfully challenging.

So was life with Polly. Full of laughter and the occasional humdinger of a fight, all the better for making up after. And the fights were getting less as they learned how not to press each other's buttons.

Now, as they hurried along, he could make out Kate nursing baby Thomas in her arms, and Joe's broad shoulders. Solo recognised more faces from his visits to the farm in recent months, keeping Ted company with a non-alcoholic beer at the pub.

And there, finally, was Ted. Looking nervous, tugging at his bow tie.

"Come on, quick, hon, before Mim arrives."

He grabbed her hand and they sprinted over to the others. The marriage celebrant smiled at them and Joe beckoned.

Polly's green gaze joined with his in an intimate moment that spoke volumes. Every day there was more trust glowing out of those bewitching eyes.

He squeezed back.

And then there was Mim, dressed in a pearly cream dress with a hat full of gold and dusky pink roses. Radiant. When he spied her, Ted's grin was big enough to split his face. He looked so proud. Here were these two, finally joining together in marriage for all to see. Celebrating a love that had weathered the storms. Celebrating the love that Mim had kept on giving, unconditionally, despite all those ups and downs.

Finally winning her Ted, wholeheartedly.

And in turn Ted had won back his daughter's love. It warmed Solo's heart every time he watched Ted and Polly wrestling hay bales onto the back of the tractor and trundling off in the ute to mend fences together.

He glanced down and saw Polly's eyes glinting with unshed tears.

Happy tears. He let his arm snake around her waist. She leaned into him, her head resting on his shoulder, exactly where it belonged.

Solo imagined that same head, in thirty years' time, the curls streaked salt and pepper just like Mim's. Somewhere inside him he knew, he *knew*, that head would still be right there by his side.

They'd be sitting talking about their grandkids in front of a fire, maybe knitting, possibly eating chocolate, Polly still complaining about her thighs and then laughing at how ridiculous that was.

He kissed the top of her curls. Soon. Very soon, he'd ask her...

They both stood to attention as the marriage celebrant spoke. "We are here today to join Ted Fletcher in marriage to his beloved partner Mim Walters... on this beautiful day, we, their family and friends come together to celebrate the abiding nature of true love..."

His girl nestled against his hip, his new family all around him, Solo sighed happily.

Amen to that.

THE ALICE EQUATION

Sometimes love is complicated

Alice Montgomery's life is like Groundhog day. Five years after graduating, she's still working in her Mum's bookshop, hiding her stash of romance novels under the bed and pining for the gorgeous guy who helped her over a panic attack before her final uni exam.

Aaron Blake, loves to party – *hard*. His idea of commitment to anything other than his legal career is strictly three months. Until landing a job with the most prestigious law firm in town means he has to convince the partners he's committed to family values.

Aaron needs a fake date fast—and who could be safer than shy, bookish Alice?

Soon Alice finds herself dating her secret crush, sporting a daring new look of vintage frocks and itsy-bitsy lace underwear.

Now the heat is notching up. Aaron's feelings for his fake date are proving anything but safe, and Alice is discovering her inner sex-goddess.

But when secrets are revealed and lies uncovered, both Alice and Aaron will have to work out the hardest equation of all — what this crazy thing called love is all about.

The Alice Equation

A KISS FOR CARTER

Carter (Carts) Wells is 6' 6 " of kind heart and seriously bad hair cuts. He's also atrocious at love. First, his fiancée leaves him for her personal trainer, next he sets his heart on book-worm Alice, but she much prefers his best mate, Aaron.

Now Carts has met Judith. She's kind and beautiful (and tall) and it seems like she's falling for him too.

But what happens when the Universe decides to throw a curved ball into Carts and Judith's path?

Is Carts destined for heartbreak and bad hair days forever? Or will Cupid finally take pity on him? Find out in this sweet and funny third novel in The Laws of Love Series.

Available mid 2021

ABOUT THE AUTHOR

Davina Stone writes romances about flawed but lovable characters who get it horribly wrong before they finally get it right. They also kiss a fair bit on the way to happily ever after.

Davina grew up in England, before meeting her very own hero who whisked her across wild oceans to Australia. She has now lived exactly half her life in both countries which makes her a hybrid Anglo-Aussie.

When not writing she can be found chasing kangaroos off her veggie patch, dodging snakes and even staring down the odd crocodile. But despite her many adventures, in her heart, she still believes that a nice cup of tea fixes most problems- and of course, that true love conquers all.

Please Review This book.

Reviews help authors to keep writing and help readers to find our books. If you enjoyed *The Polly Principle*, please consider leaving a review on Amazon and/or Goodreads. https://www.goodreads.com/book/show/57296804-the-polly-principle

Why not drop by and say hi?

Want to read the story of when Alice and Aaron first met? Sign up for my newsletter and get the prequel to the first in the Laws of Love series, *The Alice Equation* FREE. You will also get updates on new releases and a little bit of once-a-month silliness (cute pics of kangaroos may be included on occasions.)

Check out my website at htttps://www.davinastone.com/

Connect with me on ...

instagram.com/davinastone_

bookbub.com/profile/davina-stone